LaTOUR, Susan
Dead reckoning

S

DATE DUE

34611

STOCKTON
Township Public Library
Stockton, IL

Books may be drawn for two weeks and renewed once.
A fine of five cents a library day shall be paid for each
book kept overtime

Borrower's card must be presented whenever a book
is taken. If card is lost a new one will be given for
payment of 25 cents

Each borrower must pay for damage to books

KEEP YOUR CARD IN THIS POCKET

DEMCO

DEAD RECKONING

SUSAN &
PIERRE LaTOUR, JR.

DEAD RECKONING

THOMAS DUNNE
ST. MARTIN'S PRESS ✿ NEW YORK

A THOMAS DUNNE BOOK.
An imprint of St. Martin's Press.

Design by Junie Lee

ISBN 0-312-13958-6

10 9 8 7 6 5 4 3 2

PROLOGUE

From the journal of Catherine Lakey
Stonington College
September 17, 1980

Waking up this morning, very early, I had a vivid memory of my father and me sailing on Lake Ontario. It startled me because even though it was something we did every summer, I haven't thought about it for years. The boat we had was just a little fourteen-footer, and though we rarely went very far in it or did much of anything worth reporting, he kept a ship's log religiously because, he said, that's what a captain did. One never knew. Every now and then, he'd get the charts out and we'd pick a buoy or an island ten or fifteen miles away and he'd try to get us there just using his watch and his old Navy sextant, shooting the sun every few hours or so, noting our position in the log. Dead reckoning he called it, and he took such satisfaction from the times when he'd hit our target on the nose. "Cat," he'd say, rubbing those big brown hands of his together, "it doesn't always happen like this, getting where you think you're going. Not navigating this way."

But maybe it does. I'll be forty tomorrow, with nothing to report except that time is spinning by me faster than I like to think about and that each year looks like the others—another straight run out to Meacham's Point. I'm happy enough, I guess. I still love teaching and the college has been good to me, but I find myself wishing that just once before I'm through that the navigation would break down, that I'd miss my destination and end up someplace that I'd never been before.

PART ONE

D A Y   O N E

MARCH—1987						
S	M	T	W	T	F	S
1	2	3	4	5	6	7
8	9	10	11	12	13	14
15	16	17	18	19	20	21
22	23	24	25	<u>26</u>	27	28
29	30	31				

DAY ONE

Cotchpinicut, Massachusetts
Morning

Fog is moving in—a creeping, gray shroud that dampens all the seaside sounds except the cry of gulls—and a breeze, still fitful in the early morning, has come up off the ocean. It will strengthen as the day wears on, shift to the east and blow relentlessly until nightfall.

Inside Catherine Lakey's cottage, the gustings stir her curtains and waffle the flannel of her nightgown as she stands, barefooted, at a kitchen sink, gazing out over sand dunes and sea grass to the edge of the receding tide. Her hair, naturally wavy and cut short, is the color of wet sand drying in the sun. Her face, winter pale, has small, sharp features: a thin-lipped mouth, a narrow, slightly hooked nose, and deep-set eyes that are a somber, slate blue. She squints, watching a solitary gull as it hovers over the sea before a stronger current catches it and carries it away.

She leaves the kitchen and goes to shower, afterwards toweling her hair brusquely, and dressing in a cotton turtleneck, a fisherman's sweater and a khaki skirt. She makes her bed, pulling the white sheets taut, smoothing the wool blankets, then neatly folds her nightgown and puts it away in a pine bureau drawer. She carries sandals to the kitchen, sets them down next to a large leather purse on one of the chairs that flank the kitchen table. Using an old tin tablespoon, she measures coffee for an automatic coffee maker, then sets the table for breakfast: a blue mug imprinted with a college seal, a plate, a knife, a small plastic container of margarine, a crock of imported marmalade and a fresh cloth napkin.

After gathering the purse and sandals, she leaves and follows a sandy path that winds through the dunes to the beach below. Soon she stops, looks up at the sky, and returns to the house where she takes a red windbreaker from a hook beside the door and puts it on.

Back on the path again, she makes her way over the crest of a dune, then down a steep run to the beach. For a while she is out of sight, but comes into view again as she approaches the tide rim. A breaker, larger than the others, collapses on the shore. Its outwash swirls around her ankles.

She stops, glances back over her shoulder at the cottage, then turns and heads south down the beach, her footprints outlined in tiny bubbles before being erased by the next wave. She walks at a steady pace and as she moves farther down the beach and deeper into fog, her form grows indistinct—becomes a smudge of red that fades and reappears, then fades again and disappears entirely.

DAY FIVE

MARCH—1987						
S	M	T	W	T	F	S
1	2	3	4	5	6	7
8	9	10	11	12	13	14
15	16	17	18	19	20	21
22	23	24	25	<u>26</u>	27	28
29	(30)	31				

DAY FIVE

MONDAY, MARCH 30, 1987

Devon, Connecticut
Morning

Frank Simco squinted through the smeary arcs of water that his
windshield wipers made. It irritated him that he'd forgotten to
have the blades changed and it irritated him more that it was rain-
ing. In his eight years as dean of Natural Sciences at Stonington
College, experience had taught him that a smooth opening of the
term set a rhythm and a tone for the days and weeks that followed.
This term was less than three hours old and already the carefully
planned order of the day was beginning to unravel.

The light patter of raindrops hitting the windshield began to
change to the sharper cracks of sleet as Simco turned on to High
Meadow Lane and stopped in front of Catherine Lakey's small
campus house. He turned off the ignition and peered up at the
house. The windows were discouragingly dark and Catherine's car
wasn't in the driveway. Stepping out into the rain, he ran up the
short brick walk, avoiding puddles, and knocked on the door—
three hard, quick raps. He waited, listened; then hit it again, harder,
with his fist.

"Catherine," he said. Then, louder: "Catherine? It's me,
Frank." He tried the door. It was locked.

"Shit," he muttered, and turning up his collar, hurried around the side of the house to the back door. It was locked, too, but beneath the doorknob there was an old-fashioned keyhole. He bent down, put his ear to it, knocked on the door and listened. Nothing. Turning his head, he put his lips to the keyhole and tried to call through it: "Catherine, are you all right?" but it came out a muffled "Kahin, er oo ahrey?" Embarrassed, he straightened up and wiped his glasses on his sleeve. He backed himself against the door as tightly as he could, seeking the shelter of the doorway and the eaves, but a shift in the wind brought the rain in after him, soaking his raincoat, sending icy streaks of water under his collar. He turned once again to face the door, pressed his ear against it, pounded hard with both fists. "Goddamn it, Catherine," he yelled, then quickly turned around, imagining the eyes from neighbors' windows, watching. To hell with it, he thought. He'd done what he could. Now security could take over and go through the house. That's what they got paid for.

He stepped out of the doorway onto a tattered sisal mat, which gave off a sodden, squishy sound. Could there be . . .? He lifted the mat, found nothing, then ran his hand along the molding above the door. His fingers struck something small and cold which flew past his head, then jingled down the back steps to the grass. He scrambled after it, picked it up and saw that it was a badly tarnished key.

He unlocked the door and went inside. "Catherine?" he said in a lowered voice, as if she might be sleeping and he didn't want to wake her. "Anybody here?" The place was cold and quiet with that faintly moldy-musty smell that houses get when no one's been living in them for a while.

He went through the kitchen to the living room, then down a darkened hallway to a tidy, white bedroom, the single bed so neatly made that it looked as if it had been ironed. "Catherine?"

Across the hall behind him was another room, a study with a chair pushed into the kneehole of the desk, a computer tucked away beneath a vinyl cover, and books aligned precisely along the edges of the shelves.

Simco returned to the kitchen and noticed there was a calendar on the wall next to the telephone. He lifted it off its hook and studied it. Printed into the small squares were the daily details of Catherine's life: meetings, appointments, reminders to pick up the car, pay the taxes. Friday, March 20, was circled in red and below it Catherine had written with a bold exuberance SPRING BREAK!! TO COTCH! That's it, thought Simco. She'd spent the week at her cottage in Cotchpinicut on Cape Cod and had put off returning until the last minute this morning; then traffic, or maybe car trouble, had made her miss her first two classes today.

He checked his watch. It was nearly ten-thirty. By now she'd be back at the Science Center, or, at the very least, would have called in. He felt relieved that she was safe, that this disruption of his life was going to be very brief and minor, but at the edge of his relief was irritation.

He'd say something to her about cutting things too fine and let her know that he'd been out in the rain looking for her, worried, when he had so many other things to do. He put the calendar back on the wall, locked the door behind him, replaced the key on the molding and left.

When he arrived at his office, he was surprised to find no messages. He checked the time, got out the master schedule and ran his finger down the left-hand column: Mon. Per 3: Lakey, C. Intro Chem. Lab A Rm. C-12. He walked quickly downstairs to the chemistry wing, then along a brightly lit, gleaming corridor that still smelled strongly of floor wax. As he neared C-12, he could hear the high-pitched laughter and chatter of female voices. Simco opened the door and a hush fell over the room as he met the collective gaze of lab section A: eighteen young women, lounging on lab benches, goggles jauntily pushed back on the tops of their heads, waiting for Professor Lakey.

Cotchpinicut, Massachusetts
Late morning

The sign on the desk said Sgt. William Cahoon, but everyone in the small Cape Cod town of Cotchpinicut, Massachusetts, called him Billy. He was filling out an accident report when the dispatcher called out across the room, "Billy, gotta guy here from Connecticut. Maybe you should talk to him."

He reached for the phone. "Sergeant Cahoon." He cradled the receiver between his cheek and shoulder and continued to fill out the report. After a minute or two, he took a pad from the desk drawer.

"Name again?"

"Could you spell that? L - A - K - E - Y." He wrote the name on the pad.

"And the first name, you say, is Catherine?"

"Do you have an address?" He wrote "51 Pilgrim's Trace" in big, loopy letters.

"Sure. Don't blame you. Now, Mr.—sorry, missed your name—Simco. Frank Simco. Is there a number where we can reach you?" He wrote the name and number at the top of the pad.

"We'll check it out and give you a call."

He tore the page off the pad, stuffed it into his shirt pocket, then walked across the room and slapped the dispatcher on the back. "Beakey, I'm gonna take a drive out to the beach."

The main highway ran north to Provincetown, paralleling the shore, and every so often smaller roads branched off and twisted their way eastward toward the sea. Billy Cahoon turned on to one of these—Shore Road—unmarked because the sign had been stolen so often that the town had stopped replacing it.

At the Whistling Beach parking lot, the road curved, then narrowed and every now and then was striped with lines of drifting sand. Cahoon turned on to Pilgrim's Trace and followed it east to the dunes where it turned south again and ran behind them, following the shore. On the left in a sandy hollow was a small shingled cottage, its doors and windows boarded up. Cahoon slowed the car and squinted. Beside the door, a rusty 47 had stained the bleached gray shingles brown.

A mile farther down the road, another cottage stood in the dunes. This one was board-and-batten, freshly painted white with sea-blue shutters and trim. Under every window was a window box, still showing the stubble of last summer's flowers. In the gravel parking area was a white Ford Escort with Connecticut plates. Cahoon stopped behind the car and called in the plate numbers to Beakey, who said that for out-of-states it would take a few minutes. Cahoon told him he'd look around and call him back.

For the cottages on the ocean side of Pilgrim's Trace, directions were reversed. Their backs were toward the road; their fronts faced out toward the dunes and, beyond them or between them, to the dark blue line of sea. Cahoon went up the short brick walk to the back door of the house, noticing the smooth half-moons of sand that had drifted over it. They showed no footprints. He knocked on the door and waited, then knocked again. "Anybody there?" he said, in his deep, official voice. "Miss Lacey?" He reached into his pocket and took out the piece of crumpled paper. "Miss Lakey. Police."

A sandy path led along the back of the house, then curved around the side. He followed it and found that when it reached the front, it divided, the right branch running toward the dunes and the left leading to the house, to a blue screen door which gently rocked against the jamb in the freshening easterly breeze. Cahoon started toward it, then stopped. The door behind the screen was open.

"Anybody there?" He reached down slowly and took his revolver from its holster; then ducked off the path and took three running steps to the side of the house beside the door.

"Anybody there?" he said sharply. "Police."

With his left hand he grabbed the knob and flicked the door open; it swung rapidly through 180 degrees, crashed into the house, swung back and slammed closed. Cahoon waited, listened; then crouching, he swung the door slowly open and, with the revolver held out in front of him, took two quick bouncing steps inside. He was in the kitchen, apparently alone. He straightened up.

"Anybody here?"

There was a doorway across the room. He approached it slowly, then suddenly swung himself through it. It was a living room, dank and sparsely furnished. He went through a doorway to a bedroom, a bathroom, a smaller bedroom. No one was there. He returned to the kitchen and reholstered his gun. The ceiling light was on and by the window next to the door were two wooden chairs and a small round table, set for breakfast. On the counter next to the stove, the light of the coffee maker glowed red. He went over to turn it off and saw that the coffee in the pot was now a dark brown sludge. He closed the kitchen door against the dampness of the wind and went back to his car.

"Beakey, you got a make on that plate?"

"Yeah. Lakey, Catherine, Twenty-one High Meadow Lane, Devon, Connecticut."

"OK, do me a favor. Find Enfield and send him out here. Pilgrim's Trace. He'll see the car. We got a strange one."

Devon, Connecticut
Afternoon

When Cahoon's call came in early that afternoon, Frank Simco had just finished arranging to have other members of the department fill in for Catherine the next day, and, if necessary, for the rest of the week. It had occurred to him that a longer-term solution might be necessary, but he'd pushed that thought out of his mind.

In some ways, it was reassuring to hear that Cahoon hadn't found Catherine at the cottage. She wasn't the sort of person who would simply fail to come to work—unless, of course, something well beyond her control had happened, an illness or an injury. But much less reassuring—even reported in Cahoon's slow, laconic way—were the signs that Catherine had intended to return to the cottage: the coffee maker, the set table, the clothes in the closets, the open kitchen door, the car sitting in the driveway.

"Our guess is she's been gone four, maybe five days," said Cahoon. "It'd take that long for most of the coffee to evaporate, and the latest paper in the living room was Wednesday's."

Simco waited for Cahoon to continue, but he didn't. "And there aren't any signs where she might have gone?"

"Was she a walker, Mr. Simco?"

"A walker?"

"Did she take walks, up and down the beach, around town?"

"I'm sorry, Sergeant, I don't know. It isn't something we talked about."

"Reason I ask," said Cahoon, "if she was walking in the dunes or down by the rocks at the south end of the beach, she might have fallen, but if she's been out there all this time . . ." He didn't finish the thought. "And there's other possibilities we can't rule out yet, though we haven't had anything serious happen out here in maybe fifteen years."

"Serious?"

"Murder . . . kidnapping. She have enemies?"

"I don't know. I doubt it."

"Umh," said Cahoon noncommittally. "When did you see her last?"

"A week ago Friday, just before spring break."

"And she seemed OK?"

Simco thought for a moment, understanding the real question. "Yes, fine. Tired maybe, but fine."

"Sometimes they leave notes, sometimes they don't. Like I said, we don't want to upset anybody, but we have to check these things out. She have family?"

"Not around here. She's got a mother in a nursing home in Indiana, I think, and a niece or cousin somewhere out there too."

"Someone should call them, and it might be less alarming if you did."

"OK," said Simco, making a note of it.

"They might know where she is," Cahoon continued. "Could be there was a family emergency, but seeing that you haven't heard from them, I doubt it. Anyway, they need to be notified. We're checking the clinics, the hospital; I've got four guys searching the beach; I'm going into the village. And one more thing—we need a photograph, soon as possible."

"Certainly," said Simco. He added another item to the list of things he had to do, underlining it with more force than was necessary. He thanked Cahoon, told him he'd get back to him, then hung up.

He got up from his desk, went over to the window and looked out glumly at the College Common, which in the fading light of late afternoon was slowly filling in with shadow. It bothered him that his feelings of concern kept being shoved aside by a growing sense of irritation. He dismissed most of what Cahoon had said. The man was a policeman, trained, he supposed, to think in terms of the unpleasant and sensational: bad accidents, violence, suicide. But in reality, those things were rare events, and the scientist in Simco always favored the rational and likely over the exotic and bizarre.

He had to admit though that doing what she had done—going off somewhere, not showing up to teach, not telling anyone, creating just the sorts of problems that he wasn't very good at dealing with—was inconsiderate and was, for Catherine, completely out of character.

He couldn't honestly say he liked her, but he didn't dislike her, either. She made him feel awkward sometimes, just on the edge of foolish, by the way she looked at him with that air of detached bemusement. And she could be difficult. He thought of her at meetings, sitting there, saying very little, listening, and how later one of those inevitable notes in her blocky printing would show up on his desk saying: "We tried that before, eight years ago. Didn't work. Thought you should know." Or, more than once: "What you said today, was that a suggestion or was that policy?" Yet he respected her judgment and, professionally speaking, no one was more reliable.

He went back and sat down at his desk and wondered whether he should call the college president and perhaps the dean of students. Instead he called his secretary on the intercom and asked her to fax a recent yearbook photo of Catherine to Cotchpinicut.

Then he went downstairs to Catherine's office to look for her mother's phone number.

Her door was unlocked. Simco stepped inside, turned on the light and looked around. It was a small room, simply furnished: an old oak desk with drawers on either side of the kneehole, a desk chair, a filing cabinet, a lumpy but comfortable-looking easy chair. On the walls were black-and-white photographs, an abstract oil painting, a large periodic table and a bulletin board that was bare except for pushpins. The bookshelves on either side of the room's single window were full, but uncluttered. Papers were in neat piles; textbooks, reference materials, manuals were aligned in soldierly fashion. On the windowsill was an arrangement of glass beakers of various sizes, some empty, some containing pebbles.

On Catherine's desk Simco saw that the blotter was unmarked and the top was clear of all but the essentials. She had sharpened pencils in a blue coffee mug and pens in a small earthenware vase that looked like a student had made it in a beginning pottery class. There were a few books, her computer, a telephone, a Rolodex and two loose-leaf notebooks labeled "lecture notes."

Simco hesitated. He thought of offices and desks as private places, and nosing around in someone else's made him feel uneasy, almost guilty, but setting that aside, he sat down at the desk and flipped through the Rolodex. It was the first card in the *L*'s: Ruth Lakey, The Emma Singer Nursing Home, Bloomington, Indiana. He copied down the telephone number, turned out the light and left.

Cotchpinicut, Massachusetts
Late afternoon

"Yep, that's her." Priscilla Nickerson, the owner of the Cotchpinicut Variety, squinted at the photograph on the counter. "Not a good likeness, though. In season—which was generally when she was here—she'd come in most every morning, early, before eight, always for a *New York Times*. Except Sunday, when she'd get here about noon because we can't get the *Times* together before eleven."

Billy Cahoon picked up the picture, folded it carefully and put it back in his shirt pocket. "And she was in last week?"

"Yep. I saw her at the beginning. Sunday, Monday, Tuesday and I think Wednesday, too. Didn't see her after that."

Cahoon walked around behind the counter and poured himself a cup of coffee from the old blue pot on the hot plate. "Did you know anything about her? Where she's from? What she does around here?"

Priscilla Nickerson rolled her eyes to the ceiling the way his mother always did when he tried her patience. "Billy Cahoon, you've lived here thirty years and how many summer people do you know? Maybe the Pierces, but they've been coming here since your father was a boy. I didn't know a thing about her. She'd say 'Good morning' or remark about the weather. Never more than that."

"And she was always alone?"

"Oh, I suppose. I don't know." Priscilla scratched the side of her neck. "I can't swear to it, but I can't recall her with anybody."

Cahoon went over to the sink and poured out what remained of the coffee. He rinsed the mug and set it upside down on the counter. "Prissy, you ever notice how she got here? She drive? Bike?"

"Maybe she drove over, but I never saw her car—but then it's hard to see out over all that stuff in the windows. I figured she walked, because in the warm weather, sometimes, she'd be carrying her shoes and would put them on inside the store. Now why would you walk barefoot from the car to the store?"

"Don't know," said Cahoon. "Seems to me you wouldn't."

"Well, she'd probably been walking on the beach. Where'd she live? Pilgrim's Trace? Sure, you go along the beach for about half a mile, then cut over onto Seaview. In season, a lot of folks this side of the highway do it."

"And last week, is that the way she came?"

"Good Lord, Billy, now how would I know that? She wasn't carrying her shoes, if that's what you mean."

Cahoon shrugged and plunked some coins down on the counter. "Thanks for the coffee—and call me if you think of anything."

Priscilla Nickerson snorted. "Think of anything? What's there to think about out here at the end of March except taxes due, and tourists not coming back until May? Go on now and take this." She grabbed his sleeve and handed him back a quarter. "Wonder when you'll ever learn to count."

Devon, Connecticut
Late afternoon

When Frank Simco called the Emma Singer Nursing Home, he was put on hold twice, the second time long enough to finish "Falling Leaves" and to be well into "Sweet Violets" before, mercifully, the director, Elizabeth Singer, was back on the line.

"Sorry to make you wait, Mr. Simco. We're a little shorthanded here today. I have Ruth Lakey's folder in front of me now. And, as I said, Mrs. Lakey has been so ill—very disoriented for quite some time—that I'm afraid she can't help you at all. But I may be able to, if I can just find the list. Excuse me a minute."

Simco waited, heard her shuffling papers.

"Yes. Here it is. For financial reasons and for possible emergencies we have a record of her relatives. There's her daughter, Catherine; her granddaughter, Nancy Mulholland, who lives here in Bloomington." She gave the phone number. "And her son, Stephen Lakey."

Stephen Lakey puzzled Simco. He'd never heard Catherine mention a brother. He asked for his address and number.

"Washington, D.C." She paused. "That's the only address we have. No phone. Sorry."

After thanking her, Simco hung up, tore off the note that had Nancy Mulholland's number on it and went downstairs to Catherine's office to look through the *L* section of the Rolodex again, a card at a time. There was no card for Stephen Lakey.

He dialed Nancy Mulholland's number. No answer. On the chance he had misdialed, he placed the call again, but again no one answered. Wearily he put the receiver down and, looking up from the desk and out to the corridor, he became aware that he was the only one left in the chemistry wing. The sun had set, the building was silent, and apart from the pool of light cast by the desk lamp, the room was dark. He turned off the light and went back up the stairs to his office. He put on his rumpled raincoat, then went over to his desk and picked up his appointment calendar. He had missed three meetings, canceled two others and there was already a stack of course-change forms in the basket on his desk. He shook his head and stuffed a handful of them into his briefcase and went down the quiet corridor to the front door. He started toward his car, then decided he'd walk home instead. It wasn't far and the walk, he thought, would do him some good.

The sky had cleared and it was chilly—a reminder that spring always struggled into the Devon valley and sometimes didn't arrive until mid-April. Overhead, a nearly full moon caused Simco's shadow to skitter along the sidewalk in front of him. He held his raincoat closed against the cold and wished that there was some way for him to begin the day again, quietly, normally this time, with everyone exactly where they ought to be.

D A Y   S I X

MARCH—1987						
S	M	T	W	T	F	S
1	2	3	4	5	6	7
8	9	10	11	12	13	14
15	16	17	18	19	20	21
22	23	24	25	<u>26</u>	27	28
29	30	(31)				

D A Y   S I X

Bloomington, Indiana
Morning

In her dream, Nancy Mulholland saw herself sitting in a restaurant with a man whose face she could not see. He was asking her something, but she couldn't make out the words because of the noisy chirupping of the birds overhead. "Why are there birds in a restaurant?" she wondered, slowly coming out of sleep. "Why . . . "

She opened her eyes and realized that the birds were the ringing of the bedside telephone. She rolled over and looked at the clock: 7:05. Only Michael would call so early in the morning.

"Hello," she said, not trying to hide the fact that she was still more asleep than awake.

"Hello," said a voice that wasn't Michael's. "Is this Nancy Mulholland?"

"Yes." She cleared her throat and propped herself up on one elbow.

"This is Frank Simco from Stonington College in Connecticut. I work with your aunt, Catherine Lakey."

"Yes?"

"We're having a bit of a problem here and wondered if you might know where she is?"

"Where she is? Who?"

"Your aunt."

"In Connecticut, isn't she? Or are you still on break? The Cape. I don't understand."

Simco told himself to be patient. "I'm sorry to call so early, Miss Mulholland. I tried to reach you yesterday, but there wasn't any answer."

"You called yesterday?" Nancy was trying very hard to be awake. "About Catherine? I was away, on business—didn't get in until late last night. But, sorry, go on."

"Monday—yesterday—she didn't come to work. We checked her house here, then we thought that maybe she was still at her place on the Cape. We checked there—actually, we had the police check there—but no luck. Her car was there."

"Her car? But where was she?"

"We don't know. We thought that maybe you could help us. Perhaps she said something to you about plans, possibly a trip she forgot to tell us about."

"A trip?" Nancy was fully awake now, but she was still having trouble grasping the conversation. "Mr. Simpson?"

"Simco."

"Simco. Sorry. Could you hold the line a minute?"

She went into the bathroom and splashed some water on her face, then walked quickly to the kitchen and riffled through some papers on the small corner table that she used as a desk. She found a light blue envelope and brought it back with her to the bedroom.

"I got a letter from Catherine at the end of last month—February 24. Let's see." She scanned the letter rapidly. "No. Here: *in only three weeks' time, this dreary term will end and I'm off to Cotchpinicut for a bit of rest and relaxation. It's a faint hope, but by the time I return, maybe spring will have arrived.*' I think that's all." She turned the page over and scanned it quickly. "No trip. Nothing."

"I see," said Simco. He paused for a moment. "Miss Mulholland, has your aunt ever done anything like this before—gone off without telling anyone?"

"Catherine? Not that I know of. Never. It's hard to imagine."

Nancy paused, searching for a familiar handhold that would snap things into focus so that all of this made sense. "She's not at the Cape?"

"No, not at her house anyway. The police checked everything pretty carefully. She was there until last Wednesday or Thursday—the woman who runs a local store remembers seeing her Wednesday—but then nothing."

"And nobody at the college knows anything?"

"Nobody."

"What do the police say?"

"Not very much. They don't have much to go on. They're talking to people in town, checking out the places where she'd been seen. They'll call if they find anything."

"I see," said Nancy, not seeing at all.

Simco heard her bewilderment and felt he should say something solicitous, reassuring, but he wasn't good at that and usually ended up sounding unctuous or insincere. "Try not to worry," he said, and was relieved when she made no reply. "I almost forgot," he went on, "someone should call her brother. I don't have his number."

"Brother?" Nancy said. "Whose brother?"

"Catherine's," said Simco. "Stephen Lakey. Maybe it would be better if you called him."

"Stephen Lakey? Mr. Simco, Catherine doesn't have a brother."

Cotchpinicut, Massachusetts
Afternoon

Two policemen stood on the beach below the dunes, the fur-lined collars of their heavy nylon windbreakers pulled up against the raw March wind. One of them, the taller of the two, turning toward the dunes, made a sweeping gesture with his arm, then watched as the other trudged slowly through the soft sand of the upper beach to a twisting pathway that vanished into the undulating ridges.

The taller one, who was alone now on the beach, began to walk south, trying to stay on the wet, hard-packed strip of sand where the outwash of the surf ran up, paused, then disappeared, as if absorbed by a gigantic sponge. Every hundred yards or so, he stopped and scanned the water with binoculars, then wiped the lenses with a handkerchief and continued down the beach.

When he had gone about a half a mile, he suddenly stopped, looked down in front of him, kicked tentatively at the sand, then dropped to one knee and began to dig. After two or three scoops, he pulled a black and sand-caked something from the beach, looked at it closely, then carried it down to the water's edge. A large wave broke and sent a foamy sheet of ocean up to meet him. He bent down and swirled the object rapidly through the water, then straightened up and examined what he had: it had been badly discolored and some straps had pulled loose from the sole, but it was clearly the sandal of a woman.

MARCH—1987						
S	M	T	W	T	F	S
1	2	3	4	5	6	7
8	9	10	11	12	13	14
15	16	17	18	19	20	21
22	23	24	25	_26_	27	28
29	30	31				

DAY SEVEN

APRIL—1987						
S	M	T	W	T	F	S
			(1)	2	3	4
5	6	7	8	9	10	11
12	13	14	15	16	17	18
19	20	21	22	23	24	25
26	27	28	29	30		

DAY SEVEN

Boston, Massachusetts
Morning

Frank Simco felt a little foolish, standing at the gate, holding a small Stonington pennant over his head, absorbing the curious glances of arriving passengers. A thin woman, barely five feet tall, with savagely bleached blond hair came up to him and smiled. "Ida Josephson," she said, "Stonington, class of '39. A wonderful place. Haven't been back in years. Of course, things must be so different now."

"Oh, I don't know," said Simco, nodding to her politely, then scanning again the line of people moving past them toward the main terminal. Along the concourse, a woman who looked to be in her late twenties or early thirties was approaching, moving through a fresh surge of disembarking passengers with an energy that drew attention to her. She was slender, wore tailored jeans and a bulky seaman's jacket, and as she glided closer on long-legged, moccasined strides, a small duffel bag, slung from one shoulder, bounced at her side. She stopped behind Ida Josephson and looked questioningly at Simco with wide-set eyes that were green? gray? hazel? It was hard to say. Her hair, a deep, straight, shiny auburn, fell gently over one shoulder as she tilted her head to one side and gave him a faint smile.

"Miss Mulholland?" asked Simco.

Ida Josephson chuckled and shook her head. "I don't suppose that Miss Brainerd is still there," she said. "We used to call her bird-legs."

Simco tried to edge his way around the older lady. "No, I don't think so," he said. He smiled apologetically. "Could you excuse me? I'm meeting someone."

Ida Josephson seemed not to hear him. "It was a wonderful place," she said, speaking to no one in particular, and sidled off into the line that was heading for the baggage area.

Frank Simco held out his hand to Nancy Mulholland and introduced himself.

"Thanks for meeting me," she said, shaking his hand. "You've gone to a lot of trouble, driving here from Connecticut."

"It's the least I could do."

"Anything new?"

He shook his head. "Not really. I talked to the police this morning before I left. I'll fill you in on the ride down." He guided her away from the congestion of the arrival area. "You have bags?"

She held up her duffel. "Just this."

"Good," he said. "We've got to be in Cotchpinicut in two hours."

Dodging through the heavy tunnel and expressway traffic, Simco retraced the events of the previous two days. He had checked with people at the college—colleagues, students, staff, anyone who had had any sort of contact with Catherine—and no one could recall anything that might shed light on what had happened. The police had put out an all-points bulletin and had combed the beach, the nearby woods and the entire village of Cotchpinicut, but they had nothing new to report. Nancy listened quietly, looking straight ahead, following the road. As they passed the outskirts of the city, she curled her left leg underneath her and leaned back against the door.

"I just don't understand this," said Nancy. She sighed. "I

checked with the police too—after you called. Sorry I was so groggy then, but being awake hasn't done me much good. Everything seems worse." She turned to look out the window, biting her lower lip.

"I've racked my brain to figure this out," Nancy continued. "No good answers," her voice faded into her jacket as her head dropped. "It's a nightmare, really." She felt tears in her eyes and, looking out the window again, tried to concentrate on the passing countryside.

"Thanks for driving me to Cotchpinicut," she said, finally. "There was so much to do yesterday. This helps. I arranged to take some time off from work and called the one person I could think of who might know Catherine's whereabouts—left a message on his answering machine. He's Richard Weiss, a good friend of hers. I also went to the nursing home."

"About Stephen Lakey?" asked Simco.

"Yes, and I still can't figure it out. I . . ." She paused. "Would you mind if I smoked?"

Simco was startled. He didn't know anyone who smoked anymore. And he did mind. Even when he had smoked heavily, years ago, he had never smoked in the car. He rolled down his window. "Not at all," he said.

She pushed in the lighter. "I know Catherine doesn't have a brother because I know damn well that *I* don't have an uncle. There was only the two of them—the Lakey sisters: Catherine and my mother, who was six years older. My mother died ten years ago." Nancy lit her cigarette and the car filled with a blue haze. She rolled her window down and threw the cigarette out. Papers lying loose on the backseat swirled toward the roof. Quickly, she cranked the window up. "Sorry." Nancy unbuckled her seat belt and started to crawl into the back.

"Please don't bother," said Simco. "They're fine. Nothing important."

"Really?"

"Believe me. Just a lot of stuff that will get filed away and never looked at again. But continue. You said you went to the nursing home."

"Yes. After you called I went there and met with the director. She had the records. Grandma Ruth has been there seven years, since '80. She's gotten steadily worse. Doesn't recognize me anymore. Gets confused. Thinks Catherine is my mother, that sort of thing . . . Anyway, she doesn't have many visitors. Just Catherine and me or sometimes someone from the Unitarian Church—she used to be the organist there. But, about a month ago—" Nancy looked through her bag and brought out a piece of paper "—February 16, a man showed up and said he was Stephen Lakey, her son."

"He'd never been there before?"

"Never."

"And didn't someone there find that odd?" asked Simco. "An elderly woman in a rest home for seven years, very sick, and then, out of the blue, a son that no one's ever heard of or even mentioned just walks in the door?"

"They did find it odd, and they did just what I would have done. They called Catherine."

"And . . . ?"

"She wasn't at home, so they called the college. She was at a conference, in St. Louis. Next they called me. But I wasn't home either. I work in admissions at Indiana University and do a lot of traveling."

"So what did they do?"

"They watched him. He came around every day for three days. He stayed about a half hour on each visit, just sat in the room, said nothing—and that's odd."

"What's odd about it?"

"Have you ever spent any time with someone who's like that?"

Simco thought for a moment. "No, I don't think I have."

"Well, you do something—go over to the bed and squeeze a hand—and you say something. Sometimes you even try to carry on a conversation as if things were normal, and if you don't talk, you putter—fix flowers, straighten a sheet—or you sit by the bed, close enough so that you're really there. Touching distance."

"But Stephen Lakey just sat in a chair?"

"Exactly. By the window. No greeting, no touching, no puttering, no talking."

"But maybe he did some of those things in private."

"No, the door was open and the nurses watched—discreetly—but they kept tabs on him, through the door and on the room monitor. They told me he sometimes read a magazine—leafed through it. One nurse said he looked as if he were in Midas Muffler waiting for his car to be done."

"Did he say anything to the staff, other than identifying himself?"

Nancy looked down at the piece of paper, then turned it over. "Only on the last day he was there. When he came out of her room, he stopped by the nurses' station. He said that he had to leave, but he was glad that his mother was in such good hands. Then he said, 'When you talk to my sister, please tell her that I was here.' When the nurse asked him for an address or phone number where he could be reached in an emergency, he said that he moved around too much for that, but that he always knew how to get in touch with Catherine."

"Did they ever talk to Catherine about this?"

"Absolutely. She called as soon as she got back to Devon."

"And?"

"Elizabeth Singer, the director, talked to her. She told her exactly what this Stephen Lakey had said."

"And what did Catherine say?"

"She didn't say a thing, at first. And then she said, 'Would you mind not saying anything about this to Miss Mulholland?' "

Cotchpinicut, Massachusetts
Morning

"*Could* have? *Might* have? Jeez, Ben, I thought you were an expert." Billy Cahoon picked the blackened sandal off his desk, holding it between thumb and forefinger. He examined it for a minute or two, then glanced back at Ben Costa, the commander

of the North Cotchpinicut Coast Guard Station, who was standing at the wall behind Beakey's desk, studying a large map of
Cotchpinicut.

"Expert's got nothing to do with it," said Costa without turning around. "All I know and all you know is that you found it
here." He ran his finger down along the map. "Yeah, right off the
beach at the end of Seaview."

"Now, generally, *generally*, the close-in current's gonna go
north to south," Costa moved his hand upward along the coast-
line on the map, then drew it slowly down. "So the thing probably went in somewhere up here and drifted down."

"Pilgrim's Trace?"

"Pilgrim's Trace, North Cotch, maybe Provincetown. Depends on winds, tides, how long it was in the water."

Cahoon got up and went over to the map and nudged Costa's
shoulder with the sandal.

"You said it was in the water a week."

"Weeks," said Costa. "As opposed to months or days." He
turned toward Cahoon, took the sandal and held it up so Billy
could see.

"The heel's beginning to come apart—but not completely.
And the stitching's still OK." He turned the sandal over. "And
look at the buckle. It's cheap, not solid brass, and there's some cor-
rosion. Put this in saltwater for a month and the buckle's gone."

Cahoon went back to his desk. "So if Catherine Lakey went
into the water about a week ago, off Pilgrim's Trace and she lost
her shoe, this could be it?"

"Could be," said Costa, "but you don't even know the size is
right."

"It's right. Guy down at Leatherworkers said it's probably a
seven—maybe a six and a half—and I'll betcha a six-pack when I
get out there this afternoon, that's her size."

Cahoon picked up the phone and dialed.

"Prissy? Billy Cahoon. Look, when this Lakey woman came
into the store last week—remember? Yeah, well, remember you
said that she wasn't carrying her shoes? Right. Did you notice what
she was wearing on her feet?" Cahoon picked up the sandal and

began to tap it gently against his forehead. "OK," he said. "That's probably what I thought. Thanks, Priss. Sure. See ya."

He put the phone down and looked over at Costa.

"Dammit all, she didn't notice."

Cotchpinicut, Massachusetts
Afternoon

"Sandals?" said Nancy quietly, almost to herself. She was sitting in the front seat of Billy Cahoon's cruiser on the way out to the cottage on Pilgrim's Trace. She turned the sandal over in her hands, fingering the straps, her gaze drifting up, then out the right-hand window. "I don't think . . . No, I'm sure." Nancy looked down at the sandal in her hands. "I've never seen Catherine wear sandals, but we weren't together very often in sandal weather—not in Bloomington."

Cahoon looked into the rearview mirror. "How about you, Mr. Simco?"

"Me? I don't recall, but I don't really notice that sort of thing. Some of our professors wear sandals year round—with heavy socks when it's cold out. In the winter, it's sort of a look, but not Catherine's style. She's more buttoned up—more traditional. But I don't know—she may have."

"Either of you ever visit her out here?"

Simco was startled by the question. "Well, actually no, I didn't. I have a place in Maine—completely the other direction." In the eight years that he had known Catherine Lakey, he couldn't recall a single, purely social occasion with her. It had never occurred to him that she would invite him to the Cape.

"We'd talk about it every summer," said Nancy, "and then something would come up and we'd put it off another year."

Cahoon stopped the car in the parking area at the rear of the cottage. He took a small manila envelope from his shirt pocket, opened it and took out a key. "We locked up after we left—keys were hanging by the kitchen door."

They got out of the car and went to the back door. On the way, Simco stopped beside the white Escort and peered in the window. "It's hers," he said, and Cahoon nodded.

Cahoon unlocked the door and held it open for Nancy and Simco, then followed them into the small living room. He put his hands on his hips and looked around. "This is the way we found it," he said. He looked at Nancy, then at Simco. "Take all the time you want." He pointed at a doorway on the far side of the room. "Back there's two bedrooms, a bathroom." He turned and gestured with his head. "And in there's the kitchen."

Nancy turned slowly around, taking everything in. Cahoon took a few steps toward the bedroom doorway. "Before you start," he said, "Miss Mulholland, could you look at a few things in the closet here?"

Nancy followed him into the hallway and then into a small bedroom. An iron bed, painted white and neatly made, stood against the near wall, facing a row of windows which framed a sweeping view of dunes, and, between them, a glimpse of sea. On a white wicker bedside table there was an old-fashioned wind-up alarm clock—now stopped—and a book of crossword puzzles. Underneath the windows was an old pine bureau—old, but not antique—in need of refinishing.

Cahoon crossed to a door and opened it to reveal a shallow closet. "What I need to know," he told Nancy, "is whether or not the stuff in here belongs to your aunt. Tell me if you see anything that's hers, or if you see anything that isn't. We're pretty sure that she was staying here when she disappeared, but we don't know if she was staying here alone." Cahoon bent over, picked up a pair of brown loafers and took them over to the window. He turned them over, then peered inside. Size seven on the nose, he thought.

Nancy ran her hand along the short row of clothes on hangers. Two white blouses, a plain blue dress, a pair of khaki pants, a green cardigan sweater. She shook her head. "I can't tell," she said. "This dress"—she took the blue dress out of the closet and held it up in the light—"it looks familiar—it's certainly the kind of thing she'd wear, but I don't know." She turned to put the dress back in the closet and stopped.

"That's hers, I know that." She reached up to a small shelf above the clothes and removed a small, green vinyl suitcase. "Catherine prided herself on how light she traveled and whenever she came to Bloomington, this is all she brought. Carry-on. She hated waiting for bags."

"OK," said Cahoon. "That's something." He walked around the bed to the doorway, then stopped. He seemed embarrassed. "You said you last talked with your aunt about a month ago?"

"Mid-February. Valentine's Day."

"And she seemed OK?"

"Fine," said Nancy, and she shook her head. "No, I've thought of that—suicide. I asked Mr. Simco about her at school—if there was anything unusual the past few weeks. Nothing. She was tired, but that's the time of year. You don't kill yourself because you're tired."

"No, I guess you don't," said Cahoon, dropping the subject. "I'll be in the kitchen, if you need me."

Nancy went over to the bureau and opened the top drawer. There was some underwear, some heavy woolen socks, and over on the right a white sweatshirt with INDIANA in red block letters embroidered on the front. She took it from the drawer, went to the mirror and held it up in front of her. She remembered giving it to Catherine on the spur of the moment, in December, on Catherine's last night in Bloomington, two or three years ago. She had bought it for her father, who'd said he'd fly in from Los Angeles to see her, but, like so many times before, he'd called at the last minute . . . had to change plans . . . couldn't make it. Ever since he'd walked out on her mother years ago, he'd been like that, never understanding the disappointment, thinking that new promises, a call at Christmas, a birthday card would make things right.

She'd said to hell with him and had rewrapped the sweatshirt, enclosing a card: "To Cat—for those cold Connecticut winters. Love, Nannie." When Catherine had torn off the tissue, she'd looked at Nancy in surprise and had said in that cautious, puzzled way of hers, "Why thank you, Nannie, but what on earth am I going to do with a basketball uniform?" Basketball uniform! Only Catherine . . . Nancy began to laugh, shrilly, sucking in her breath. She buried her face in the sweatshirt and let herself cry.

In the kitchen, Cahoon sat at the table trying to compose his report of the investigation. He didn't hear Simco enter the room and was startled when Simco said, "Sergeant?" just above his shoulder. He looked up. Simco motioned toward the kitchen door, then went over and opened it. Cahoon followed him outside. They walked down the path to the edge of the dune and looked out at the ocean, gentle today, small waves crumping against the beach.

"I need to know what you really think," said Simco.

Cahoon shrugged. "Hard to say. Don't know much about the woman. Don't have much to go on."

"How about the sandal?"

"It's something, not conclusive." He turned to Simco, studied him a moment. Simco met Cahoon's gaze head-on and waited. "But often," Cahoon continued, "we don't get conclusive. We guess the best we can. And what we think boils down to that."

"And?" said Simco.

"I think she's gone for good. Don't know what happened. Maybe some creep found her walking alone, maybe she had something happen in her life that nobody knows about and she just walked into the sea. But I do know that when someone's missing, if they're gonna get found, it's generally in a day or two. She's been gone a week. That's too long."

"OK," said Simco. "Two days ago I wouldn't have agreed with you, but now I do." He turned and walked back to the cottage.

Simco found Nancy in the living room, sitting on the sofa. He noticed that her eyes were red, that along one cheek there was a faint gray streak of eye shadow. "Find anything?" he asked.

She shook her head. "Not much. You?"

"Books," he said. "One on oil painting, some chemistry texts,

mysteries." He tried to think of something else to say. "It's difficult," he began, his voice trailing off.

"Yes," said Nancy, looking down at her hands folded in her
lap. When she didn't raise her head or say anything else, he cleared
his throat.

"I don't know about you, but I could do with something to
eat!" Simco winced. He sounded like his father at the lake, those
many summers ago, after long days of rain, handing him the damp
towel, telling him not to mind the weather, that they were going
for an early morning swim.

"Maybe a cup of tea," said Nancy, starting to rise from the
sofa.

"Stay put," said Simco. "I'll see what's in the kitchen, or if
Sergeant Cahoon is done, we can go into town."

"No," said Nancy, "Let me. I need to get up and do something." She left the room, and Simco, debating whether to follow
her, took a few steps toward the kitchen, then decided he should
stay where he was. He found an old *National Geographic* and, with
a sigh, sat down with it.

When Nancy walked into the kitchen, Cahoon was still at the table
filling out his report. He put down his pen and watched her as she
crossed the room to the stove where she put water on to boil. In
a canister, she found tea bags and in the bread drawer an English
muffin, which she divided and put in the toaster.

"Want to split an English muffin?" she called through the
doorway.

"That's fine," said Simco from the living room.

Nancy turned to the table, saw the single place setting in front
of one of the chairs and looked at Cahoon.

"She left it that way," he said. "We put some stuff in the refrigerator." Nancy nodded. Her gaze moved from Cahoon, back
to the table, to the silverware, the blue mug, the cloth napkin that
had been folded into a triangle. Solemnly she surveyed the room,
wall by wall, stopping when she came to a dark blue overcoat that
was hanging on a peg by the door.

"That's hers," she said softly.

"What?"

"The coat. By the door." Cahoon turned to see what she meant. When he looked back to Nancy she was at the sink, staring out the window, her back to him. Cahoon waited. Nancy was aware that he was watching her, but for a long moment couldn't say anything. "Nice view," she said, at last, her voice ragged.

Cahoon coughed, elaborately shuffled papers. Nancy turned on the cold water, and cupping some in her hand, took a drink and ran wet fingers across her forehead. The kettle began whistling. Cahoon got up, took it off the burner, then put a tea bag in the mug that was on the table. As he was pouring the boiling water, the muffin halves popped up, their edges singed black. Smoke wisped from the toaster. "Damn," said Nancy. She took them to the table and sat down. Cahoon handed her the mug.

She took a sip of tea, eyed the blackened muffins on the table top in front of her and shook her head. "Maybe if we put something on them," she said.

Cahoon went over to the refrigerator. "There's jam and margarine in here," he said, opening the refrigerator door, bending down to look inside. He pushed aside a carton of eggs and reached for the round plastic container and the white crock. "There's fruit here, too." He freed two fingers to pick up an apple. Using his hands, his fingers and forearms to carry everything, he turned and bumped the door with his hip. But as the door slammed shut, he began to bobble his armload. Nancy sprang to her feet, took the apple from him. Everything shifted. The plastic container slid; the jar slipped. Cahoon caught one, but his grab for the other missed. The jar fell to the floor and shattered. Both of them jumped back, Cahoon cursing.

As Cahoon stepped over the mess on the floor to put the margarine on the table, Nancy knelt down to begin picking up the larger pieces of glass. She stopped when she saw that the jam oozing over the white, opaque shards wasn't red, as she had expected, but orange. She daubed at it with a finger, tasted it, then quickly picked up the largest piece of the broken crock and turned it over in her hand. She saw the words "Est'd 1797," and below that, in bold black letters: "Dundee Orange Marmalade." She looked stunned. "My God," she murmured.

"Cut yourself?" asked Cahoon, moving swiftly toward her, a look of concern on his face.

Nancy put a hand to the floor to brace herself. "No, fine. I'm just . . . just glad you didn't get hurt," she said, finishing her sentence in a rush. She stood up and handed Cahoon the piece of glass she'd picked up. "Was this the jar you found on the table?"

"Yeah," he said, a snort of a laugh escaping from him. "What's left of it. Jeez. Don't poke around in that any more. I'll get a mop, if I can find one."

Nancy watched Cahoon go to a closet and disappear into its dark interior. She heard him groping for the string that hung from the overhead light, saw that Frank Simco had entered the room. She motioned him to the sink, where she sponged off her hands and rinsed them under a flow of cold water.

"I've changed my mind," she said to him, her voice just audible above the water. "I'm going to stay, at least tonight."

"What?" he said. "What for?"

Nancy turned around, looked across the room to the clatter that was coming from the open closet. Cahoon was bent over, muttering to himself, reaching deeper into the closet, a vacuum cleaner hose draped over his shoulder.

Nancy turned off the water. She squeezed out the sponge, began wiping the counter. Simco watched her, puzzled. "I'd like to look around some more. Get some of her things in order, just in case," she said, her voice low, but conversational.

"How will you get to Devon?"

"Her car's here. I don't think she'd mind."

"Suit yourself," said Simco. There was weariness in his voice and a slight edge. One minute Nancy Mulholland needed consoling and the next she was completely in control. He didn't like being off balance or seeing that all his gestures of the day—meeting her at the airport, driving her to Cotchpinicut—had added up to nothing except a three-hour drive back to Devon, alone. He started to leave the kitchen, but Nancy caught him by the wrist.

"You've been very kind," she said. "The least I can do is buy you dinner before you go." Nancy looked back over her shoulder. Cahoon had emerged from the closet, a mop in hand. "Sergeant," she said, "is there a restaurant in town you'd recommend?"

Cotchpinicut, Massachusetts
Evening

At the Ebb Tide, Cotchpinicut's only year-round restaurant, Nancy Mulholland and Frank Simco sat opposite each other in the semicircle of a dimly lit booth. She watched him inch the menu closer to a small glass lantern on the table, trying to find enough light to read by, his forehead wrinkled in concentration.

"What looks good?" she said, amused by his earnestness.

"Fish, I suppose. Maybe swordfish." Simco turned the menu over, was squinting at it when the waiter appeared. He took their orders and Nancy asked for a bottle of wine. After he'd left, she opened a pack of cigarettes, removed one and leaned toward the candle to light it, then stopped and looked up at Simco. "Mind?" He made a gesture with his hand which she took to mean he didn't. She lit the cigarette, took a puff, then exhaled the smoke through the side of her mouth, trying to direct it away from him. "Thanks for coming to dinner. I know you must have other things to do."

Simco looked down at the table, thinking that, yes, he certainly did, but torn between wanting to be tactful and not wanting to lie, he only mumbled, "Well . . . ," taking refuge in the blandness of the word.

The waiter returned with the bottle of wine and filled their glasses. Nancy took a sip and then crushed out her cigarette. She wasn't at all sure how to tell him what she wanted to say, but her instincts told her that, with Frank Simco, directness was probably the best approach.

"Whatever's happened to Catherine, she's made it happen to herself," she said, finally, keeping her voice even, calm. She stopped, watched him, giving him time to say something. Simco slowly looked up and studied her. "All right," he said, then folded his arms in front of him and waited for her to continue. His reaction was unsettling. She had expected something more emphatic—an exclamation, or at least some questions that would carry the conversation forward. She lowered her gaze to the table, taking a moment to consider how she should continue.

"This afternoon," she began again, "in the kitchen, the jar that broke. It was marmalade, the same one that the police found on the table." She looked up at Simco. He still said nothing, but she could tell by the way he was looking at her that he was interested.

"Catherine hated marmalade." Nancy paused. "But it's more than that. Some years ago—I'm not sure how it came up—I think Catherine and I were talking about little surprises and disappointments we'd had. Catherine told me about the first time she tasted marmalade—how she had been sure it was going to be wonderful because marmalade looks so delicious—has that beautiful color—she called it sunshine orange. But when she tasted it, it was awful—gritty and much too sweet, not at all what she'd expected." Nancy smiled, remembering the look on her aunt's face. "Anyway, marmalade became a sort of code word. She used it to describe anything that was different from what you'd expect."

The waiter reappeared, balancing plates and a basket of bread. Nancy stopped talking and kept her eyes on Simco as the food was served. He took a piece of bread, tore it in half, buttered both halves carefully and bit into one. He chewed slowly, then wiped his mouth with the corner of his napkin. The waiter asked if everything was all right. Simco nodded.

"Do you see what I'm getting at?" Nancy asked, when the waiter had left.

"I don't know. But I think you're asking why she'd put marmalade on the table if she didn't like it."

Nancy leaned forward and rested her elbows on the table. "No," she said. "I think I know why."

Simco gave her a faint smile. "Please explain."

"I'm Catherine," said Nancy, "and I'm going to disappear, and—"

"Why?" interrupted Simco.

"No," said Nancy. "Let me continue."

Simco nodded. "All right."

"I'm going to disappear and I want to make it look as though something's happened to me. So I set the table, put on the coffee maker, leave the kitchen door open—everything to suggest I'll be right back." Nancy stopped to take a sip of wine. "But before I go, I want to leave a message for my niece, telling her I'm OK— or if not OK, that I haven't been murdered or gone off and killed myself. That message has got to be clear and, just as important, it's got to be only for my niece, no one else. And so I leave a jar of marmalade."

"Interesting," said Simco. He looked at her, then picked up the buttered half-slice of bread and pushed it absently around his plate. He said nothing.

"What's the matter?" asked Nancy.

"The matter?"

"Is there something wrong with what I've said?"

"Not wrong," said Simco. "Could I go back to my original question?"

"Which was?"

"Why does Catherine want to disappear? She's a perfectly normal, ordinary, responsible chemistry professor in a small New England college. As far as I know, she's happy, she's not in any trouble, none of the things that would make someone do something like this, disappear and leave her classes, her friends, relatives, without a word."

"I can't answer that, but she didn't leave without a word. She left the marmalade." Nancy looked at Simco carefully. "How well did you know her?"

"Well enough. We've worked together for eight years."

"I mean personally. You said that, as far as you knew, she was a perfectly ordinary, happy woman."

"I don't know," said Simco. He remembered Cahoon's question that afternoon, about visiting Cotchpinicut. "Not terribly well, I suppose."

"I know her very well. She's my aunt, my friend, and for ten years she's been like a mother to me," said Nancy, "and I agree with you. I can't imagine why she'd want to do something like this, but she has."

Simco said nothing. Nancy, busying herself with her food, which had gone cold, could feel him looking at her, could sense that he wasn't satisfied—that he wanted to say something, but was too polite or too shy to say it. She put down her fork. "You're making me feel stupid."

"Stupid?"

"You don't agree with me about the marmalade, but you're not telling me why, like I've missed something terribly obvious that any schoolgirl could pick up. I give up. What is it?"

"I don't think you've missed anything," he said. "I've got another question, though. Why the marmalade? That's awfully subtle. And how could she have known that you'd come all the way to Cape Cod to find it? As it is, it was just the dumbest luck that Cahoon took it out of the refrigerator this afternoon. Why not a letter or a phone call?"

"I don't know exactly," said Nancy. "The thing about the marmalade is that it can be left out in the open and mean nothing to anyone but me. Catherine would be pretty sure that I'd be called. And she knows me. She knew I'd come to Cotchpinicut."

Simco smiled and slowly shook his head. "So convincing, but it's bad science."

"You're doing it again," said Nancy, her irritation showing.

"Miss Mulholland, I'm sorry. What I mean to say is that everything you say makes perfect sense only if you accept your basic premise, which is wildly improbable. If Catherine, as you say, has decided to make herself disappear, then everything follows. But neither of us can come up with any sort of plausible reason why she'd do it."

"Isn't the fact that she's disappeared wildly improbable?" said Nancy. "That's something that doesn't happen to most people, does it? What do you suppose the odds are?"

Simco sighed. "I'm not talking about chance or odds, that kind of improbability. I'm talking about something happening for no discernible reason. Making yourself disappear isn't a walk around the block, it's a big deal and I think Catherine or anyone would have to have some pretty powerful reasons for doing it." Simco leaned forward until his face was directly above the lantern. "Be honest, don't you find it odd that you and me, two people who have known her for years, don't have an inkling, not a hint, of what those reasons might be?"

Nancy looked at him for a long moment, then slowly nodded her head. "I do. But since your phone call yesterday, everything's been odd. Anyhow, I know she left the marmalade for me. Call it intuition if you like."

"Shouldn't you tell the police, then?"

"No," she said. "If Catherine had wanted the police to know, she'd have left a message they could read, and for whatever reason, she didn't want them to know and went out of her way to make sure they didn't. I have a feeling that she'd be very disappointed, maybe very angry, if I told the police anything . . ." Nancy's voice trailed off. Lowering her head, she stared at the napkin in her lap, smoothed it with an absent-minded stroke of her hand, then sat perfectly still. Suddenly she looked back across the table, directly at Simco. "Sergeant Cahoon thinks she's dead, doesn't he?"

Simco was surprised at the directness of her question. "Well," he said. "He doesn't think that she's . . . he thinks that it probably isn't a good sign . . . and the sandal, if it's hers, it isn't . . . "

"He thinks she's dead," said Nancy, matter-of-factly. "I don't blame him. This afternoon, I did too. She did a good job."

"I suppose." said Simco, steering away from an argument. "Maybe we should be getting back. I've got a three-hour drive to Devon and it's almost nine."

She opened her purse, fished around inside. "You go ahead. I'll get a cab."

He laughed. "In Cotchpinicut? I doubt it."

She found her wallet and the credit card she wanted. "What?" she said, looking up at him.

"You won't find a cab. I'll drive you back."

"Are you sure? It's late." Turning in her seat, she raised her hand and waved to catch the eye of the waiter. When he appeared with the check, Simco reached for his pocket.

"We'll split it," he said.

"You've done enough," said Nancy, studying the check, adding up the numbers in her head. "What's fifteen percent of thirty-eight?"

"Make it six," said Simco, "or at least let me."

Nancy shook her head and signed the slip.

"What will you do now, after tonight?" asked Simco.

"First I'm going to go through the cottage carefully, room by room. If she left one signal, she might have left another. I might not find anything, but I think I will. Then I'll go back to Devon, probably tomorrow, and look through her house and her office. If you don't mind, of course." She stood up from the table. "Ready?"

Simco took a last sip of wine and glanced up at her, surprised at how disappointed he was that the evening was ending. He got up and followed her through the dining room and out the front door, nodding at the waiter, who held the door open for them.

When they had gone, the waiter returned to the table, picked up the credit card slip and examined it carefully, holding it close to the lantern. He looked around the dining room, then folded the slip, put it in his pocket and walked out to the lobby. Standing at the front window, he watched the twin red dots of Simco's tail-lights turn left out of the parking lot and disappear around a curve in the road. He crossed the lobby to a phone booth, entered, took the credit slip from his pocket, and closed the door.

Cotchpinicut, Massachusetts
Night

There was very little conversation in the car as Simco drove slowly along the dark, deserted roads of Cotchpinicut, trying to remember the way that they had come. After only two wrong turns, he found the beach road, then Pilgrim's Trace. At the cottage, he parked his car alongside Catherine's and turned the engine off.

Nancy got out and walked around to the window on the driver's side. Simco rolled it down. "Thanks for everything," she said.

"You're welcome," he said, aware of the awkwardness he always felt when he was around attractive women.

"When I get to Devon . . . " Nancy laughed. "I don't know how to get to Devon. I don't even know the general direction."

Simco leaned across the front seat and opened the glove compartment. "Maybe I've got a map," he said, sorting through the credit slips, the repair receipts and other papers that were there. "Here," he said, then "no, that's Maine." He sat up. "I'll write out directions."

Simco got out of the car and followed Nancy up the walkway and into the cottage. He stood in the living room as she went around turning on lights, then disappeared into the kitchen.

"Found something you can write on," she called out. "Would you like some coffee?"

He followed her voice into the kitchen. She handed him a small pad and a pen. "Coffee would be fine," he said, sitting down at the table. He began to write out the directions, looking up from time to time, watching Nancy as she tried to figure out the logic of Catherine's storage scheme, opening and closing drawers, standing on her tiptoes, peering into cabinets.

"If you take milk, you're out of luck," she said, closing the refrigerator door.

"Black's fine." He tore the page of directions off the pad and put it on the table. "These are pretty simple," he said. "But just in case, I've put my home and office numbers at the bottom."

Nancy brought the coffee to the table, picked up the directions and studied them.

"You might want to stop and get a map," he said, looking up at her.

"These are fine." She put the paper back on the table, then looked around the room, turning slowly until she had completed a full turn. She walked over to the doorway to the living room, turned, and swept the kitchen once more with her eyes.

"What are you looking for?" he asked.

"I don't know," she said. "Another jar of marmalade, some

sign from Catherine that might tell me something more, like why she's gone or maybe where. My guess is that she wouldn't leave it at just the marmalade: that things aren't what they seem. I don't know."

"Does that make sense?" asked Simco. "If she wants to disappear, that means she doesn't want anyone to know where she is, doesn't it?"

"It might. It might not. If she wants me to know, there has to be something else, doesn't there? And I won't find it unless I look."

Simco got up from the table and went to the kitchen door. He peered through it out into the night. "And what if you do find something?" he said without turning around. "What if you find out where she is? What do you do about it?"

"I go to her."

Simco turned and looked at her. "Go to her? Maybe she doesn't want you to."

"Mr. Simco, are you married?"

For the second or third time that evening, a question of hers had swooped down at him out of nowhere, taking him completely by surprise. "Divorced," he said.

"Children?" she asked.

"No children."

"Brothers, sisters?"

"One of each. Why?"

"If this weren't Catherine, if it were your sister, and you knew or you discovered where she was, wouldn't you go to her?"

"I don't know. That would depend, I guess, on . . . " he paused. "What I would do, even in an extremely hypothetical situation, isn't the point."

"You're right. It isn't. I'm the one who has to decide and until I know more, this is an extremely hypothetical situation. But what was it you said earlier—that disappearing isn't a walk around the block. You're right. You don't do it because you're feeling happy and secure. I'm afraid Catherine's in trouble, and I'm going to find her."

She left Simco, walked out of the kitchen into the living room.

After a moment, he followed and stood watching as she again did her slow turn in the middle of the room. When she had gone halfway around, she stopped and went over to the bookcase. She bent down and ran her index finger along the spines of the books. "Did you touch any of these this afternoon?"

"Touch?" He didn't really know what she meant, but was beginning to feel guilty anyway.

"Take them out, move them around?" She was still studying the books.

"Just the one on oil painting. I looked through it, then put it back."

Nancy stood up and walked to the other side of the room. She put her hands on her hips and stared at the floor, concentrating. It was obvious to him that she was very much in her own world, one that he wasn't part of. He glanced at his watch. "I've got to get back," he said.

She looked up and gave him a blank stare, as though she couldn't remember why he was there. "That's right," she said. "It's a long drive."

He went to the living room door, the one that opened to the parking area. He put his hand on the knob and stopped. "Maybe you better try to start the car before I go. It's been sitting out there for a while."

"Good idea. I'll get the keys." She went into the kitchen. He waited, heard drawers opening and closing. "Did you see the keys this afternoon?" she shouted.

Simco went to the kitchen doorway. "Just the ones Cahoon had."

"Those were house keys," she said. "Where the hell would she put them?"

"Check the bedroom. I'll check the car. Out here, maybe you leave them in the ignition."

He went to the car, tried the door. It was locked. He peered through the side window. It was too dark to see much, but he decided that didn't matter. Catherine Lakey would never lock her keys inside her car. Back inside, he found Nancy waiting for him expectantly. "Nothing," he said.

She went over to an upholstered chair and threw herself into it. "Goddamn it all," she said with surprising vehemence. "What the hell do I do now?"

Simco said nothing, hoping that she would answer her own question. When she didn't, he sat down on the sofa across from her. "I'll have to drive you back to Devon," he said, tentatively.

She looked at him with a tired smile. "That's very nice of you, but—" she made a sweeping gesture with one arm—"I still have to go through the other rooms, and you need to . . . " She slapped the arm of the chair. "Shit," she said softly.

"I'll help you look around," said Simco. "We could stay here tonight and leave early in the morning."

Nancy hesitated, then shook her head. "That isn't fair. You've got things to do."

"Not at ten o'clock at night, I don't. If we leave early enough tomorrow, I can be in Devon for my first appointment. Anyway, without a car you're stranded out here."

Nancy stood up. "Thank you," she said softly. She looked around the room. "All right. I'll do the back of the house, the bedrooms and the bathroom. You do the little places—the kitchen drawers and cabinets, the closets."

"What am I looking for?"

"A note, a letter, anything in Catherine's handwriting." Nancy paused and thought. "Anything that's out of place. You know how organized she is. A screwdriver in the silver drawer—something like that."

"A screwdriver in the silver drawer," he repeated, and went into the kitchen.

Two hours later, both of them having gone through the entire cottage, they sat again in the living room. Nancy in the chair, fighting sleep; Simco on the sofa. Nancy yawned. "I'm surprised," she said. "At dinner, I would have bet you that I'd find something else in here."

"That's not what you said."

"Of course not. You didn't think much of the marmalade. I wasn't going to set myself up for 'I told you so.' " She leaned back and looked at him through half-closed eyes. "You still don't think much of the marmalade, do you? And you're afraid I've latched on to it to deny she's dead."

"I think," said Simco, once again startled by her directness, "that—understandably—it's difficult to face the possibility you may never see her again. And," he paused, wanting to choose his words carefully, "I think there might be other reasonable explanations for the marmalade."

"Such as?"

"I don't know. Tastes change. There was a time when I wouldn't touch artichokes. I like them now. Or perhaps she had a guest—or was expecting one and that's who the marmalade was for."

She got up and smiled at Simco. "Those are not reasonable explanations, and I will see her again. What time should we leave?"

"No later than six," said Simco, looking up at her.

"I'll set the alarm for five-thirty. You take the small bedroom, the one on the left. Good night, and again—thanks."

Lying on the too short, too narrow guest bed, staring at the ceiling, Simco wondered how long he had until five-thirty. His hand reached out and groped along the surface of the bedside table, found his watch and lifted it close to his face. Dimly glowing in the dark, it said 2:15.

He put it back on the table, rolled over on his side and finally felt sleep coming on, like a slowly rising tide. He thought of Nancy Mulholland in the other room and smiled to himself. Vague, disjointed memories of an old Doris Day movie were coalescing into the beginning of a dream: a wakeful, yearning Rock Hudson, tossing fitfully, only one thin door away from sweet and lovely Doris Day, asleep among an avalanche of pillows.

		MARCH—1987				
S	M	T	W	T	F	S
1	2	3	4	5	6	7
8	9	10	11	12	13	14
15	16	17	18	19	20	21
22	23	24	25	<u>26</u>	27	28
29	30	31				

DAY EIGHT

		APRIL—1987				
S	M	T	W	T	F	S
			1	(2)	3	4
5	6	7	8	9	10	11
12	13	14	15	16	17	18
19	20	21	22	23	24	25
26	27	28	29	30		

DAY EIGHT

THURSDAY, APRIL 2, 1987

Cotchpinicut/Devon
Morning

They drove along, not saying much, as the new day overtook them. Simco fiddled with the radio, settling, finally, on an all-news station from Boston which whined and crackled every time they went beneath an overpass. Nancy had wedged herself into the corner formed by seat and door and nodded off from time to time. There was no traffic.

In Rhode Island they found a truck stop and got coffee and greasy doughnuts at the take-out counter. Nancy bought a Providence paper. Back in the car, she riffled through it noisily. "Nothing here," she announced, and promptly fell asleep. At a little after nine, when they passed the sign Devon Welcomes You, Simco reached over and shook her awake.

"House or office?" said Simco.

"Whichever's best for you," said Nancy, yawning, stretching.

Simco looked at his watch. "Office then. I've got the president in fifteen minutes and then the goddamn press." He swung the car onto College Avenue, then in behind the Science Center, nosing it up to a sign that said Reserved for Dean.

*   *   *

Inside Catherine Lakey's office, Nancy walked around the room, noting what was on the walls, the shelves, the desk. Simco told her that the oil painting had been done by a student who had graduated the previous June. Not much of a chemistry student—not much of a painter, either, for that matter—but charming and energetic. She had been a favorite of Catherine's.

Nancy went over to the bookshelves and ran her hand along the bookbindings, noting titles. She rounded the room again, taking in the photographs, the periodic table, the empty bulletin board. "Neat as a pin," she said, touching the bare cork. "Even the pushpins are in lines." She ran her fingers over them, then paused. "Is this the way it always looks?"

Simco looked around. "More or less, though maybe this is a little sparse. Except for the other day, I've never been here unless Catherine was in, and she'd have papers on her desk, more stuff out. But most people clean up before vacation. She always did."

Nancy was listening, but as Simco spoke she continued walking around the office, running her hand over things—books, the chair, a wall peg—as if she were reading braille. At the computer she studied the numbers on a note stuck to the face of the screen.

"Could I use this?" she said, gesturing at the computer.

"Go right ahead. If you need anything, my extension is 56 and my secretary's name is Georgia Whitney. She knows more about this place and how it works than I do." He walked toward the office door. "And, if you want to go to Catherine's house, Georgia will drive you. The house key is on the molding over the back door." He saw that she was already seated at the desk, punching keys, glancing at the monitor. "I'll check with you later. Perhaps we could have lunch."

She looked up and smiled at him absently. "Lunch," she said vaguely. "That would be fine."

As he went down the corridor toward the stairway, he heard the old bell in Memorial Tower chime the end of the first class period; doors opened and he was surrounded by a swirl of young women whose perfume-shampoo smell blended oddly well with the faint odor of chemicals coming from the laboratories. For a moment, everything seemed exactly as it should be and then he felt a hand on his arm. He looked down to see a young woman, blond and pretty, but wide-eyed with worry. "Dean Simco," she said, "we're hearing things. Has something happened to Professor Lakey?"

When Simco returned at twelve-thirty, he found Nancy sitting at Catherine's desk, the phone pinched between her shoulder and her ear, writing numbers on a yellow pad. She nodded at him, held up one finger, wrote something else, said, "six forty-eight. OK, thanks," and hung up.

"Have a good morning?" he asked.

"Better than that," she said, gathering up her jacket and her purse. She turned off the desk light and the computer, folded several sheets of yellow paper and stuffed them in her pocket, then walked past him toward the door.

"Better than what?" he said, following her.

"I'll tell you over lunch. How long will it take me to get to Hartford?"

He stopped. "Hartford? What's in Hartford?"

"The airport. I've got a flight to Pittsburgh at a little after four."

Devon, Connecticut
Midday

The student union was crowded and noisy, and the only seats that Nancy and Simco could find were side by side at one end of a long, Formica-topped table. Across from them sat two young women who had learned how to carry on a conversation without looking at one another. They glanced around the room and both of them, from time to time, stopped and looked at Nancy, then at Simco, and smiled as though they expected an introduction. Nancy peeled the plastic wrap from around her sandwich, removed the top slice of bread and with her finger probed the grayish paste inside.

Simco turned and leaned toward her so that he wouldn't have to shout to be heard. "Tell me about Pittsburgh."

"Do you remember me mentioning Richard Weiss?" said Nancy, holding up the sandwich, studying it as though it were a fish that she had caught.

"Someone you called? A friend of Catherine's?"

The students across from them got up to leave. Nancy turned in her chair so that she and Simco could talk with a bit more privacy if someone else joined their table. "More than just a friend, I think. She met him five or six years ago at a conference. For a while, things between them were fairly serious, but then cooled down. They stayed friends, though. When Catherine came to Bloomington, sometimes she'd stop in Pittsburgh to see him."

"And you talked to him this morning?"

Nancy nodded. "I called him on Monday, in Bloomington, after you called me. I left a message on his machine, but then I came out here and forgot about it. When I was going through her Rolodex this morning, I saw his name and remembered. I called him at work. He teaches something or other at a medical school."

"That's right," said Simco. "I remember at the dedication of the Science Center, Catherine had a friend. I thought he was a doctor."

"I don't think so. Not an M.D.," said Nancy. "This morning I told him who I was and what had happened, and asked him if he might have any idea what was going on."

"And he did?" Simco sounded interested, but skeptical.

"Well, he didn't exactly say that. Not in so many words," said Nancy. "He was strange on the phone. When I told him that Catherine was missing, he didn't say anything and I assumed he was in shock. When I began to apologize for breaking the news so bluntly, he told me not to worry, that he understood, and then he said that he was in the middle of something and would call me back within the hour."

"Is that so strange?"

"Not what he said, but his voice. It was absolutely normal, as though I'd just told him that Catherine's plane had been delayed."

"I take it he called back."

"About an hour later. But this time he was different—very businesslike, almost brusque—or perhaps just rushed. He told me that he wanted to help me but that he couldn't do it on the phone. He asked if I could come to Pittsburgh, and when I said I could, he gave me a flight number and told me that he'd meet the plane. Before I could ask him anything, he hung up." She looked at Simco, who was staring straight ahead across the room. "What do you think?"

"Why couldn't he tell you on the phone?"

"I don't know. I told you, I didn't get a chance to ask."

"I'm astounded," said Simco without looking at her. "It sounds as if this Mr. Weiss knows exactly what's going on and, apparently, it doesn't concern him very much." Simco grabbed his napkin and wadded it into a ball. He shook his head. "So you were partly right. Maybe she has gone off somewhere, but it doesn't sound like she's in trouble, does it?"

"I don't know."

"From what you said about his voice it doesn't." Simco, tight-jawed, faced Nancy. "Do you know how I spent my morning?" he said, irritation rising in his voice. "I sat in a room with four reporters talking about poor Catherine Lakey and her mysterious disappearance. Then I met with a group of students, several of whom were crying. And the president, of course, has asked me—told me, really—that I've got to handle this thing for the college. Too bad you'll be in Pittsburgh, I'll be on the news tonight."

Nancy quickly gathered the bits of torn cellophane, her napkin, the leftover pieces of her sandwich and jammed them into her Styrofoam cup. Coffee slopped onto her tray. "You make it sound like Catherine's done this simply to inconvenience you," she said, the warmth gone from her voice.

"I'm sorry it sounded that way, but it has inconvenienced me and everybody else around here. If she's in Pittsburgh, I hope like hell there's some good reason."

Nancy pushed her chair away from the table, stood up and grabbed her tray. "I've got to go pack and call a cab." She started to leave, then stopped. "I hope like hell she is in Pittsburgh," she said, clearly angry, "or any place else where she's safe. I'll call you, if I find anything, not because you really care, of course, but just so you can stop putting yourself out."

Abruptly, she turned her back on Simco, crossed the dining hall, dropped her tray in the return bin and disappeared through the doorway. Simco threw his wadded napkin at the table. He was angry at Catherine Lakey, but even angrier with himself.

Pittsburgh, Pennsylvania
Evening

As the plane taxied up to the gate, it occurred to Nancy that in the tumble of flight times and numbers hurriedly conveyed in the morning's phone call, she had never met Richard Weiss and hadn't any idea what he looked like. She closed her eyes and tried to ignore the jostling of the man next to her, who was already standing, rummaging through the overhead bin, handing her a pillow with an offhand "Could you hold this?" What sort of man would Catherine Lakey find attractive? Trim, Nancy thought, maybe five ten or so, and nice-looking in a plain sort of way, not model-glamorous.

When she came off the ramp into the gate area, she stepped to one side to get out of the stream of passengers and scanned the waiting area behind the railing. It seemed to be a lean night for welcomes: a few women, about Nancy's age—wives, she assumed—standing on tiptoes, waving, greeting their husbands; a clutch of men in business suits, glancing at their watches, smoking, laughing easily with one another; and a family of four—a mother, father, little girl, older brother—looking anxious until the little girl, screaming "Gramma!" ducked under the lower rail and wrapped her arms around the legs of a white-haired lady, almost knocking the woman over with the fierceness of her hug.

After a few minutes the last of the passengers had disappeared down one of the tunnel-corridors beneath the signs that showed the way to baggage claim. The flight attendants, chattering happily, still perfect-pressed even after serving meals and drinks to 147 people in little more than an hour, came up the ramp, pulling suitcases on little wheeled carts. As they went by, one of them looked at Nancy and stopped. "Everything OK?" she asked. "Need some help?" Nancy smiled and shook her head. "No, fine," she said.

She followed the attendants into the concourse and was about to begin the long walk to the main terminal when she saw a man—dark, mid-forties, nice-looking—standing at a pay phone and, she thought, looking at her. She stopped, returned the look and smiled. He said a few more things into the receiver, hung up, bent down to pick up his briefcase, then came toward her. They spoke simultaneously. "Rich——" she began. "Bon——" he said. They stopped, laughed.

"Richard Weiss?" she said. His smile faded.

"You're not Bonnie Adams?" She shook her head. "No."

"Too bad," he said, his smile returning.

He returned to the telephone booth and Nancy made her way back to the gate just in case Richard Weiss had somehow slipped past her. She found it deserted except for a man who was posting departure information for a later flight. She sighed and began the long walk up the concourse to the main terminal.

Once there, she looked around, hoping to see at least one man looking as puzzled as she did, but everyone seemed to be scurrying someplace, looking purposeful. She found the passenger service agent and had Weiss paged. She waited at the counter, then had him paged again. A few minutes later, the agent asked if Nancy would like the page repeated. Nancy told her no, looked through her purse, found the paper with Weiss's address and number, then crossed the terminal to a bank of phone booths. She dialed the number. After the fourth ring she heard a beep followed by Weiss's voice asking her to leave a message.

"Hi, Mr. Weiss. It's Nancy Mulholland. I'm at the airport at, ah," she looked at her watch, "six-forty. I'll be here for another forty minutes or so. You can reach me by calling the passenger service agent. U.S. Air. Sorry, I don't know the number. Thanks. Bye." She glared at the receiver, surprised and a little disappointed in herself that she had so deftly managed to conceal the anger she felt. She hung up and stood for a moment, staring at the telephone, her fingers drumming on the metal shelf that held the directories, then she went back to the passenger service counter. She wrote her name on a piece of paper and told the agent that if anyone was looking for her, she'd be at the bar across the way.

She ordered a beer and took it to a tiny table back in the corner, by the big plate-glass window which looked out at darkness punctuated by rows of small blue lights, tracing out the runways. The silence of the nearly empty bar was broken now and then by the electronic beeping of the cash register and the muffled thunder of faraway jet engines.

Nancy lit a cigarette and tried to map out her next moves. But where the hell was Weiss? She told herself to calm down, that the way to do this was to take things a step at a time. She'd finish her beer, smoke one more cigarette, then she'd call him again. If she couldn't reach him, she'd find a place to stay, take a cab to the hotel, check in, call him again—at least leave a message telling him where she was. And if she didn't hear from him? She didn't know. She didn't want to think about it.

She finished the beer, stubbed out her cigarette and went out to the phone booths. She dialed and was puzzled when the machine failed to intercept the ringing. She waited, promising only five more rings, then five more after that, then ten. She hung up. Had he come back, turned the machine off—and what? Did he get her message? Had he tried to reach her and she'd missed the page? She hurried back to the passenger service counter. The agent looked up from the paperback she'd been reading, gave Nancy an apologetic smile and shook her head.

"Nothing?" said Nancy.

"Sorry."

Nancy had the agent page Weiss one more time, and while she waited, she asked the woman's advice on hotels near Weiss's neighborhood. She suggested the William Penn Charter House and gave Nancy the address, wishing her good luck. Nancy thanked the agent and followed the signs pointing the way to ground transportation.

She gave the taxi driver the hotel's address, then changed her mind and gave him Richard Weiss's address. She flicked on the cab's small overhead light, took out a piece of paper and, trying to write between stretches of bumpy roadway, composed a note. "Dear Mr. Weiss," she wrote, then paused, flirting with the temptation of beginning: "Where the hell were you?" deciding instead on: "I'm sorry we missed one another. I'm staying at the William Penn Charter House. Please call me when you get in—I don't care how late it is. Nancy Mulholland."

The cab stopped in front of a squat, blocky building, with the number 371 illuminated by a row of lights above the front door. After asking the driver to wait, Nancy hurried up the walkway, opened the door and found herself in a small, square vestibule. On the left-hand wall was a row of narrow brass slots, each one containing a nameplate. Next to each was a black button. Nancy ran her finger down the row until she found R. WEISS 2C. She pressed the button and waited. She pressed it again, then began looking around for a place to leave her note. On the opposite wall were rows of mailboxes, also brass, also with nameplates. Above the nameplates were small, decorative grilles. She considered sticking the note in the mailbox grille, but decided that, late at night, he probably wouldn't check his mail, so she folded the paper in half, wrote RICHARD WEISS in large block letters, and wedged the note between the inside door and the jamb at what she guessed would be his eye level. She pressed the button again and, without waiting, went out the door, back to the cab.

At the hotel, she changed into her nightgown, sat on the bed and smoked a cigarette. Absently, she played with the buttons of the television remote control that was bolted to the bedside table. A point of light appeared in the center of the screen and spread slowly toward the edges, finally resolving itself into an image of a heavyset man in goggles, running a piece of wood through a table saw. She found the volume button and turned it all the way down. She looked at her watch. It was almost ten.

She considered calling Frank Simco and asking his advice, then thought of the conversation in the student union. The hell with him, she said to herself. She clicked through all the channels, hoping to find something that would absorb her, but she found it hard to concentrate.

She went through her conversation with Richard Weiss that morning, trying to replay every word of it in her head. He had given her the right flight number, she was sure of that, and he had said that he would meet the plane. If something had come up, and something must have, that still didn't explain why he hadn't left a message.

She decided that there wasn't any point in worrying about it now. She had done everything she could, and, anyway, she was sure that he would call tomorrow. She called the front desk to ask for a seven o'clock wake-up call, then turned up the volume on the TV and very quickly fell asleep.

	MARCH—1987					
S	M	T	W	T	F	S
1	2	3	4	5	6	7
8	9	10	11	12	13	14
15	16	17	18	19	20	21
22	23	24	25	<u>26</u>	27	28
29	30	31				

DAY NINE

	APRIL—1987					
S	M	T	W	T	F	S
			1	2	(3)	4
5	6	7	8	9	10	11
12	13	14	15	16	17	18
19	20	21	22	23	24	25
26	27	28	29	30		

D A Y   N I N E

FRIDAY, APRIL 3, 1987

Pittsburgh, Pennsylvania
Morning

The phone was ringing. Nancy opened her eyes and, for a moment, couldn't remember where she was. She sat up and blinked at the television screen where Big Bird was dancing with someone in uniform. Pittsburgh, she remembered. Weiss! Grabbing the phone, she blurted a hello into the receiver, afraid that he might hang up. There was a faint whir, then a click. "Good morning," said a metallic voice, "It's 7 A.M. Have a nice day."

Not very gently, Nancy dropped the receiver into its cradle and looked around for the piece of paper with Weiss's number. She found it and dialed, waiting through seven rings before she hung up. She checked the number and dialed again. Still no answer. It didn't make any sense and the irritation she felt was only slightly dissipated several minutes later when she stepped into the shower and under a cascade of hot water thought out her plan for the morning: she'd go downstairs for breakfast, then, just as soon as the college switchboard was open, she would call Weiss at work and, if necessary, she'd go to his office and demand to see him.

* * *

There were signs in the lobby of the William Penn Charter House that pointed the way to the dining room, but at seven-thirty they weren't needed. Though the lobby was quiet, almost empty, from down the left corridor came a clatter of dishes and a din of voices. Already the dining room was crowded and Nancy had to wait in line in front of a sign that said: THE HOSTESS WILL SEAT YOU. The hostess, a faded but flamboyantly made-up woman of indeterminate age, was struggling with the logistics of trying to distribute too many solitary diners among too few tables. Nancy slipped out of line and went up to the cashier's desk where there were stacks of morning papers. She chose a Pittsburgh daily, left a quarter on the counter and resumed her place in line. After glancing at the weather forecast (mostly cloudy, milder), she scanned the front page and began to read an article under the headline: Cuomo Says No to '88 Bid.

"How many, please?"

Nancy looked up at the hostess and noticed that the woman's bright red lipstick had been applied with almost no regard for the location of her lips. It was hard not to stare. "One," said Nancy.

"Oh, cheesh," said the hostess, looking anxiously around the room. "Mind sharing a table?"

Nancy did mind, but not enough to stand in line for another twenty minutes. "Fine," she said, and followed the hostess on a meandering trip to a table in the middle of the room where she was seated opposite a man who was hidden behind an open newspaper. Nancy glanced at the menu, then beckoned to a young waiter who was circulating through the room, pouring coffee. He filled her cup and left her with two small plastic containers of cream. She emptied one into the coffee, stirred it with her teaspoon and looked for the sugar bowl, but couldn't find it.

"Excuse me," she said in a small voice to the open newspaper. When nothing happened, she cleared her throat and tried again, louder. "Excuse me." When again there was no response, Nancy leaned forward and tapped the newspaper with her teaspoon. On the second tap the paper slid slowly down, revealing first some sandy-colored hair, then a broad expanse of forehead and, finally, blue eyes that weren't entirely friendly. However, as the eyes took in Nancy Mulholland sitting only a few feet away across the table, their expression changed and the paper continued to slide down until it lay flat between them, a lumpy second tablecloth.

"Would you have the sugar?" asked Nancy pleasantly.

"Sugar?" The man stared at her, then looked quickly down in front of him and handed her the bowl. Nancy accepted it, thanking him, and bringing her hands together under her chin, cocked her head to one side. "But now I can't seem to find my coffee."

He looked puzzled, then caught on, and in a flurry of crumpling and folding, took the newspaper off the table. "Sorry."

As she was spooning sugar into her coffee, a waitress appeared. Nancy ordered orange juice and an English muffin, then unfolded her paper and returned to the Cuomo article. She was aware that the man was staring at her from across the table and decided to ignore him. She also decided that she didn't want to pursue the story to A29 and pulled out the second section—MetroRegion.

In the top center of the first page was a large picture of a fireman giving mouth-to-mouth resuscitation to a little girl, soot-stained, her head drooping back, looking limp and lifeless. The caption, though, said that she had recovered. Nancy was relieved. She was about to turn the page when a headline in the lower right-hand corner caught her attention. She scanned the story, her eyes racing through its three brief paragraphs. "Shit," she whispered, and read the story again, vaguely aware that the man across the table was talking to her, asking her something. She looked up at him blankly, then found a five-dollar bill in her purse and slid it across the table. "I'm sorry—would you mind paying my bill. I've got to make a phone call." She grabbed the newspaper, put it under her arm and hurried to the elevator, leaving the man at the table gaping after her.

Back in her room, Nancy swore at the announcement telling her that her call could not be completed as dialed. She dialed again, this time remembering to include the area code. Simco answered after the first ring.

"Hello."

"Professor Simco? This is Nancy Mulholland."

"Where are you? I'm glad you called. I wanted to apologize about yesterday. I didn't mean—"

"I'm in Pittsburgh," she interrupted. "Richard Weiss is dead."

"What!"

"He's dead," said Nancy, fighting to keep her voice under control. "He didn't meet me at the airport. I left messages for him. Then, this morning, it was in the paper."

"What the hell happened?"

"He was shot, mugged." She unfolded the paper and read him the story:

> The body of Richard A. Weiss, 49, a professor of pharmacology at Collina Medical College, was found early yesterday evening in Hopedale Park by two teenaged girls.
>
> According to police, Weiss had been shot once in the chest at close range with a small-caliber weapon. His wallet, containing no cash, was found in the underbrush a short distance from where the body was discovered.
>
> Hopedale Park abuts Collina Medical College on the west and a residential area on the east where Professor Weiss, a bachelor, lived in the Wright Hill Apartments. Police surveillance of the park has been increased in recent months following a rash of muggings.

"Jesus," said Simco.

Nancy brushed a tear from one eye. "I never got to talk to him. Goddamn it."

There was silence on the line.

"Are you OK?"

"Yes. Maybe . . . I don't know. Shit! What am I going to do?"

"Were you planning to fly back to Connecticut today?"

There was another silence on the line.

"Nancy?"

"Yes?"

"Did you book a return?"

"Yes." She reached across the bed to her purse, removed her ticket and studied it. "I get into Hartford at 3:05 this afternoon."

"What's the flight?"

"U.S. Air 1017."

"I'll have Georgia meet you. I would, but I absolutely can't get away then. Will you call me when you get back? We should talk."

"OK." Her voice was flat. "Bye," she said and hung up before Simco could say anything else. For several minutes she didn't move, just sat on the edge of the bed and stared at the carpet. Then she lit a cigarette, picked up an ashtray and began to pace the room. Halfway to the window, she stubbed it out, rushed back to the bed, sat down, picked up the phone and dialed. No one answered. Figuring that Frank Simco was on his way to work, she packed her duffel and made sure she wasn't leaving anything behind before she called him at the Science Center.

"Frank Simco's office," said a pleasant, beautifully modulated voice.

"Is Professor Simco in?"

"He's in a meeting right now. May I take a message?"

"Is this Georgia Whitney?"

"It is." The voice became hesitant. "May I ask who's calling?"

"I'm sorry. This is Nancy Mulholland. I spoke with Professor Simco earlier this morning and told him the flight I'd be on today."

"Oh yes." The voice brightened immediately. "He told me about that. It's U.S. Air 1017, from Pittsburgh. I'll be there."

"Thank you so much, Ms. Whitney, but that won't be necessary. My plans have changed and I'll be taking a later plane."

"Do you know the flight number?"

"Not yet, but please tell Professor Simco I'll call as soon as I do."

Pittsburgh, Pennsylvania
Morning

Nancy Mulholland paid the cab driver with a ten-dollar bill, then tried to calculate the tip in her head, but gave up. "Keep it," she said, and got out. In the daylight the apartment building looked more massive and brooding than it had the night before; the dull brown bricks and the deeply recessed windows gave it the look of a fort or a police station.

There was nothing outside the apartment building to suggest that a resident had been murdered, but there could be people inside—police, reporters, relatives. She took her time walking to the front door of the entrance vestibule and opened it cautiously. The vestibule was empty and the main door to the building was shut and bare. The message she'd left the night before was gone. She tried to remember what the paper had said about the time of Weiss's death, but couldn't. Had he returned and found it, then gone out again? Or was he already dead by the time she'd left it? If so, who would have taken it, and why? She decided that she couldn't think about that now, that she had more urgent things to do. She went over to the row of nameplates on the left-hand wall, checked each name, then crossed the vestibule to the mailboxes. As she was studying them, she heard a door open. Turning, she saw a man dressed in a business suit and carrying a briefcase hurry by her and out the front door. Nancy ran to the door, catching it before it closed. "Excuse me," she shouted. The man stopped and turned around, his look of mild curiosity changing to one of more than casual interest. "Yes?" he said.

Nancy came down the walkway, smiling apologetically. "I'm sorry, but I'm looking for the superintendent, the custodian."

He laughed. "Aren't we all."

Nancy's smile faded. "He's not here?"

"John?" he said with a shrug. "Who knows? John's always here when you don't need him, but when you do . . ."

Nancy coaxed her smile back. "Right," she said, "but how do I get hold of him—or at least try?"

With his briefcase the man motioned toward the front door. "In the entryway, on the right, above the mailboxes, you'll see a phone. Pick it up. Press the button. Hope."

"And if he's not there?"

The man shook his head. "Never have figured that one out. He has a home phone, but he never answers. Leave a note in the door. That's what everybody does."

Nancy thanked him and returned to the vestibule. She found the phone and saw that on the back of the receiver was a piece of embossed plastic tape that said J. Lovecchio—Super. She pressed the button. Very faintly, perhaps coming from the back of the building, a bell rang. She waited, then pressed again, this time making it ring longer. Finally, there was a click, then a voice. "Yeah, this is John."

"Hello, John. Mr. Lovecchio. I'm a friend of Mr. Weiss. Did you hear what happened?"

"Yeah," he said, his voice matter-of-fact. "Saw it in the paper."

"Well," she said, sounding upset, "I need to ask a favor."

"Ask."

"I'd feel better if you'd come out here. It's rather private."

There was a long silence. "OK," he said, and hung up.

He came through the inside door, a large, unkempt man in a dirty flannel shirt and blue jeans. There was a huge ring of keys jangling at his belt. Nancy gave him a large, sad smile, then looked at the floor. "I need to get into Mr. Weiss's apartment."

He looked at her, expressionless.

"I—we were friends." She was stammering, unable to tell what this man was thinking. "I stayed here now and then. There are things—some of my things—in there. It would be embarrassing if . . . I'd rather get them before . . . " Her shoulders sagged and she felt a blush creep up her neck. "Clothes," she said. "Underwear, things like that."

He looked at her steadily. "Don't remember seeing you before."

She stepped closer to him, looked around, and held up her left hand. The small gold ring with a narrow band of tiny rubies, a gift from Catherine several years ago and usually worn on her right ring finger, now glinted on her left. In a very low voice she said, "Mr. Lovecchio, I'm married. I need to get those things. Would you please help me?"

A look of distaste came across his face. He rubbed the stubble on his chin with the back of his hand.

"If you don't trust me," she said, "you can come with me if you want."

"What the hell do I care," he muttered, turning toward the door. "Come on," he said to her. "The shit that goes on here," he said to no one in particular, leading Nancy upstairs to Apartment 2–C.

He unlocked the apartment door, then showed her how to re-lock it when she left. "Get your stuff and get the hell out," he said. "I don't want nobody finding you in here, then finding it's me who let you in."

"Thanks," she said.

She closed the door behind her and stood for a moment with her eyes closed, not quite believing what she had just done. When she opened them, she saw that she was looking at a living room flooded with light from two windows on the opposite wall. It had leather strapped chairs, a black leather, deep-cushioned sofa and a large, round brass coffee table.

She entered and looked around. In one corner was a large TV piled high with papers and magazines. To her left were French doors, which opened to a small dining area and a kitchen beyond. To her right was a dim hallway, which she presumed led to bedrooms. There was a small pair of binoculars on the coffee table and beside them a crumpled paper napkin and an empty beer bottle.

Running the width of the room, underneath the windows, was shelving that was crammed with books and stereo equipment and a jumble of tapes. Nancy poked through some of them—James Taylor, Beethoven, Charlie Parker—then knelt on the carpet and examined the books. There were novels, good ones, and science texts, several biographies, a book on sea serpents, all shelved together, in no apparent order. There was a very large dictionary and two books of poetry and, at the end of the top shelf, what looked like a red loose-leaf notebook. It had nothing written on its spine. She slid it out and opened it and saw right away it was a makeshift photo album. Two or three snapshots fluttered to the floor and when Nancy picked them up she saw that one of them was a picture of Catherine standing on a dock, a blue lake in the background. She had the same bemused, laconic smile she seemed to wear for all her pictures, as though the idea that anyone wanted to photograph her she found silly, but amusing. Nancy thumbed quickly through the pages and saw that Catherine was a frequent subject. Without thinking much about it, she decided that, despite its bulk, the album was worth taking. She could conceal it under her jacket when she left.

She put the album on the coffee table, went to the hallway and flicked on the light. There were three doorways at the end of the hall, two of them open. Through the left doorway was a rumpled double bed, a terry cloth bathrobe slung over its footboard; a long oak bureau, matching bedside tables with lamps, a clock radio and a small TV. In front of her was a bathroom and on her right—another bedroom? Nancy opened the door. A sofa covered by a plaid blanket was pushed against one wall, a recliner chair beside it. Books were stacked on the floor by the chair and to one side of an immense desk that took up most of the room. She went in and sat down at the desk. The top was littered with magazines, a checkbook, a stack of bills held together with a rubber band, a roll of stamps. She went through the drawers rapidly, sifting through pads of paper, envelopes, rolls of tape, pencils. When she opened the large file drawer she was surprised to find it empty.

She sat there for a moment, thinking. She had to hurry, couldn't ransack the place. What was she looking for? Things that had to do with Catherine. Would she have written letters? Of course she would, she was a wonderful correspondent who much preferred a letter to the telephone. Would Weiss have kept them? She didn't know, but if he had, where would ... A loud buzz sounded, then another. The doorbell? Nancy realized the apartment door was unlocked.

She reached down, removed her shoes, ran on tiptoes across the hallway to Weiss's bedroom. Her eyes darted around the room. Not the bed. The closet! She opened it, stepped in, arranged herself behind some clothes, closed the door as quietly as she could and waited in the musty darkness, straining to hear, dreading to hear, the click of a door, footsteps. She wished to hell she hadn't turned on the hall light. Faintly, she heard another buzz, then nothing. Slowly she counted to 300, then 350, hoping that whoever had been there was, by now, out of patience and had left. She opened the closet door a crack, heard nothing, then holding her shoes in her hands, she tiptoed to the bedroom doorway, stopped, leaned forward just enough to peek down the hall. It was empty.

She ventured down the hall, stopping with each step to listen, careful about every footfall, afraid that a floorboard would give her away. Nearing the end of the hall, she held her breath, listened intently, then forced herself to step into the living room. No one was there. She put her shoes down on the floor and stepped into them, noticing that her fingers had left damp marks on the leather.

Quickly, she went through the open French doors into an L-shaped kitchen/dining area which had only one window. Some chairs and a table were in front of the window. The rest of the room, the long part of the L, was a dark labyrinth of drawers and cabinets which stretched back into the interior of the apartment.

On the table an opened book lay face down. What had Weiss been reading? As Nancy leaned over the table to see, a shrill ring made her jump. She lurched forward, lost her balance and clutched a chair to steady herself. Turning around, she saw the phone on the counter and the machine beside it, blinking at her, its message light flashing a red 18. The phone rang just once more—an unnerving ring that was much too loud. Eyeing the phone and keeping a safe distance from it, as if it were an animal that shouldn't be disturbed, she jabbed a bar on the answering machine. The tape ejected. She put it in her skirt pocket, then hurried into the living room where she grabbed the photo album.

At the apartment door, she took a deep breath, wiped her hands on her skirt, then cautiously opened the door. Remembering to lock it, she closed it quietly behind her and, as casually as she could, went down the corridor, looking straight ahead. When she got to the stairwell, she removed her jacket and folded it over the album.

In the vestibule, something caught her eye. Someone had taped a manila envelope to Weiss's mailbox. *Dr. Weiss* it said in an awkward, backward-slanted script. Nancy looked around and, on impulse, tore the envelope from the mailbox and slipped it under her jacket. She opened the door, went down the pathway to the sidewalk, and turned toward the hotel. As she moved down the street, she forced herself to breathe deeply, to push her shoulders down away from the knot they had formed, and to keep walking, though the urge to run was almost overwhelming.

Hartford/Devon, Connecticut
Evening

The flight to Hartford took off as the sun was setting and Nancy, resting her head against the window, watched the lights of Pittsburgh, just coming on to meet the night, grow faint and vanish as the plane climbed above cloud cover. It was hard to believe that Pittsburgh was real, that what she had done was real. Weiss was dead. The shock she'd felt was gone, replaced by frustration and sadness. And the excitement of the morning had faded, too, leaving her with a weary suspicion that the risks she had taken weren't worth it.

There was still the tape, which she hadn't had an opportunity to play. It was tucked away in an inner pocket of her purse. The envelope, carefully opened, was in her duffel. The ten-page paper inside had been written by one of Weiss's students. Grad students know enough to make copies, she told herself, but she wished she hadn't taken it. There was no return address on the envelope.

"Excuse me." The voice belonged to a stewardess who had arrived with the beverage cart. Nancy paid for white wine and accepted a silver packet of peanuts. She was glad the flight was nearly empty. It gave her the luxury of having one row entirely to herself. She lowered the tray table of the middle seat, put her wine and peanuts on it, then raised the armrests and, turning her back to the window, stretched her legs out over the two empty seats and turned her attention to the photo album.

She had looked at it briefly back at the hotel, had gone through it again at the airport, as best she could, while waiting for her flight to be called. She opened it again, no longer expecting much. Whatever else he may have been, Richard Weiss had not had the instincts of an archivist or a librarian. There was no pattern to the arrangement of the photographs and Catherine appeared far less frequently than the quick inspection in the apartment had originally promised. There were long stretches of pages where the photos were of places and people that Nancy didn't recognize, and all of the pictures were undated and unidentified.

The Catherine photos seemed to come in clumps. There were some that had been taken in Weiss's apartment, oddly formal, Catherine sitting stiffly on the sofa, an awkward smile frozen on her face; another batch, showing Catherine at a lake, with forest-covered mountains in the background; Catherine in a motorboat, waving; Catherine by a swimming pool; Catherine standing next to a horse, holding reins, stroking its nose. In many of the photographs there was a man, shorter than Catherine, maybe five feet four inches, squarely built, with a broad expanse of forehead and brown, curly hair. In most of the pictures he was smiling shyly, engagingly, and in the shots of him and Catherine there was a sense of easy familiarity between them; it seemed that they knew each other well, and what they knew they liked. While Nancy couldn't be absolutely certain, she assumed the man was Weiss.

There were two sets of pictures taken in Cotchpinicut. The pictures themselves were unremarkable: beach shots, sunsets, a tanned Catherine entering the water, Weiss putting up a beach umbrella, and in another photo, Weiss painting the side of the cottage. What surprised Nancy was that he had spent time there. Catherine had never mentioned it and she wondered why.

It would have helped if he had bothered to write brief captions in the album or on the backs of photographs like her mother always had. Nancy thumbed through the album until she found the set of pictures that intrigued her the most. They seemed to have been taken at a party: the people had glasses in their hands and wore the slightly fuzzy smiles of celebration. In two of them, Weiss and Catherine stood on either side of a strikingly handsome man who had his arms around their shoulders while the three of them smiled broadly at the camera. Nancy held the album up closer to the light. In both pictures, there was a woman, small and blond and fragile looking, standing off to one side, a foot or so from Weiss, as if she wasn't sure whether she was part of the group or not. She wasn't looking at the camera, but instead seemed to be studying the handsome man between Weiss and Catherine. She wasn't smiling, either. Nancy closed the album and turned off the overhead light. She tucked her feet underneath her, rested her head against a pillow and wondered who the woman was and why she wasn't smiling. In the middle of her wondering, she closed her eyes and fell asleep.

As the plane descended into Hartford, she awoke and began gathering her things and thinking about arranging transportation to Devon. She had called Simco's office earlier in the day, leaving word with Georgia Whitney about her new arrival time, and had learned that Simco would be at the faculty senate until at least half past seven that evening. Coming out of the ramp into the waiting area, she was surprised to see a stocky young man, in blue jeans and a red-and-black-checked woolen jacket, holding above his head a cardboard sign that said, in blue marker: Stonington/Mulholland.

Nancy went over to him and introduced herself. He seemed awkward, almost embarrassed, as he took her duffel. He told her he was Bill Tull from the Maintenance Department and that Professor Simco had asked him to meet the plane. It wasn't what he normally did, he told her, "But I'm happy to," he added, grinning shyly at her.

He guided her through the terminal, out to the parking area to a dark blue van that had Stonington College written on the doors. He put her bag in the backseat, then with an easy competence which Nancy admired, he maneuvered the van through a maze of ramps and roadways. Nancy saw a green sign pass overhead: 86 East—Boston. She leaned against the door and closed her eyes. The hum of the tires and the barely audible whisper of the radio were soothing.

Bill Tull cleared his throat. "Mr. Mahoney, my supervisor, he told me you're related to Professor Lakey, the one who disappeared."

"That's right. I'm her niece."

"I'm sorry."

Not quite sure how to respond, Nancy said nothing. They drove along in silence for a while.

"Must have been a shock," said Tull, finally.

"Yes."

"I read in the papers that the police out on Cape Cod don't have a clue. Nothing."

Nancy didn't feel like having this conversation, but Bill Tull had gone out of his way for her. "That's not quite so. They found a sandal on the beach. Her size, but no one can be sure it's hers."

"That so?" he said. "I only met her once."

"Met her?"

"Early this year. The disposal in her kitchen jammed and I went over. Nice lady."

There was another green sign: Devon. Next 2 Exits. He eased the van on to the exit ramp and soon they were in the dark Connecticut countryside. "You have any ideas?" he said, after they had driven several miles.

"Ideas?" said Nancy, wearily, thinking that the conversation had ended.

"About what happened to her."

"No, I don't," she said, with some finality. She made a show of yawning, then said into the darkness, "It's been a long day." Bill Tull glanced over at her and seemed to understand. He turned up the volume of the radio and they finished the trip without further conversation.

Nancy let herself into Catherine's house through the front door and moved cautiously in the darkened living room, bumping softly into furniture, looking for lights. She took her bag into Catherine's bedroom and opened her purse, unzipping the inner pocket to remove Weiss's tape. She put the tape in her skirt pocket, then went to the kitchen where she hoped she'd find not only an answering machine, but food. She had slept through the in-flight dinner service and, aside from the peanuts she had on the plane and a candy bar she bought at the airport, she had had nothing to eat all day.

There wasn't anything appetizing in the cupboards. Opening the refrigerator, she saw it was almost empty. There was a jar of mayonnaise, a few bottles of salad dressing, ketchup and a can of coffee. Giving up on food for the moment, she looked for the answering machine but found only a phone, on the wall by the back door. She thought for a moment about the logical place for one and remembered Catherine's study.

When she switched on the overhead light there, she saw it right away, on the desk, next to the telephone. It had been turned off. The first thing to do was to see if it had any messages. She turned it on, pressed the play button. There weren't any.

Next she called Simco, reaching him at home, and fended off his questions about her delay in getting back by telling him she would explain things later. She told him she had some things she wanted him to see and when he said he could come by tonight, she asked if he'd mind picking up a pizza for her. He said he'd be by in about half an hour with pizza and beer, which meant she'd have more than enough time to play the tape.

She removed Catherine's cassette and replaced it with the one from Weiss's machine. She pressed the rewind button, drummed her fingers impatiently on the desk, then when the tape stopped, pressed PLAY. The tape turned slowly. She heard a beep, then a voice too faint to understand. She stopped the tape, looked for the volume control, found it, turned it up to maximum. She rewound the tape and started it again. This time the voice was clearly audible:

"Hi, Professor Weiss? Bill Fahey. I tried to find you at school this afternoon. My data's a mess and I need to talk with you about an extension. Could you call me at 473-3311? Thanks."

Nancy stopped the tape. Fahey? Wasn't that the name of the

student who had left the envelope taped to Weiss's mailbox? She went to Catherine's bedroom and took the manila envelope from her duffel and returned with it to Catherine's desk and took out the neatly typed paper.

At the top was the title: "Stress-Induced Hypersensitization to Certain Classes of Pharmaceuticals," and under that . . . yes: "William Fahey." Now, at least, she had a phone number.

She pressed the play button again, and listened.

Twenty minutes later she was startled by the doorbell. She stopped the tape and put her pen down on the pad that she'd been writing on. At the front door she found Simco, balancing a pizza carton on one hand, holding a six-pack of beer in the other. She showed him the way to the kitchen, where he opened the carton, tested the temperature of the pizza with his finger, and gave it to Nancy to reheat. While she put the pizza in the oven, he opened a beer for each of them and sat down at the kitchen table.

"On the phone," he said, "you sounded mysterious."

She smiled. "I didn't mean to."

"What is it you wanted to show me?"

"Wait here," she said, and left the room. When she returned, she put the photo album and the tape cassette on the table in front of him.

He opened the album, turned two or three pages, then looked up at her.

"Where did you get this?"

"Weiss's apartment," she said, trying to sound matter-of-fact.

"Weiss's apartment? I don't understand."

"After I talked with you this morning, right after I found out, I couldn't just come back here without at least trying to find the connection between Catherine and him, about what he knew." She shrugged. "The only thing I could think of was his apartment. So I went there."

"You went there?" he said, incredulity clear in his voice. "You just walked in? You had a key?"

"No key," she said, lifting herself up onto the counter, sitting there, legs dangling. "I found the super, made up a story, said I was

Weiss's married lover and needed to get some stuff out of the apartment to avoid embarrassment." She looked at Simco.

He stared back at her, astonished. "You lied to the super . . . " he began, and then his voice trailed off. He pointed to the album. " . . . and then you just helped yourself?"

"I didn't think of it quite that way." There was a coolness in her voice and she watched Simco, appraising him as she spoke. "I had to look. I knew I wouldn't get another chance."

"But you can't do that. You can't just go barging into people's apartments, taking what you want."

Nancy looked up at the ceiling, exasperated. "The man's dead."

"And that makes it all right?"

Nancy slipped down from the kitchen counter. She opened the oven, took out the pizza, slapped it down on the counter and frowned at it for a moment, then turned to Simco. "I didn't ask you here to lecture me."

"And I didn't come here to lecture you. But I can't believe you broke into that apartment." Simco took a long swallow of beer and looked up at Nancy. She was staring at him, seemed about to say something, then turned her back on him and yanked opened the large drawer next to the stove.

"Has it occurred to you," said Simco, careful to keep his voice modulated, "that Weiss wasn't mugged? Doesn't it seem a bit too obvious, the coincidence: he talks to you, says he'll help, invites you to Pittsburgh and then six hours later he's dead?"

"Of course it has." Nancy rattled noisily through utensils, found a sharp knife.

"Jesus," he said. "And you still . . . " He shook his head in wonderment. "You know, it isn't smart not to be scared." Nancy shut the drawer, then stood there, her back to him, saying nothing. "Nancy," he persisted, "you've got to take this stuff to the police."

"Why?" she said, facing him.

"Because it's evidence, if what we think is true. And, anyway, you've got to tell them what you know—the marmalade, and then let them go from there."

Nancy turned back to the counter, concentrated on the pizza, sawing at it with the knife. "No," she said, finally.

"What the hell do you mean, no? Nancy, Miss Mulholland, I'm agreeing with you that something very strange has happened, that Catherine has made herself disappear, that Weiss knew why or where, or both, and someone killed him." He stopped. Nancy wasn't cutting pizza any more. She wasn't doing anything except looking at him, her arms folded. "What I'm saying," he continued, his voice much softer, "is that this is no place for you or me."

"I thought of that," she said and Simco thought her voice seemed warmer, that she was looking differently at him. He began to hope he'd made his points.

Nancy went to the sink, picked up her beer and drank some of it. "What's there to tell the police? The marmalade? And what else? I thought you'd be the first one to see that I don't have any evidence, not one single thing, for them to go on. Just an aunt who's disappeared, my story about the marmalade, and a report that a guy who was her boyfriend was mugged and killed in Pittsburgh."

"Do what you want," said Simco, rising from the table, sounding tired.

"Do you want to hear the tape?"

"What tape?"

Nancy pointed at the cassette. "It's from Weiss's answering machine. I've heard it."

"No," he said. "I'm not going to play detective."

"So you're not going to help."

"I'm not going to help you get into trouble."

"All right. What do I owe you for the pizza?"

"Nothing," said Simco, moving toward the door. "Good night."

When he had left, Nancy finished her beer, put two slices of pizza on a plate and went back to Catherine's study. She pushed the rewind button on the answering machine, intending to listen to the tape again, but then decided not to. It would take too long. She was tired and was feeling discouraged. She wasn't even hungry anymore, but began eating the pizza because she knew she should.

She wasn't discouraged because of Frank Simco. She didn't really care that he had refused to listen to the tape—was rather glad he'd refused, because there wasn't much there. Nor did she care that he'd walked out on her tonight. What bothered her was that she had so little to go on and that too much of what he'd said made sense. Maybe with some sleep, things would look better in the morning.

She glanced down at the pad and read what she had written earlier: "Catherine. Storm? Gil Bennet." She turned off the desk lamp and went to bed.

MARCH—1987						
S	M	T	W	T	F	S
1	2	3	4	5	6	7
8	9	10	11	12	13	14
15	16	17	18	19	20	21
22	23	24	25	_26_	27	28
29	30	31				

DAY TEN

APRIL—1987						
S	M	T	W	T	F	S
			1	2	3	(4)
5	6	7	8	9	10	11
12	13	14	15	16	17	18
19	20	21	22	23	24	25
26	27	28	29	30		

D A Y   T E N

Devon, Connecticut
Morning

Nancy was usually up by seven-thirty—even on weekends she never slept past nine—but when she awoke in Catherine's bedroom it was already twenty of ten. Even at that hour, lying there in the soft bed, the house quiet except for the hum of the furnace, she felt herself drifting backwards toward sleep and had to force herself to sit up, to swing her legs out from under the covers, to put her feet on the cold floor. She went to the window, and as she pulled up the shade, bright, white light flooded the room. It had snowed overnight.

She scurried to Catherine's closet, found an old, quilted bathrobe and put it on, smiling at the fit: big enough to wrap around her nearly twice, the hem and sleeves far too short. But it was warm.

In the kitchen, she made coffee and debated for a moment whether to take a shower, but decided that that could wait for later. She poured coffee into a large blue mug and padded down the hallway to Catherine's study where she sat down at the desk and pressed the play button of the answering machine. She listened for a moment, then sped the tape forward. She pressed play again and heard her aunt's voice:

"Richard. It's Catherine. There's a big storm out on the ocean and it made me want to talk to you. Call me, if you can."

There was a click. Then the machine's singsong voice said: *"Tuesday, 9:52 p.m."*

The tape played on: someone canceled a squash game; a plumbing supply company said Weiss's order was in. Then:

"Richard. It's me. Very stormy at sea. I'd hate to be out on a night like this. I hope it stops because I must go out tomorrow. Please don't worry."

Again the click, then:

"Wednesday, 11:41 p.m."

Nancy stopped the tape, rewound it and listened again to Catherine's two messages. There was something about them that wasn't quite right. Catherine's voice: there was something oddly flat about it as though she were reading baseball scores or stock quotations. It was not the voice of someone who was thrilled by ocean storms, who had, in fact, some years before called Nancy late at night to describe a storm in Cotchpinicut with such vividness and excitement that Nancy could almost hear the wind and the crashing of the surf against the beach.

And midway through the second message, Catherine's voice changed, grew softer, warmer. *"I hope it stops because I must . . . "* (her "must" was almost whispered and the emphasis was clear) *" . . . go out tomorrow."* And her final words: *"Please don't worry"* . . . she said that sadly, as though she knew Weiss would worry, and had reason to.

Nancy got up from the desk and went over to the window. Clumps of snow, dislodged from the tree branches by small gusts of wind, were hitting the ground with muffled *whuffs*. She wondered whether she was making too much of Catherine's voice. Maybe ocean storms had lost their fascination for her, or maybe she'd simply been tired. Or maybe, it suddenly occurred to Nancy, there hadn't been a storm at all.

She hurried into the bedroom; took from her wallet the card that Cahoon had given her; dialed the Cotchpinicut police and asked for him. He wasn't in, but the dispatcher was able to give her the information she needed: the week Catherine had disappeared the weather had been fair and mild until Thursday, when clouds had moved in and the temperature had dropped. But there hadn't been anything dramatic—no high seas, no gale-force winds, no downpours—just some cold weather, annoying in late March when everyone was restless for spring, but otherwise unremarkable.

After the phone call, Nancy paced the living room, trying to figure out what Catherine's messages meant. Was she talking to Weiss in some kind of code? Saying that things were what? Bad? Unsettled? Dangerous? She tried to think of other synonyms for stormy, but couldn't.

Nancy thought again about Catherine's final words: *"I must go out tomorrow"* and said them softly, out loud to herself. The message had been recorded late Wednesday. Thursday, from everything they knew so far, was probably the day Catherine disappeared, so it seemed very likely that Catherine was telling Weiss that she was leaving—leaving Thursday. It fit—very nicely—but explained nothing. She still had no idea where Catherine had disappeared to or why.

Nancy went back to the kitchen. There wasn't anything to eat for breakfast except cold slices of leftover pizza and she wondered how she would get to a store. She didn't have a car, and after last night, she couldn't call on Simco. It occurred to her that little things, like getting groceries, were going to present problems.

She took a slice of pizza to the study and pressed the PLAY button on the answering machine. The tape droned on through several more beeps followed by silences, then came a call from a woman about a paper that Weiss was going to deliver and after that the message that had caught her attention last night:

"Dick? Gil Bennet. Could you call us at the Potomac number? Thanks."

Then: *"Monday, 1:54 p.m."*

Gil Bennet? Why was that name familiar? She knew she'd seen it or heard it recently, but she couldn't remember where. Had Catherine mentioned him? She couldn't be sure, but she doubted it. She let the tape play on; heard a message from some printing company, next one from a woman who seemed to be

Weiss's secretary, and then there was Gil Bennet again, but sounding different this time:

"Dick? Gil. We're a little concerned that we haven't heard from you. There are some things that have come up that we really need to discuss. I think you should call us at the Savannah number."

"Wednesday, 11:38 p.m."

His voice wasn't that of someone who was a "little concerned." It was an angry voice, controlled, but not trying to conceal what lay just beneath the surface. Why hadn't Weiss called him back and why did that upset him—or them? Who was the "we" that Bennet was talking about and what was the Savannah number? The hints and glimpses were tantalizing, but nothing more than that.

She picked up her slice of pizza, pulled off the top layer of cold mozzarella, and put it in her mouth. It was tasteless and tough, like a wad of old chewing gum. She finished her coffee and then went into the bathroom to take a shower. Afterwards, she told herself, she would begin to search the house.

Devon, Connecticut
Morning

Frank Simco hated winter. As early as the second week of January, he was aware of the slow, almost reluctant lengthening of days and throughout February and March he read the signs of the approaching season with the satisfaction of a weary traveler who notes more and more familiar landmarks the nearer he gets to home. An early April snow was not, to Simco, a shoulder shrug or a shake of the head or a New England weather joke; it was a setback, an interruption of progress and of order and it put him in an even worse mood than he'd been in the night before.

He put on his old tweed overcoat, then struggled with his black galoshes, which he didn't bother to buckle. One of his blue wool gloves had a hole at the base of the thumb and no matter how carefully he tried to put it on, his thumb popped through like a curious cat finding an open cabinet door.

He went out the back door and squished along the walkway to the garage. The sun was out, at least, and already there was a slow dripping from the eaves. He opened the overhead door and took the orange snow shovel from its hook and began scraping grimly at the driveway.

It would have been a relief if the work had taken his mind off last night, but it didn't and Simco found it difficult to move his thoughts very far away from Nancy Mulholland and the scene in Catherine's kitchen. The word that kept running through his mind was reckless: something which, apparently, Nancy was and something which he decidedly was not. The disappearance of Catherine Lakey, which had seemed, at first, a puzzling inconvenience, and which had then slowly taken on the shape of ordinary tragedy—random violence, perhaps, or suicide—now was clearly something more. And, whatever it was, it did not—should not—invite the amateurish nosing around of people who didn't know what they were dealing with. He had been absolutely right in telling Nancy that he wouldn't help her.

The trouble with that decision, though, was that it seemed to have accomplished nothing. It hadn't caused her to turn things over to the police and it hadn't in the least discouraged her from persisting in her own investigations. What it had done was to cut him off from her and, more than anything, that was why he felt as unhappy as he did. For nearly fifteen years, ever since the dissolution of his marriage to a woman who had nagged him into marrying her and who had nearly nagged him into giving up his studies, Simco had found it easy to maintain pleasant, but distant relationships with women. He was content with his ordered academic life and enjoyed his freedom to lead it as he chose.

Nancy Mulholland was threatening that. She had about her an energy, a self-assurance and a recklessness that both discomfited and attracted him. He liked nothing about the Catherine Lakey mess—it was confusing, dark and unfamiliar—but he was being pulled back to it by Nancy.

He finished the driveway, then cleared the front steps and

saw from there that his efforts had been unnecessary: the snow was melting quickly now and the streets and sidewalks would soon be as clear as the places he had shoveled.

He went into the house, kicked off his galoshes and tossed his coat and gloves onto the sofa. He stared at the phone on the table beside the armchair and thought of calling her. He could apologize—no, apologize was not the word; he could say that he had thought things over, had reconsidered and that he would try to help, if he could, as time permitted, of course, provided that she understood that certain things were out, like breaking into places and walking off with things. But since she'd gone to all the trouble to get the tape, he'd listen to it, if she still wanted him to. In his head he liked the sound of the conversation. He wasn't really compromising his position, but only offering to do what he could and, furthermore, if he were around, he could probably prevent her from doing something rash and dangerous like she'd done in Pittsburgh. What she would say was harder to imagine. She might be very pleased, but it was entirely possible, he knew, that she saw their differences too clearly and that she'd prefer to work alone. What would he say then? He didn't know and he wasn't eager to confront the possibility. He looked at his watch and thought about the piles of paperwork sitting on his desk, the leavings of the past fractured week, which had given him almost no time to spend on the business of running the department. He could go to his office, put in a solid afternoon of work. The snow would melt, his mood might change, and then he could decide what he should do about Miss Mulholland, who had not once the entire week asked him to call her Nancy.

Devon, Connecticut
Midday

Nancy found something right away. It was in the antique wood box in the living room, on top of a stack of magazines and newspapers, wrapped in thick, canary yellow paper and tied with orange ribbon. Taped to one corner was a card with a drawing in black ink:

It was what Catherine called the C-cat and she used it as her signature on all her letters to Nancy.

Nancy unwrapped the package carefully and was puzzled to find a small red loose-leaf notebook which said on the front, Dinner In Devon. It was a cookbook, but the very one that Catherine had already given her for Christmas. She opened the front cover. On the title page was an inscription written in Catherine's precise, blocky printing:

April 14, 1987
Dear Nannie,

Happy Birthday and thank you for the times you
were my gracious hostess last year.
Enjoy the recipes—I hope you find some favorites!

Love, C.

Another marmalade? April 14 was her birthday. The C-cat was obviously for her and only she would know that Catherine had already given her the book.

She read the inscription again. Four words were underlined: "the times" and "last year." "The times last year," said Nancy, musing aloud, concentrating. "The times last year when I was her hostess." Nancy closed her eyes, tried to remember when Catherine had visited. Just before Christmas and, before that, sometime in the summer—July or August, she couldn't be quite sure. What was Catherine saying? That there was something about those visits that was important? That they tied in with why she disappeared or where she was?

Nancy went to the front window. The snow was melting rapidly in the early April sunshine; already the walks and roads were bare, mist wisping from them as they dried. Staring out the window, Nancy tried to recall Catherine's visits to Bloomington. What had they done together? What had they talked about? *Books . . . movies . . . Grandma Ruth . . . the nursing home . . . me . . . my restlessness . . . my penchant for getting into relationships with men who let me down.* She was still seeing Michael then, still involved, but had begun to have her doubts and to feel corralled . . . Nancy shook her head. Wrong track. She tried another approach—tried to visualize Catherine being with her last year—the meals they'd shared, the walks they'd taken—but the images were like out-of-focus photographs.

She returned to the sofa, picked up the cookbook by its spine and held it so the pages hung straight down. She blew between them and gave the book a shake, hoping to see a note or card flutter to the floor. That one didn't was no surprise to her. Catherine seemed almost obsessed with subtlety, with leaving messages that only Nancy would be able to read. But somewhere in the book there had to be something.

Nancy sat down, opened it to the beginning and began turning the pages slowly, studying each one carefully: the acknowledgments, the preface, the table of contents, then the title page of section one. It said "January" in large bold type that ran along the top of the page. Below it was a line drawing of a house, snow-covered, a curl of smoke coming from the chimney. She turned the page to the first recipe. It was Betty Putney's Roast Beef Stew. She stopped. That wasn't right. She could have sworn . . . She remembered that shortly after Christmas she had tried the first recipe in the book and it wasn't roast beef stew. It was a chili recipe: Let It Snow Chili. She had made it for friends for a New Year's supper and now it wasn't there. She flipped back to the index, ran her finger down the *C* column, found Let It Snow Chili, and she was right: it was, or should have been page 7, the page where the recipes began. She flipped back to Betty Putney's Roast Beef Stew. It was page 9. The 7–8 page was missing.

"Favorite," she said suddenly, remembering that in her thank-you she had told Catherine about the supper party, that the chili had been a big hit and that the recipe had quickly become a favorite. And in the cookbook inscription Catherine had written: "I hope you find some favorites."

What other favorites? What others had she tried and liked and mentioned to Catherine? Another winter dish, she remembered. A stew, an Irish stew. What was its name? B something. She turned to the index and found it: Ballybunion Irish Stew, page 176. Nancy quickly thumbed through the pages: 169, 171, 173, 177. She stopped. Pages 175–176 were gone.

"It isn't here," she said to herself and repeated the message, slowly: "I hope you find some favorites." Find them where? "Goddamn it, Catherine!" Nancy got up from the sofa and went into the kitchen, where she poured herself more coffee and tried to think clearly.

If I were going to hide those recipes, thought Nancy, where would I expect someone to look for them? What place is logical, but not too obvious? A card file? She hadn't seen one in the kitchen, but . . . Nancy turned and looked across the kitchen to the counter that ran from the refrigerator to the stove. There, between two wooden bookends, was a tidy row of cookbooks. "My God," said Nancy, "of course."

She hurried to the counter, grabbed the first cookbook and shook it. A shower of papers, cards, clippings fluttered to the floor. Nancy dropped to her hands and knees and began going through them one at a time.

Forty-five minutes later the kitchen floor was littered with cookbooks and papers and index cards. Nancy, still sitting on the floor, surveyed the mess and felt keenly disappointed. She had been sure she was on the right track, but had found nothing. What had Simco said? That this was no place for her?

Wearily she got up from the floor. Maybe she should go for a walk, see how far it was to town; or go to Catherine's office and look around some more.

She went to the bedroom to get her jacket and, as she went through the living room, there was *Dinner In Devon* lying on the coffee table. She picked it up, hefted it in her hand as though she were testing its weight, and felt the urge to hurl it as hard as she could into the fireplace.

Devon, Connecticut
Afternoon

Nancy turned on the overhead light in Catherine's office and tossed her jacket over the back of a chair. On the windowsill there was a stack of paper towels and she used one to wipe the perspiration from her forehead. The day had turned warm and the walk to Devon Center had been much longer than she had expected.

Thursday morning, before she'd called Weiss, she had gone through the office, looking for something that Catherine might have left for her. Then she'd started searching the desk and had begun by flipping through the Rolodex. Was that where she'd seen it? She sat down at Catherine's desk, picked up the Rolodex, found the tab marked *B*, and began going through the cards. Bailey, Barnetti, Belsen, Bennet. She removed the card. "Bennet, Gil" was typed at the top. Below it there was only a telephone number with an area code that didn't look familiar. The card was soft and smudged around the edges, suggesting that it had seen its share of use.

Nancy pushed back her chair, began opening the desk drawers. She found a telephone directory, thumbed through the front pages, stopping when she came to the map of area codes. Tracing her finger down the East Coast, she found Bennet's, 301. It was Maryland. She dialed the number, waited, heard a click, then a man's smooth metallic voice saying that she had reached Gil Bennet's office and that if she'd please leave a message, he'd get back to her as soon as he could. She decided not to, but made a note to call again on Monday.

She put the card in her purse and lit a cigarette. She was fairly sure now that Catherine hadn't left anything in the office for her, yet there might be something that would be another clue, like

Bennet's name and number on the Rolodex. She decided that she should go through the desk carefully, drawer by drawer, and after that, the computer disks. She slid the coffee mug across the desk so she could use it as an ashtray, then opened the lower left-hand drawer and removed a stack of folders. She folded her legs underneath her and began to read.

She had read through three or four when a voice from the doorway startled her. "I thought I saw a light down here." She looked up and saw Frank Simco squinting at her through the smoke. She gave him an embarrassed smile, went over to the window and opened it.

"I didn't know it was so bad in here," she said.

Simco shrugged. "I was going to call you. I thought you might need a lift to town. For groceries."

"I went to town. It's quite a hike."

"Why don't you take my car." He reached in his pocket and took out some keys and tossed them to her. "It's an easy walk home for me from here. You can call me when you're done."

She held the keys in the palm of her hand. "Are you sure?"

"Absolutely."

"Thanks," she said. "You've been . . . you've made things much easier."

Simco looked at the floor. "I'm not sure I have. I think last night—"

"Don't worry about it," said Nancy. "I'm not sure I blame you. You've got enough to do around here without getting involved in this."

"What I mean to say is that if there's something I can do— though maybe there isn't—that I'd be willing to do what I can." He paused. "I want to find Catherine, too."

"Thanks," said Nancy. "I'll let you know."

"All right," said Simco. He stood in the doorway awkwardly, his hands in his pockets. "Do you still want me to listen to that tape?"

"It's back at the house. I'm not sure it's worth your while." She glanced at her watch. "When do you need your car?"

"Whenever. No hurry."

"I thought I'd go through some things here, then go into town. Is five OK?"

"Fine. Well, I should go get some work done."

"Thanks again," said Nancy.

He turned to leave.

"Professor Simco?"

"Please. It's Frank. Students call me Professor."

"OK," said Nancy. "Frank. Did Catherine ever mention a Gil Bennet to you?"

Simco thought for a moment. "I don't think so. It doesn't ring a bell. Why?"

"It's just a name that's come up, but don't let me keep you. I'll call you when I'm back."

After Simco left, Nancy went over to the open window and lit another cigarette. The snow had nearly disappeared; there were only odd white patches in some shady spots. She was surprised at Simco's conversation, at his suggesting that he had changed his mind and now wanted to help. Last night in the kitchen she would have welcomed him, but now she wasn't sure. She needed help, she knew that, but not if it meant a long string of arguments with him to justify what she knew she had to do. She might be better off being on her own. She didn't know. She'd have to think about it.

Devon, Connecticut
Evening

She didn't do it easily, but on the drive back to Catherine's from the shopping center Nancy finally decided to accept Simco's offer. Her experience that morning—her failure to solve the puzzle of the cookbook—had persuaded her that she couldn't continue on her own. The trick, she knew, was to use Simco to her advantage, to consult him as a resource only when she needed to; she wasn't looking for a guardian or a partner.

* * *

In Catherine's kitchen, she arranged the groceries neatly along the counter because she didn't know where her aunt kept things and she didn't want to disrupt what she was sure was a meticulously thought-out system. Nor did she want to violate a superstition that had developed twenty years earlier when her mother had gone into the hospital the first time, desperately ill. Shortly after the sitter had arrived, she had begun rearranging everything—putting the spice tins in alphabetical order, moving the kitchen canisters to another counter, closer to the stove ("more efficient," she'd said). Nancy had felt a terrible anxiety, then rage, and had ordered the woman to stop, to put everything back. Though Nancy had been only thirteen at the time, the sitter had obeyed, and a few weeks later her mother had surprised everyone by getting better. She had come home and had lived on in that house for ten more years; and while it wasn't anything Nancy could prove, she'd felt, ever since then, that by leaving things the way they were she'd reserved a place for her mother, a place that, otherwise, might have been lost. Now she was doing it for Catherine, hoping it would work again.

She dropped two ice cubes in a glass, poured herself some of the wine she'd just bought and thought about the offer she was going to make to Simco. She called him. When there was no answer, she left a message on his machine, then went into the living room to the sofa and picked up the cookbook. She opened it and reread the inscription. " . . . I hope you find some favorites."

"Why the hell did you have to hide them?" said Nancy out loud. The telephone rang. She put down the cookbook and went to the kitchen to answer it. It was Simco.

"Your car's back," she said. "If you'll give me directions, I'll deliver it."

"It's easier if I just come and get it. It's an excuse to get outside. I've been cooped up all day."

She laughed. "I wish you'd let me do something for you. I'm feeling like a burden."

"Don't worry about it."

She wasn't sure what to say to him next. The telephone silence was lengthening, beginning to get awkward. "I could give you a drink."

"That's nice of you." His voice was brighter, warmer.

"I don't know what I have, what Catherine has. I bought some wine."

"Anything is fine."

"If you have time, I'd like you to listen to the tape."

"Good. Can I bring anything?"

"Bring your brain. Mine's not working very well, and there's something else I want to show you. Another marmalade, I think."

"Really?" He sounded surprised, a little skeptical. "When did this happen?"

"This morning. It's a message from Catherine, but I can't figure out what it's saying. It's been driving me crazy all day."

"All right," he said, "see you in twenty minutes."

She played the tape for him once, all the way through, then replayed the two messages from Catherine and the two from Bennet. She had decided that she would say nothing about her own conclusions, but would wait instead to hear what he might think. He asked her to play Catherine's second message again. He scratched his forehead with his thumb.

"Well?" she said.

"Was this the Wednesday and the Tuesday of the week she disappeared?"

"I'm almost positive. If you go backwards from the end of the tape—the last message is mine, last Thursday night—there's at least one message every day going back to the Monday of the week she disappeared."

"I don't remember any storms," he said, "but then, of course, I'm not on Cape Cod."

Nancy smiled to herself, but said nothing.

"And that thing about having to go out 'tomorrow.' That's the day the police think whatever happened, happened. Was she telling Weiss what she was going to do?" He shrugged, almost to himself. "That would account for the way he sounded on the telephone with you, why he wasn't surprised. And another thing that strikes me is that Catherine doesn't come out and say anything on the telephone. Neither did Weiss with you. It's as if they thought someone might be listening."

Nancy hadn't thought of that, but Simco was right. It was odd that Weiss had said that he wanted to help, but he couldn't do it on the telephone, that she had to come to Pittsburgh.

He looked at her a little anxiously, like a pupil at a teacher in the middle of a recitation, trying to read how he is doing. "I don't know," he said. "I guess that's about it."

"And what about the things from Bennet?"

He shook his head. "You must know something I don't know. I'm trying to figure out why you singled him out. He calls, asks Weiss to call him back, then calls again with the same message. So what?"

"You didn't hear anything odd?" she said, a note of disappointment in her voice. She pressed some buttons on the machine and moved the tape back and forth until she found Bennet's second message. She played it again.

"He's mad?" said Simco, uncertainly. "I don't know."

"Very," said Nancy.

"All right, but I get mad too when people don't call me back."

"Wait a minute," said Nancy. "I do know something you don't know." She got her purse, rummaged through it, found the card with Bennet's name and phone number and handed it to Simco. "I found that in Catherine's Rolodex this afternoon."

Simco looked at it. "So that's why you asked me if she'd mentioned him."

"I called him."

"You called him?" said Simco, surprised.

"No answer, just a machine. Probably a business number."

"I'm not sure you should have done that."

"Why not?" said Nancy, puzzled. "He's a link between Catherine and Weiss, maybe the only one I've got. Why wouldn't I call him?"

"Maybe you should let the police talk to him."

"The police? Why would the police talk to him?" Nancy didn't like the turn the conversation had taken.

"Because he's a link. Because he seems to be a friend—at least an acquaintance—of a woman who's disappeared and of her friend who was murdered. I think the police would want to talk to somebody like that."

Nancy sighed. "There you go again." She tapped a finger against the side of her head. "The link's up here for you and me. We've got a jar of marmalade, a very brief conversation with Weiss, a few messages on an answering machine—some hunches, really, but not evidence. The police wouldn't be interested."

"Look at it another way, then," said Simco, persisting. "What if you're right—in the worst sense—that this Bennet is a link between Weiss and Catherine, that—"

"What do you mean, worst sense?"

"That he had something to do with what's happened." He looked at Nancy and saw the skepticism on her face.

"That's not what I was thinking," she said.

"For argument's sake, let's say he did. Right now he's probably never heard of you, but if you pick up the phone and call him, he'll not only know who you are, he'll know what you're up to."

"I hadn't thought of that," she said quietly, surprised she hadn't and angry with herself. What Simco was suggesting was unlikely, but she knew she couldn't discount it entirely. At least she hadn't actually reached Bennet. No harm had been done. "But what do I do?" she said. "Just sit here and make believe I've never heard of him?"

Simco gave her a thin smile. "No police?"

"No police."

"Lie then. You seem to have a gift."

"Lie to who?" she asked, ignoring the remark.

"To Bennet. Tell him you're a friend of Catherine's; tell him you're anybody but who you are. Tell him you're just checking everybody she knew to see if anyone has any idea what might have happened."

"And what about Weiss?"

Simco looked at the floor. "I don't know."

Nancy stood up from the desk. "I'll think about it," she said.

She didn't think very much of Simco's strategy, but she didn't want to argue. "Let me show you what I was talking about on the phone."

She led him into the living room and handed him the cookbook. He looked at it briefly, turning it over in his hands, then he looked at Nancy questioningly. She bent down and picked up the yellow wrapping paper from the floor beside the armchair. She found the small card, opened it and held it up for him to see. "The book was wrapped in this," she said, "and see this card?"

Simco nodded.

"Her C-cat," Nancy said, "the way she always signed her name on her letters to me. That's why I assumed the present was for me." Nancy tossed the paper onto the chair. "Open it."

Simco opened the front cover.

"See the inscription?" said Nancy.

Simco studied it, looked up. "Well, it is for you."

"It certainly is," she said, then she paused for effect. "Even though she gave me the exact same thing for Christmas."

Simco went over to the sofa and sat down. He looked at the book again. "So this is another marmalade?"

"It's more than that . . . the inscription, that thing about finding my favorites? Take a look at the first recipe."

Simco leafed through a few pages, then stopped. "Betty Putney's Roast Beef Stew?"

Nancy shook her head. "The first recipe is missing. It was a recipe for chili, a favorite of mine. I wrote Catherine about it, telling her how much I liked it." Nancy went over to the sofa and sat down next to Simco. She took the book from him and leafed through it to the index. "And another one she knew I liked, this Irish stew, it's supposed to be . . . ," she turned some pages, " . . . right here." She handed the open book back to Simco. "But it isn't."

He turned back to the title page and looked at the inscription. " 'I hope you find some favorites.' I see."

"But I don't." Nancy got up and went over to the fireplace. "Where would she have hidden them? I thought this morning that it would have to be someplace where I'd think of looking, not in a hollowed-out table leg or behind a chimney brick. Where's a logical place to put a recipe?"

Simco seemed startled by the question. "You're asking me?" he said.

"Where would you look for a recipe?"

"The kitchen? Where she keeps her recipes?"

Nancy smiled at him. "Exactly what I thought. I went through every cookbook I could find. Nothing."

Simco looked up at her. "On the phone, did you say something about a drink?"

Nancy looked at him blankly, then tossed her head back and looked at the ceiling. "I'm sorry. You give me your car, you drive me all over New England, and I can't even remember to offer you a drink." She went into the kitchen and soon Simco heard the clinking of bottles, liquor bottles he presumed. "What would you like?" she shouted.

"Bourbon, if you have it. Some water," said Simco. He put the cookbook on the coffee table and began leafing through it absently.

"Got it," said Nancy from the kitchen. "Short or tall?"

"Short," said Simco, almost to himself. He had leaned forward and was studying the book intently.

Nancy came to the doorway. "Sorry, didn't hear you."

Simco didn't look up. "Let It Snow Chili?" he said.

"That's right."

"Here it is."

"Here what is?"

"The recipe." He held the book up for her to see.

She crossed the room quickly and took the book from him. She looked at it and laughed. "The only cookbook I didn't look in." She sat down in the armchair and studied the recipe. After a minute or two, she looked up at Simco. "It's just the recipe."

"What do you mean?"

"Just that. It's the recipe. Nothing's changed. There's nothing new here." She turned the page, then turned it back. "What the hell is she doing?"

"Let me see," said Simco, extending his hand. Nancy passed the book to him, got up and went back to the kitchen. Simco looked carefully at the recipe, then turned to the index at the back of the book. He nodded his head slowly and leaned back on the sofa.

Nancy returned from the kitchen, a drink in each hand. When she saw Simco, she stopped. "What is it?"

He smiled at her. "I don't know why," he said, sitting up straight, "but she's changed the page number." He tapped the book with his index finger. "Look here. She's whited out the original and written in a new one in black ink. It's hard to tell the difference."

Nancy handed him the drink and sat down next to him on the sofa. She leaned over and looked at the page. "You're right."

"It's supposed to be page 7, but she's changed it to 21. Anything special about that number?"

Nancy thought for a moment. "No, not that I can think of."

"All right," said Simco. He leaned forward, began turning the pages slowly. Nancy got up and went into the kitchen. A few minutes later, she returned, smoking a cigarette and holding a green bowl that she was using as an ashtray.

Simco looked up, glanced briefly at the cigarette, then motioned for her to come and sit beside him. "I think I've got the other," he said. "Ballybunion Irish Stew?"

"That's it." Nancy crushed the cigarette into the bowl, went behind the sofa and leaned over his shoulder.

"And that page number's been changed too," he said, "from whatever it was to 14. Does 14 mean anything to you?"

"No. I don't think so."

Simco stood up and rattled the ice in his empty glass. "May I?"

"Sure," said Nancy, "let me."

"No. I'll help myself," said Simco. "Did you have any other favorites? Recipes, I mean."

Nancy shook her head. "There wasn't time. I might have tried one or two others, but I don't think I told Catherine about them."

Simco picked up the book and handed it to her. "Start right at the beginning," he said. "Just look at the numbers on the bottom of the page. Take your time. Can I get you some more wine?"

"Thanks," she said and gave him her glass. She walked around the sofa and sat down on the floor beside the coffee table. She put the book in her lap and began going through the pages one at a time. Almost immediately, she raised an arm and shouted, "I've got another one!"

"Be right there," said Simco from the kitchen. He appeared a minute later, carrying two glasses.

"Chicken Curry Bombay," she said. "Right up here at the beginning. Page number's changed to 8."

"A favorite?"

"No. Never tried it."

"Keep looking."

"Let's alternate sections," said Nancy. "You do one, then I'll do one."

"What sections?"

Nancy turned to the orange divider page that said "February" and pointed to it. "The book's arranged by months," she said. "If you're looking for something for a beach picnic, you look in July or August. Nice idea."

"By months?" Simco said, looking at her. A smile began to spread across his face. "I think I see."

"See what?"

"Quick," he said. "Tell me the first thing you think of that's arranged by months."

"Date book. Calendar. Oh my God, a calendar."

"Maybe," said Simco. "She's moved the recipes to new months. Let's see." He thumbed forward to the chili recipe. "Chili's in May, and the new number, that could be the date. May 21." He thumbed forward again. "And the stew. That's in July. July 14."

"And the curry's been moved back to January," said Nancy. "January 8."

"Clever," said Simco, admiringly. "So we have three dates."

"But what year?" said Nancy. "This year, at least the January one? Last year? Five years ago?"

"What did you say?" said Simco suddenly.

"What? What year, this year, last year, five—"

Simco grabbed the book and turned to the front of it. He slapped it hard with his hand. Nancy jumped. "Ha! She's telling you. Last year."

"Where?"

"The inscription," said Simco. "The underlined words, 'the times last year.' The time is last year."

"January 8, 1986. May 21, July 14. What happened then? What's so important about those dates?"

"I don't know," said Simco, "but there may be more. You said a section at a time. I'll do February."

Almost an hour later, Simco closed the cookbook with a sigh. They had gone carefully through every page, looking for the telltale change of numbers, but had found nothing more. Simco got up from the sofa, stretched and yawned. He looked over at Nancy, who was curled up in the armchair, a legal pad in her lap, its top sheet covered with doodles and numbers.

She finally looked up at him. "We're missing something. She wouldn't have gone to all the trouble of giving me those dates if she wasn't going to tell me what they meant. Did something happen to her last January 8, or did something simply happen that she wants me to know about?"

Simco looked at his watch. "I think you should back away from this for a while. Let it sit overnight, come back to it in the morning when you're fresher. It's something I do all the time. It works."

Nancy kept writing on the pad. "I suppose," she said, absently. "But I'm not sure how I simply stop thinking about it."

"Maybe by having some dinner," said Simco, "maybe with me."

Nancy stopped writing and rubbed her eyes. "Thanks, Mr. . . . Frank, but I'm not really very hungry. You go ahead."

"I feel guilty, you alone in a strange place, no car, not very much to do."

Nancy smiled at him. "There's plenty to do. I appreciate your concern, but please don't worry about me. I'll try to do what you said. I'll clean this place up; make some calls back to Indiana, see if they'll let me take next week off; maybe watch TV."

"You're staying, then?"

"I've got to now that I've come this far. It seems that Catherine wants me to find something. Maybe she wants me to find her."

"You're sure you won't join me?" The disappointment in Simco's voice was clear.

"Another time," said Nancy, as gently as she could. "And thanks for the car and for all your help tonight. I'm not sure I ever would have found those recipes or seen the page numbers."

"I'm sure you would have, eventually," said Simco. He put his glass down on the coffee table. "I guess I need my keys."

Nancy went into the kitchen and came back with them. "Call me if you have any ideas."

"I'll call tomorrow whether I have any ideas or not, if that's all right."

"That's fine."

Simco went to the front door, turned to her and started to say something, but reconsidered. He gave her an awkward smile and a small wave of his hand, then he left.

For a moment, Nancy stood there, staring at the closed door, then she went back to the armchair and lit a cigarette. She smiled to herself and shook her head. Working with men was always complicated.

MARCH—1987						
S	M	T	W	T	F	S
1	2	3	4	5	6	7
8	9	10	11	12	13	14
15	16	17	18	19	20	21
22	23	24	25	26	27	28
29	30	31				

DAY ELEVEN

APRIL—1987						
S	M	T	W	T	F	S
			1	2	3	4
5	6	7	8	9	10	11
12	13	14	15	16	17	18
19	20	21	22	23	24	25
26	27	28	29	30		

DAY ELEVEN

SUNDAY, APRIL 5, 1987

Bethesda, Maryland
Morning

The polished, oval conference table could easily accommodate ten people, but on this Sunday morning only three men were seated at it; two facing each other, one at the head. Their attention was directed to the center of the table, to a tape recorder that wasn't much larger than a deck of playing cards. The three men eyed it warily, as though it were some sort of insect, unpredictable and possibly dangerous.

One of them, rumpled and round-shouldered, leaned forward and pressed a switch on the machine. The tape spun. He stopped it. "The sound's OK, but a little tinny," he said, "especially through this speaker. Let me know if you want to hear anything again."

"Remind us again, Woody. When was this recorded?" The question came from across the table, from a man whose age was difficult to determine. Though his face was lined and craggy, his arms and chest, visible beneath his tight-fitting polo shirt, were those of an athlete not very far past his prime.

"Yesterday, Tony. The first call was in the morning. The last one was in the evening. You want to hear this now?" Woody glanced at Tony, who said nothing, then looked to the head of the table, and receiving a nod, pressed a switch on the recorder. At first there was only tape hiss, then, very faintly, a voice. Woody fiddled with something on the side of the machine. The volume improved.

"Hello, Sergeant Cahoon please." It was a woman speaking, her voice clearly audible, but as Woody had warned, amplified by the small tape recorder it sounded thin and metallic. As the tape played on, Woody rolled a pencil in his fingers, consciously avoiding the glances that might be coming from the other two. They weren't looking at him. Tony was staring at the recorder, his face grim. Woody's boss, seated at the head of the table, had turned his swivel chair and tilted it back so he saw only the blank wall in front of him.

After several minutes, there was a click on the tape followed by a hollow hum. Woody leaned forward and turned off the recorder. "That's it." He looked at the table and waited. He heard the swivel chair turning, then the polite command: "I wonder if we might hear that part about the tape again. And that last business about the message."

Woody fiddled with some switches. The tape spun backwards, stopped, then ran forward:

"If you have time, I'd like you to listen to the tape."

Woody stopped the machine, then, receiving a nod to continue, pressed another switch and the tape sped forward, then slowed:

"Bring your brain. Mine's not working very well, and there's something else I want to show you. Another marmalade, I think."

"Really? When did this happen?"

"This morning. It's a message from Catherine, but I can't figure out what it's saying. It's been driving me crazy all day."

Woody turned off the machine; again waited in his chair. He felt hands on his shoulders and heard the voice behind him, again speaking politely: "Fill me in on a few things. I take it the woman is Mulholland?"

Woody nodded without looking up.

"And the man?"

"Simco. Frank Simco."

"I see." Woody's shoulders were released and as his boss returned to the head of the table, Tony and Woody watched him. A man in his late thirties or early forties, he moved with the unhurried confidence of someone who was comfortable with command. When he had seated himself, he reached across the table to the recorder, picked it up and held it out in front of him. "And this was recorded at Lakey's, I presume."

Woody nodded.

"Now," he said, "first things first. Could you tell me—us," he corrected himself, glancing at Tony, "exactly what tape they were talking about?"

Woody shook his head. "Don't know. At least I can't be sure. I think it's a tape off Weiss's answering machine."

"Why do you think that?"

"We know she went to Weiss's apartment last Friday. When she left, we checked it out. The answering machine was open. The tape was gone."

"I thought we had gone through the apartment."

"We did," said Woody.

"And didn't you tell me that you had removed everything that may have been of interest? Didn't you tell me that the place was . . . how did you put it? . . . sterilized?"

Woody ran a finger over the stubble above his upper lip. "We—I—thought it was," he said, straightening up in his chair. "Look, I didn't have much time and you said to leave the place like I found it, no mess. Anyway, why should I take the goddamn tape? We've got our own."

"Yes, we've got our own, but now they've got their own." Woody's boss put the recorder on the table, flicked it with his finger and watched it slide, spinning, down past Woody to the far end, stopping just inches from the edge. "Goddamn it," he said.

"What the hell," said Woody, his voice rising. "Who'd have thought, first of all, that Mulholland would fly to Pittsburgh to see some guy she's probably never heard of; then, second of all, when he doesn't show, that she'd break into his apartment; and third of all, that she'd walk off with the goddamn tape?" He looked at the other two men, one at a time. "What do you think the god-damn odds are on that?"

"Worry about the odds at the track," said Tony. "You're sup-posed to do your job. And stop thinking so much."

"That's enough." The command brought silence immediately. "What was on the tape?"

"Depends," said Woody. "We don't know when Weiss last cleared the thing. She picked it up Friday morning. That means calls coming in Thursday night are on it for sure, maybe all day Thursday, Wednesday. Who knows?"

"I don't suppose . . . Is there any chance that the tape could have picked up earlier calls—say Monday or Tuesday?"

"Like I said, it depends," said Woody. "It's possible, but most people clear those things more often than that."

There were a few short raps on the conference room door, and a small, blond woman, her hair loosely curled, poked her head in-side. "Can I get you anything," she asked, looking to the head of the table.

"Thanks, Maggie," he said. "Could we have some coffee and something to eat, if you can find anything."

"I'll do my best," she said, smiling, closing the door.

Woody looked at the tape recorder on the table. "You know I don't think this is such a big deal," said Woody. "I mean when you think about it, they don't really know anything. This guy Simco's a professor and Mulholland, what the hell is she any-way?"

The door to the conference room opened quietly. Maggie en-tered, carrying a tray with cups, a silver carafe and two bags of su-permarket cookies. She was thin, delicately pretty, and walked slightly stooped as if she was trying to be as unobtrusive as pos-sible. Tony raised his hand at Woody, trying to signal him to stop talking, but Woody was looking toward the head of the table.

"Look, Woody, I think we can hear this later."

Woody swung around to Tony. "Why later? I was just say-ing—"

Tony glared at him and nodded slightly, toward Maggie.

"OK. What the hell," said Woody.

Maggie set the tray down. "It's all I could find," she said apologetically. "The stores will open in an hour. I could send out."

"This is fine, Maggie," said the man at the head of the table. He rose, put an arm around her shoulders, thanked her and told her to take some time off later in the week. When she had left, he poured coffee for Tony and Woody and waited for them to settle back into their chairs.

Tony pointed a finger in Woody's direction. "When the hell are you going to learn to keep your mouth shut?"

"What?" said Woody, a puzzled look on his face. "What'd I do?"

"You don't talk in front of her," said Tony, making a vague gesture toward the door.

"Maggie?" said Woody. "For Christ's sake, Tony."

"Quiet! Both of you." He held up a hand to silence them, then turned to his right. "Please, Tony." His voice was soft and soothing. "Maggie's fine."

"She's a secretary," said Tony.

"She's my secretary and she's got the same clearance that you do."

"Maybe she ought to sit in on the meeting, then."

"I'll make those decisions, thank you." Their boss stood, placed his hands on the table and leaned slightly forward toward them. His voice was even. "But I don't think that what we say or do in front of Maggie Dacey is really much of an issue right now, is it? Don't we have more pressing things to talk about? He picked up the carafe, took his time filling his own cup, then returned the carafe to the tray. He looked at Woody. "I agree with you. The tape probably isn't a big deal. What is a very big deal is that your Miss Mulholland seems to have received a message from Catherine Lakey."

Woody sighed and shook his head. "Yeah," he said. "I don't know."

"What don't you know?"

"I don't know what the hell she's talking about. No phone calls. The mail's been stopped and she hasn't gone to pick it up."

"And the reference to marmalade?"

"No idea."

"Could Lakey have left a message in the house?"

"The Devon house?" said Woody. "No goddamn way. We spent half a day in there, went over everything with a fucking microscope."

"Cotchpinicut, then?"

"That was clean, too," said Woody without much conviction.

"Clean! When? You didn't get to Cotchpinicut until Mulholland, Simco and the local police had been nosing around for . . . what was it? Four days?"

"Three," said Woody.

"Three days!" The words, spit out, were followed by a pause. "Tony," he continued, speaking in a lowered voice, "How many people do we have looking for Lakey?"

Tony took a piece of paper from his shirt pocket. "Five," he said.

"And they're still reporting nothing?"

"Nothing."

"Not surprising, is it, given we didn't even know she was gone for almost a week." He looked at Woody, then spoke again to Tony. "Pull everyone off the Lakey search and put them on Mulholland and Simco."

Woody shook his head. "I think my guys and me can handle it."

"Whatever you think, you and your guys haven't handled it and it seems to me that your thinking hasn't gotten any of us very far. As I recall, you told me that you thought Weiss would never say anything; you thought that Lakey wouldn't do anything; you thought that no one would make any connection between them and us. We simply can't afford that kind of thinking because if this balloon ever goes up . . . " He stood up, looked hard first at Woody, then at Tony. He walked to the door, opened it and, without turning around, said, "Woody, I want you in Connecticut this afternoon."

He went down the carpeted corridor, stopped at a paneled door, fished in his pocket for a key, unlocked the door and entered the office. He went to the window, raised the blinds and spent a long moment looking out at the rolling Maryland countryside, then turned and lowered himself into a large leather chair. He picked up a silver-framed photograph. A long-legged, tanned woman, her blond hair windblown, and two children in bathing suits smiled at him from the deck of a sailboat. He studied it for a moment, then returned it to its place on the desk just in front of the small brass nameplate that said Gilbert Bennet—Director.

Devon, Connecticut
Morning

It had been one of those interminable nights that Nancy hated: long periods of wakefulness punctuated by short, uneasy bouts of sleep. Two or three times she had gotten up to read and once she had even fixed herself a small tumbler of bourbon, straight, but nothing seemed to work. Finally, at a little after six, she gave up, took a shower and got dressed. In the kitchen she made some coffee, then remembered that it was Sunday and decided that she would walk to town to get a newspaper.

Devon News & Drug was just opening when she arrived a little after seven; a teenaged boy was hauling bales of papers off the sidewalk and assembling them inside. Nancy took a *New York Times* and sat on a stool at the counter that ran the length of one side of the store. From a thin lady who called her "Dearie" she ordered coffee and a toasted bagel.

The counter stools began to fill with other early morning customers. To make room for them, Nancy slid the *Times* off the counter and held it on her lap. She flipped through the sections, looking at the headlines and the lead stories. The Sports section trumpeted the opening of the baseball season and the Travel section had a dramatic picture of a skier hurtling off a ledge, a plume of snow like the contrail of a jet trailing behind him. "Skiing South America" said the headline, "Chile and the Andes." Nancy looked closely at the picture. "Let It Snow, Chile," she thought, and smiled to herself, amused at her play on words. She flipped forward to the next section, Business, then stopped. Let It Snow Chili. It hadn't occurred to her that the chili of the recipe was pronounced the same as the name of the country. But if she thought of it that way, she saw that something interesting happened: Let It Snow *CHILE,* Ballybunion *IRISH* Stew, Chicken Curry *BOMBAY.* The three transposed recipes all contained the name of a place. There was something important about Bombay and January 8, 1986, about Chile and May 21, about Ireland and July 14. Something very important. Some link.

Nancy put some money on the counter and slid off the stool. The store was crowded now and she had to pick her way through people who were standing in line waiting to be seated or to pay for their papers. Outside, the sun was already beginning to feel warm and she noticed that the wooden planters along the main street were filled with daffodils that had begun to bloom. Suddenly Nancy felt better than she had all week.

When she arrived back at Catherine's, she sat down in the armchair with the cookbook and a cup of coffee. She turned to the index and counted the recipes: there were 274. Of that number, only nine contained the names of places. It seemed unlikely that Catherine had chosen the recipes at random and just happened to pick three with place names in their titles. That two of them were her "favorites" (although with the Irish stew that was stretching it a bit) was just a matter of luck and had made the inscription more important, yet more innocuous at the same time. Once she'd understood the pattern, the message of the curry recipe was clear, even though it was one she hadn't tried.

Nancy looked at her watch, then went into Catherine's study and looked up Simco's telephone number. She dialed, waited.

"Hello, Frank. It's Nancy." She smiled. "Fine. No, really. I've been to town already and got a paper." She listened for a minute and rolled her eyes. "That's nice of you," she said, finally, "but what I really called about was the library. The college library. The main one. What time does it open on a Sunday?" With a pencil she wrote "12:00" on the calendar above the phone. "No, I just need to look up some things. No, I can do it by myself." She nodded absently. "So you'll be in your office all afternoon? OK, I'll come by if I find anything important. Frank? Wait! Where is the library?" She jotted some notes on the calendar and hung up, then returned to the living room where she sat down on the sofa and lit a cigarette. The *Times* was on the coffee table, three inches thick, imposing. Nancy knew that Catherine read it like the Bible because, as she had often told Nancy, if anything important happened anywhere, that's where you could find it—in the *Times*. Nancy smiled to herself. It would be the first place she would look.

Devon, Connecticut
Afternoon

Nancy removed the photocopy from the bin at the bottom of the machine and turned off the microfilm reader. She rewound the reel of film, replaced it in its box, then went through the library lobby to the main reading room to a table where she placed the copies of the articles side by side in front of her and read them once again:

> *The New York Times,* Jan. 8, 1986
> *Madras, India*—The Council for Cultural Relations announced yesterday that the city of Madras will host a week-long international festival of the arts in August and will dedicate the festival to the late Moraji Narayan, who had been instrumental in organizing the event. Mr. Narayan, 38, who had headed the Madras office of the Council for Cultural Relations, was found dead in his Madras apartment last week.

> *The New York Times,* May 21, 1986
> *Antofagasta, Chile*—Unrest in troubled northern Chile is growing as the Pinochet government drags its

feet on filling several Regional Council vacancies, some dating back more than four months, the latest of which is the result of the unexpected death last week of an Antofagastan banker, Cesar Valenzuela, 51, local sources said.

The New York Times, July 14, 1986
Dublin—Angry Dubliners took to the streets yesterday to protest the bus strike, now in its fifth day, that has crippled Dublin's public transportation system. Responding to criticisms of mismanagement, officials of the Irish Transport System (CIE) said they had halted talks with the drivers' union because of the recent, sudden death of CIE liaison Joseph Dunlop, 41, and promised negotiations would be renewed by the week's end.

Her initial excitement was beginning to cool. Her biggest fear had been that she would find nothing—no reference to Bombay or to India on January 8, or to Ireland and Chile on the other two dates. Therefore, she'd been relieved and encouraged when she'd found the three small articles: one—and only one—for each country on the date Catherine had given her. But what did they mean? Three men had died, apparently suddenly, but their deaths were separated by several months and thousands of miles. They were all officials—although minor ones—and that was where the common thread seemed to end.

As far as Nancy knew, Catherine had never been to any of the countries, and the men were neither scientists nor academics, so it was unlikely that she would have known any of them personally. Why did Catherine call attention to them and what had they to do with her disappearance? And what, if anything, connected them to Richard Weiss's death? She folded the copies of the articles, put them in her purse and looked up at the large clock that was on the paneled far wall of the reading room. Since it was nearly two o'clock, she doubted that Simco would mind if she interrupted him at his office.

* * *

She had to knock three times before she heard a gruff "Come in."
She opened the door and found herself in a small, cramped square
of a room with a desk, two wooden chairs, each bearing the college seal, and a bank of filing cabinets along one wall. On the desk
was a nameplate: Georgia Whitney.

"Frank?" said Nancy, looking around.

"In here," came a voice through the open door at the other side
of the room.

Nancy crossed over to it and looked in. Simco's office was
large and well appointed. Afternoon sun slanted in through small-
paned leaded windows, showing off the muted colors of the faded
Oriental rug and the two comfortable-looking leather wing chairs
that sat facing the mahogany desk. Stacks of folders were spread
out in front of Simco, who started to rise from his chair when he
saw Nancy enter the room.

"No. Don't get up," she said, waving him back down. "I'll just
stay a minute. Don't want to bother you."

"No bother." Simco tilted back in his chair, folded his hands
in his lap and gave Nancy a smile. "You found the library?"

"Yes. It's very nice. Actually, the reason I came by was to ask
you if Catherine ever mentioned Chile."

"The recipe?"

Nancy laughed. "No, the country."

"The country? I don't think so."

"How about Ireland or India?"

"Ireland or India? No, not that I recall." Simco gave her a long,
appraising look. "This is about the recipes, I take it."

She nodded. "All of a sudden it occurred to me this morning
that the important thing about the recipes wasn't that they were
my favorites—that was just to get my attention—it was the places
in their names: Chile, Ireland, Bombay or India. What she was saying was that those places and the dates she indicated were somehow important."

"And so you went to the library to look them up. *The New
York Times?*"

"I did."

"And?"

Nancy reached into her purse and took out the folded articles. "Here's what was reported about each of the countries on the day she gave me." She handed the copies to Simco, who read each one twice, slowly, then looked up at her. "Well?"

"The problem we're having," said Nancy, "is that every time we think we've found something, we end up saying 'well?' I was hoping you'd see something I'd missed." Nancy sat down in one of the wing chairs and watched Simco as he slowly leafed through the articles.

"Moraji Narayan. Cesar Valenzuela. Joseph Dunlop. They all seem to have died."

"Suddenly," said Nancy.

"Suddenly, then. But I don't see the connection and I don't see what it would have to do with Catherine."

"They were all officials of some sort."

"All right," said Simco. "Does that help?"

"I don't know." Nancy drummed her fingers on the arms of the chair. "I need to find out more about those stories. Can I call the *Times?*"

Simco glanced at the articles. "I don't think so. They're wire service stories. This one's Reuters. The others are AP. You could call them, I suppose, but you'd have to call the bureaus where the stories originated. Even then, you might not get very far. These things are old news."

Nancy stood up and walked over to the windows and looked out at the College Common. Suddenly she turned around. "Is there a blackboard I can use?"

"A blackboard? Pick any classroom."

"I just want to write down everything I know in one place where I can see it all at once. Maybe I'll see a connection."

Simco got up from his chair. "Follow me," he said and led her through his secretary's office and across the corridor. He opened a door and switched on some lights. It was a small classroom— tiny by Indiana University standards—with twenty or so large-armed writing chairs arranged in a U around three sides of the room. A green blackboard ran the width of the front wall.

Nancy picked up a piece of yellow chalk and drew a single horizontal line across the board. Above it, on the left, she wrote 1986 in large numerals, and then, at intervals: JAN—India, MAY—Chile, JULY—Ire. She made a thick vertical line that crossed the horizontal one and to the right of it she wrote 1987, then, again at intervals: FEB—S. LAKEY, MAR—STORMS, GONE, MARM, WEISS, CKBK, BENNET. Simco watched her from the back of the room. When she finished, she put the chalk down and walked back to where he was standing.

"It's not very much," he said.

"I don't agree. Look." She pointed to the left part of the board. "In 1986, three men in three countries suddenly turn up dead." She moved her arm slowly to the right. "Six months later, someone posing as Catherine's brother and calling himself Stephen Lakey shows up in Bloomington and hangs around for three days. When Catherine finds out, all she says is: Don't tell Nancy. A month after that, she leaves the messages with Weiss about the storms, about having to go out, and then she disappears, making it look like something happened to her. I call Weiss, who seems to know what's going on, but before I can talk to him he's dead—killed. I come back here and find the cookbook, which leads me to the articles . . . "

Simco had turned away from Nancy toward the doorway. "What was that?" he said.

"What?" said Nancy.

Simco put a finger to his lips, cocked his head to one side and listened. From the hallway came a faint squeaking sound accompanied by the soft *squish-squish* of rubber soles on tile. "Hello," said Simco.

"Yo!" said a voice not very far away. The squeaking grew louder. At the doorway, a round face appeared, smiling. An even rounder body followed it into the room. The squeaking came from the wheels of a bucket, stuffed with mops, which the man pulled behind him. "Thought I heard voices," he said, grinning. "Didn't know you guys worked Sundays." His blue twill pants sagged beneath his beach ball of a belly and his matching zippered jacket, with "Al" stitched on its left breast, had ridden upward, exposing a six-inch swath of denim work shirt, buttons straining.

"We don't usually," said Simco. "We're almost done."

The man waved limply at him, looked at Nancy. "Take your time," he said. "Got all night. Plenty of rooms to do." He turned around and began pushing the bucket toward the door. "Don't worry about the lights," he said over his shoulder, "and you can leave the blackboard, if you want. Got to wash it, anyway. Night."

Nancy looked back at the blackboard. "There are huge holes, but don't you begin to see the outline of a story?"

"I'd like to, but what I think I see is a dead end. I don't see where you go from here."

"I do," said Nancy, walking back up to the blackboard. She picked up the chalk and drew a circle around the name BENNET. "Right here."

"Oh," said Simco without enthusiasm. He looked like he wanted to say more but decided against it.

Nancy put the chalk down and smiled at him. "I'll let you get back to work."

"I'm about finished. Can I give you a lift back to Catherine's?"

"No trouble?"

"None. Let me just pick up some papers in my office."

When they reached the parking area behind the building, Simco stopped.

"What is it?" said Nancy.

"The blackboard. I ought to go erase it. What if that guy forgets to wash it? I don't want a room full of undergraduates reading that stuff tomorrow morning. I'll only be a minute."

He loped off toward the building and went up the back stairway three steps at a time. The hallway was dark except for the pool of light coming from the classroom he and Nancy had just left. Through the doorway came the sound of whistling, shrill and without much melody.

Simco entered the room and saw the custodian, bent over, his back toward the door, vigorously mopping the floor. "Hello again," he said, moving toward the blackboard.

The man straightened up slowly and rubbed his back. "Hey," he said, "thought you were gone."

Simco picked up an eraser.

"You don't need to do that."

"No problem," said Simco. "Hate to have people cleaning up after me."

The custodian watched him move the eraser across the board in long, even arcs. When Simco finished, he shrugged. "Suit yourself," he said.

Simco put the eraser down and walked toward the doorway, brushing his hands together to remove the chalk dust. "Night."

The custodian nodded and watched him leave, then turned to face the empty blackboard. He took a crumpled piece of yellow paper from his jacket pocket, smoothed it out against his belly, studied it, then stared again at the blackboard. "Shit," he said quietly to himself.

PART TWO

Yesterday, while I was walking in the park, I saw a woman who re-minded me of me when I was younger. It wasn't how she looked, but what happened and what she did. She was sitting on a bench, read-ing, when three boys, who were playing nearby on the grass, got into a fight that deteriorated into bullying: two of them picked up pebbles from a gravelly path and began throwing at the third, who started to cry and to run in circles, dodging and ducking. For some reason, he didn't run away. Perhaps he couldn't. Perhaps he didn't know where to go, or, maybe, he'd been told to stay with them. At any rate, when the young woman saw this, she marched straight over to them and spoke to them sharply. They stopped and backed off, the bullied boy retreating with them at a safe distance; and even though I couldn't understand the French they spoke, I could tell from the backward glances they gave her that she was a stranger and that they resented her intrusion.

She was right, of course, and I recognized in the swiftness of her action a certainty I once felt. Everything is upside down now and I don't think I've ever felt so alone. Certainly, I never dreamed that I would face the choices that I have. I know that when I was the age of that young woman in the park, I never could have imagined being where I am, doing what I'm doing, but then, at her age, I didn't know how tough the world could be, or how complex.

I wish so many things: that all of this had never happened; that the choices of what to do had not been left to me; that there was some other option, but there isn't one. I'm sailing in uncharted waters and have gone too far for wishing. I must stop looking back. I must concentrate. It isn't a matter anymore of merely doing the best I can. There is no longer any room for failure.

MARCH—1987						
S	M	T	W	T	F	S
1	2	3	4	5	6	7
8	9	10	11	12	13	14
15	16	17	18	19	20	21
22	23	24	25	<u>26</u>	27	28
29	30	31				

DAY TWELVE

APRIL—1987						
S	M	T	W	T	F	S
			1	2	3	4
5	(6)	7	8	9	10	11
12	13	14	15	16	17	18
19	20	21	22	23	24	25
26	27	28	29	30		

DAY TWELVE

Paris
Morning

The hotel lobby had the look and feel of a spacious living room that belonged to someone who had had money for a very long time. The floral-patterned chintz of the sofas and armchairs, the floor-to-ceiling window drapes and the Oriental carpets softened the room, rounding off its corners and its edges, muffling its sounds.

At its far end, facing the main entrance and in front of the two elevator doors, was the concierge's desk, marble-topped, gilt-legged. A telephone burbled quietly, and the concierge lifted the receiver carefully, as if it were made of porcelain, spoke softly into it in French, then shifted smoothly into English. From time to time guests stopped at the desk to ask him something and the concierge, placing one hand across the receiver, gestured with the other, smiled and nodded.

From a large wing chair in the corner of the lobby, a woman watched him. She wore a white blouse, a charcoal gray skirt and a dark wool coat that was plain but new, and she held a newspaper up in front of her so that when guests walked by and glanced toward her all they could see were her slate blue eyes and her curly, jet black, shiny hair. At 7:45, she saw the concierge glance at his watch, get up from his desk and walk across the lobby and out the front door of the hotel. She took a small pad of paper from her purse and checked a list of notes. The first one said: "7:40–7:45 to Rue du Bac kiosk for play reviews: 8–10 mins."

She put the notepad back in her purse, folded the newspaper carefully and placed it on the polished mahogany table in front of her. She stood up, removed her coat, draping it neatly over one arm, then walked to the elevators, keeping her head tilted very slightly down and away from the reservation clerks and cashiers behind the counter on the right side of the lobby.

She pressed the button and waited, glancing up from time to time at the brass needle over the doors as it swung smoothly through its arc in the half-moon dial that marked the elevator's downward progress. The needle stopped and the doors glided open. She pushed back the brass latticework of the inner door, then closed it behind her and pressed one of the buttons.

The elevator sighed into motion and the walls of the shaft slid slowly by the lattice door. Between floors she gently opened the inner door an inch or two and the elevator shuddered to a stop. She closed her eyes, counted silently, then shut the door again and resumed the ascent.

When the elevator stopped at the eighth floor, she got out and walked briskly down the hallway, rummaging through her purse, as though looking for her key. Her pace slowed. She stopped, turned, listened. She was alone in the hallway. Quickly she went to the door at the end of the hall, opened it, and walked down several flights of stairs before she entered another hallway and followed it to the elevators. Two men stood, waiting. One smiled at her and she smiled back. When the elevator arrived, the men waited for her to enter. She moved to the rear of the car and stood, looking up at the ceiling, as the men stepped in beside her and the doors closed.

When the elevator reached the lobby and the doors opened, the men stepped aside so she could leave first. She mumbled a soft, almost inaudible, "Merci," then went through the lobby and out the main entrance to the street. To her left, a half block away, she saw that the concierge was returning. She turned right and crossed the street to a sidewalk café, where she sat at a small, round table and ordered coffee and a croissant. When the waiter left, she opened her purse. She took out her pen and notepad, flipped to a clean sheet, entered the date and beside it wrote: "It can be done."

Chevy Chase, Maryland
Morning

He sat in the kitchen, in the early morning half-light, slowly tapping the piece of paper on the tabletop in front of him. It was another invitation, an insistent one, for him to return in June for the twentieth reunion of the Academy's class of 1967.

Two decades was a long time, but he had no trouble remembering the details of that last day: hearing his name, Gilbert Edward Bennet, come rumbling from the loudspeakers, bouncing back and forth across the stadium as if he were the only one the crowd had come to see; looking for his parents after the ceremony, and, when he'd found them, how they had looked—his father already frail from the effects of the illness that would kill him soon enough, but smiling and shaking his head in mock disbelief; and his mother, biting her lower lip, tear tracks streaking the powder on her face, looking as if she wanted to throw her arms around him but holding back for fear that she would embarrass him in front of his friends.

Gil Bennet was not a man given to regretting things, but he could not help feeling that on that sunny, humid day in Annapolis twenty years ago, things were, or at least had seemed, much simpler. There were his parents and there was the Navy, and from both he had learned the truths of duty, honor, country. At least that is the way they had been presented to him, without a trace of ambiguity. It would have been nice if things had turned out that way. He remembered a conversation with his mother that he'd had not long before she died. It was early in the morning, about this time, and she had sat with him at the same table where he was sitting now. She had said to him that everyone back in Crystal Lake, Missouri, still asked about him all the time, wanted to know what Gillie was doing in Washington, and she had said she really didn't know what to tell them because, since he'd left the Navy, she didn't really know herself. What did he do?

The question had surprised him because, like his father, she had always seemed more interested in how he was than in the details of his life. He had not missed the touch of anxiety in her voice. He would have told her, but he knew that she couldn't possibly understand. No one on the outside did. They saw the world in the starkest shades of black and white: only Russians shot down airliners, only Libyans or Palestinians lurked in the shadows, planning acts of terrorism, while we acted like John Wayne, tall and handsome, saying nothing worse than "shucks," always there in the open, always fighting fair. Bennet could remember a time when he'd believed that too, before Naval Intelligence taught him better, and he'd come to understand that his country's only chance for survival was to learn to beat them at their own dirty games.

But he couldn't say that to his mother, to his children, or to his friends in the House or the Senate either, so he just said "Special Projects" and let it go at that. His mother had looked at him a long time, her eyes searching his face, and finally she'd patted his wrist and had said, "All right, Gillie," and she never brought it up again.

Getting up from the kitchen table, Bennet took his suit jacket off the back of a chair and put it on. On a pad by the telephone he wrote a brief note to his wife, saying that he hoped he wouldn't be late, but things at the office were a bit hectic. He went down the stairs to his basement study and called his office. "Maggie?" he said, "It's Gil. I'm on my way. Would you call Tony on my phone, have him there by eight-thirty."

On his desk, beside the framed photograph of his wife and children, he saw his watch and remembered that he had put it there the night before. He picked it up. The crystal was chipped, a crack ran diagonally across it, and the gold plating, if that is what it was, had worn away around the edges. "Not a Rolex," his father had said when he'd given it to him for his high school graduation, "but it'll keep good time." Bennet turned it over and read the inscription:

> To GIL,
> WITH LOVE AND PRIDE.
> POPS AND MOTHER
> JUNE 14, 1963

He reminded himself, again, that the watch needed a new band, then he set the time, like he had to every morning because it lost nearly five minutes a day. Nothing works the way it should, he thought.

Devon, Connecticut
Morning

By the time the doorbell rang, at a little before nine, Nancy had already been up for two hours. She had spent a better night than the one before—at least a little better—but she still had had trouble shutting down the parade of things that marched across the insides of her eyelids. Toward morning, the thought that troubled her the most was the one concerning money.

If Catherine had disappeared by her own design, she would have done her planning carefully and that would have included setting aside enough money to take care of her living expenses for as long as she thought she might be gone. What intrigued Nancy, and what made her finally abandon the idea of sleep altogether, was whether or not Catherine could have managed to provide herself with enough cash for at least several weeks of living without leaving an obvious trail of paper. While the coffee was brewing in the kitchen, Nancy started through Catherine's desk in the study, drawer by drawer, one piece of paper at a time.

She found the banking records for 1987 in a neatly labeled manila envelope in the bottom right-hand drawer. Catherine had a checking account at the Devon branch of the Essex Bank & Trust Company and there was nothing particularly unusual about any of the transactions recorded between January 2 and March 16, the period covered by the statements. What caught Nancy's eye, however, was that the deposits, made with precise regularity on the sixteenth of each month, were so small—$1,800 in January, $2,000 in February and $1,650 in March. She had very little notion of what a place like Stonington paid someone of Catherine's position and seniority, but she knew it had to be more than that.

Nancy was not surprised to see Simco when she answered the door. He stood on the front steps expectantly, looking more animated than he usually did, Nancy thought.

"Hi," he said. "I was on my way to the office and I needed to ask a favor."

"Come in," said Nancy. "Coffee?"

He held up his hand. "No time, I'm afraid. Last night I thought about what you said, about wanting to call the *Times*."

"You said I shouldn't bother."

"I know. But I think your idea of trying to find out more about what happened is a good one. I went through a list of people at the college, most of them in the Political Science Department, who might know something or someone that would help and then I remembered that my college roommate, sophomore year, works at the State Department. I don't know what he does, but he might know people who could help. I thought it might be worth calling him."

"You wouldn't mind?"

"Not at all. I need the articles, though. He'll want names and dates and places."

"They're in the study. If you have a minute, there's something else I want to show you."

He looked quickly at his watch. "Well," he said, "all right."

Nancy led him down the hallway to the study and handed him the articles, then the envelope with Catherine's bank statements.

"What's this?"

"Catherine's banking records so far this year. Take a look at the deposits."

Simco sorted through the sheets of paper. "Yes?"

"When does the college issue paychecks?"

"For faculty and administration, on the fifteenth."

"And what was Catherine's salary?"

"I don't know exactly. I'd have to check."

"Roughly?" said Nancy.

"Probably fifty, maybe fifty-five." Simco looked at the bank records, then back again at Nancy. He gave her a small smile. "I see what you're thinking. Even with deductions and withholding, she was getting paid a good deal more than this."

"It's not perfect," said Nancy, "but it's pretty good. She knew that anyone snooping through the records would be looking for withdrawals, so she buried the money in the deposits instead. She could have set aside more than five thousand dollars—enough to keep her going for a while."

"It would be interesting to know how she worked it, how she made the deposits. Can you call the bank?"

Nancy sat down in the chair behind Catherine's desk. "She could have done it a number of ways. The easiest would be to deposit only part of the check and take the difference in cash. Anyway, the bank won't release that kind of information. They can't."

"They can with a court order," said Simco.

"No. Not yet. We're doing fine so far without the police. I'd rather wait until we really need them."

"And when will that be?"

"I don't know," said Nancy. "It isn't now."

Simco looked at his watch. "I'm late," he said, putting the bank records down on the desk.

"Thanks for calling this friend of yours," said Nancy, getting up. "Let me know what he says." She followed Simco out to the front door.

"I'll call you. You'll be around?"

"I won't be far. I'm going into town, to the post office, to pick up her mail. Then I'll call Bennet."

"Be careful what you say to him." Simco started down the steps. "Want the car?"

"No thanks. I like the walk." She watched Simco get into his car, ease it away from the curb and drive slowly down the street. She thought about waving, but decided that that would be silly. She went back into the house and began to think of what she would say to Bennet.

Bethesda, Maryland
Morning

Anthony Edward O'Connell—Tony—always took one lump of sugar in his coffee. He would never simply drop it in the cup, but would place it on his teaspoon, lower it carefully until it was half submerged, then watch as it turned a milky-brown and began to crumble, its edges and corners breaking off like parts of a building under a wrecker's ball, until it was just a jumble of disappearing granules in the center of the spoon. Only then would he stir.

Bennet watched the ritual, waited until he saw Tony's spoon swirl slowly through the coffee. "I'll give you the facts as they were reported to me," Bennet said, his voice matter-of-fact. "Yesterday afternoon, Mulholland went to the college library, to the microfilm section, where she apparently spent a couple of hours looking at back issues of *The New York Times.* From the library, she went to the Science Center to meet Simco. They went to an empty classroom and stayed for about an hour."

Bennet, seated at his desk, leaned forward, shuffled through some papers and found the note he wanted. "Maybe it was a strategy session—we can't be sure—but they put notes up on the blackboard. Looked like things they know, or at least think they know."

Bennet watched Tony's face carefully, surprised that it showed neither excitement nor any particular curiosity. "Our man didn't get everything down—Simco walked in on him, erased the board—but his memory is pretty good. Most of the stuff on the blackboard we know about, but some of it's new."

Tony leaned back on the leather sofa and crossed his arms. Bennet looked at the note in his hand. "They know about Stephen Lakey," he said. He paused, looked up at Tony, but when there was no response, continued. "And two other things: they know about me, they know about Chile, Ireland and India."

He put the paper down, got up from his chair, went over to the credenza and poured himself a cup of coffee. He turned toward Tony, held out the carafe. Tony shook his head.

"What do you mean they know about you? What do they know?"

"That I know Catherine. Probably that I knew Weiss."

"That's all?"

Bennet shrugged. "Very hard to tell."

"And about Chile and the other places?"

"I assume they know what happened."

"What really happened?"

"I suppose it's possible."

"Jesus Christ," said Tony. It was almost a hiss. "What else?"

"Some stuff we don't understand very well." He looked back at the note. "The letters CKBK." He looked up at Tony.

"Have no idea. Checkbook?"

"They also wrote "MARM.""

"That goddamn marmalade again. Anything else?"

"No."

"Okay. But why didn't you call me last night?"

"I thought about it," said Bennet, "then decided to give you a good night's sleep. And I wanted to think things over, by myself." He went back to his chair and sat down. "And so?"

Tony shrugged. "You know what I'm going to say."

Bennet smiled, leaned back in his chair. The tilt directed his gaze to the ceiling. "A man who comes directly to the point."

"You asked me."

Bennet came forward, looked directly at Tony. "You're right, I did."

"A week ago," said Tony slowly, "Mulholland and Simco knew nothing. Absolutely nothing. By Wednesday, they knew a little something—probably very little—and by Saturday they had Weiss's tape. By yesterday they knew about you, they knew about the incidents abroad. That's not a bad week's work for amateurs."

"Go on," said Bennet.

"And what will it be today, Gil? Or tomorrow? When do you think they'll have enough pieces to begin putting them together? Maybe they already have. And then what will they do? More to the point, what will we do?"

"And so we do things your way. We just eliminate them."

"Does that offend your sensibilities? Cut the crap, Gil. You're not running Woolworth's."

"It's stupid and it won't work."

"Is it?" Tony stirred what remained of his coffee and pointed the spoon at Bennet. "Do you remember our conversation—when was it—five months ago? You came to me about Weiss, didn't you, and said that somehow he'd found out about the field tests. And do you recall what I said then?"

Bennet nodded.

"But we didn't, did we? 'No need,' you said. And so here we are." He dropped the spoon with a clatter into the coffee cup, went to the desk and spun the nameplate around so it faced Bennet. "You're the boss."

Bennet looked up at him. "I don't believe that killing people is always the best solution."

Tony smiled at him. "Really? You picked a hell of a business, then, didn't you?"

"Sit down, Tony. If we go your way, we create more problems than we solve. With Lakey gone, the hornets have been buzzing. Weiss dies and Mulholland makes the connection. Don't you think that she and her friend Simco have told people? Now imagine how it looks if they suddenly have an accident. Everybody will jump into this thing—police, maybe even the FBI."

"And they'll find nothing."

"Really? We're that good, are we? Not quite good enough to fool this Nancy Mulholland and her college professor, but good enough to fool the FBI? Can't we learn from our mistakes?"

"Those weren't our mistakes," said Tony dryly. "Those were Woody's. When you rely on a fool . . . "

"It doesn't matter whose mistakes they were. The point is that the Weiss business has done exactly what I was afraid it would do: attract the attention of anyone who took the time to notice."

"Weiss was absolutely clean. No one raised an eyebrow. And what do you suppose would have happened if Weiss had met with Mulholland? You think they'd talk about the weather?"

Bennet shook his head, got up and went over to the window. "Aren't you forgetting our objective in all of this?"

"Find Lakey."

"But we haven't been doing very well at that, have we? If we eliminate Mulholland and Simco, we probably remove the only people who might know where Lakey is. But even if they don't, if Lakey hears about it, wherever she is, she could come out screaming before there's a thing we can do about it."

Tony went back to the sofa and sat down. "I'd rather worry about one than three," he said.

Bennet turned and smiled at him. "I don't think that's a choice we have."

The telephone on Bennet's desk buzzed. He picked up the receiver, listened for a moment, looked over at Tony. "I'm tied up, Maggie. Get a number and I'll call her back." He put the receiver down. "Nancy Mulholland," he said.

Tony took the elevator from Bennet's office directly to the underground parking garage. He sat in his car for several minutes before starting it, then drove slowly up the ramp to the street. A few blocks later, he turned down a residential street and eased the car to the curb. He punched some numbers into the telephone between the two front seats and waited until he heard the familiar voice.

"Service center."

"Woody," he said, then hesitated, his fingers drumming slowly on the steering wheel, "everything under control?"

"Fine. She called Bennet."

"I know."

"She's got balls. I'll say that for her."

"Or she's shooting blind. Make sure she doesn't get out of your sight."

"No problem."

"I mean that. Not out of your goddamn sight."

"What about Simco?"

"I don't give a shit. He's not the problem, at least not yet."

"OK."

"Call me if anything happens. I'll be at the Savannah number."

Tony clicked the phone off and sat staring through the windshield. The phone call hadn't reassured him; they could watch her closely—even Woody could manage that—but he sensed more strongly every day that watching wouldn't be enough.

Devon, Connecticut
Evening

When Simco called to ask her out to dinner, Nancy said yes because she didn't know how to say no without seeming to be unkind to a man who had done so much for her. Besides, she wanted to tell him about Bennet and hear about his conversation with his friend at the State Department. She was also tired of eating packaged meals all by herself.

Simco arrived at Catherine's at a little before seven, looking less rumpled than Nancy had seen him. He had combed his hair carefully so that it lay neatly over the thinning spot at the back of his head and his gray tweed jacket looked new, or at least freshly pressed. Nancy was surprised—and relieved—that he had not brought flowers.

In the car on the way to the restaurant she thought it odd how different the atmosphere had become. They had spent a lot of time together over the previous week: they had traveled from Boston to Cotchpinicut to Devon; they had spent hours talking; they had argued; they had become, if not old friends, then certainly colleagues. But now they were dressed up, going out to dinner, on a date (although Nancy cringed at the word) and conversation sputtered from one banality to the next. Simco talked about the weather. Nancy remarked that Connecticut reminded her of Indiana. Simco even told her how nice she looked. They seemed reluctant to begin to talk about what each of them had discovered that day, as though they feared that serious conversation—about Bennet, about the State Department—might not be enough to last through dinner and, if started now, would surely leave them in an awkward silence over coffee and dessert.

The French River Inn had been doing business more or less continuously in the same building since the middle of the eighteenth century. Inside it was all age-darkened posts and beams and the waiters and waitresses were costumed in colonial dress. A restaurant that looked very much like this one had just opened outside Indianapolis, but Nancy didn't tell Simco that, instead she commented on the fresh flowers, the beeswax candles, the pewter butter plates and noticed that every time she pointed out a new detail Simco looked very pleased in a way that was endearing, but which also put her on guard.

When they had ordered their meals and drinks had arrived, Simco lifted his glass and looked at her seriously, intently. "Well," he said, too softly, Nancy thought, "to . . . " He paused, searching for just the right toast.

"To Catherine," interjected Nancy, quickly. "To Catherine and to finding her." They touched glasses and Nancy gave him a smile, which she tried to make generic.

"All right, to Catherine," said Simco.

Nancy took advantage of the slight change of mood. "I spoke with Bennet this morning."

Simco raised his eyebrows. "You did?"

Nancy gave him a broader, warmer smile. "I thought about what you said, about making up some story about who I was and what I was doing, but I finally decided against it. I'm really not a very good liar, you know."

"So you told him who you were?"

She nodded. "I did, and he'd heard of me. From Catherine."

Simco leaned forward slightly in his chair. "All right, who is he?"

"Gil Bennet is an editor. Actually, he's more of an editor-agent. He works with academic types to get their books or articles or what have you in shape for publication. Once that's done, he shops them around to publishers."

Simco looked puzzled. "Really? I didn't know there were people who did that sort of thing, at least not for academics. But I still don't see the connection with Catherine."

"Let me back up," said Nancy. "Bennet met Catherine through Richard Weiss." She stopped to see what effect her statement would have on Simco. When he only nodded she went on. "Weiss was one of Bennet's first clients. About five or six years ago, he mentioned to Bennet that he had met someone who was thinking of writing a textbook, but didn't know how to begin."

"Catherine?"

"Catherine."

"That's odd," said Simco, studying his drink, swirling the ice with his finger. "I didn't know that Catherine was ever thinking about a book. She didn't mention it to me."

"Anyway, Weiss arranged an introduction and Bennet began to work with her. It makes sense that Catherine never mentioned it to you because Bennet said that she was the only client he'd ever had that he hadn't been able to help."

"No book?"

"No book. No nothing. Catherine kept focusing on the hard parts, even though Bennet told her not to. She'd produce a chapter and Bennet would edit it into decent shape and send it back to her. After a few weeks, she'd call and say it wasn't good enough, that she'd have to start over. That went on for three or four years, until Bennet finally agreed to drop it. It was simply taking too much time."

"When did that happen?"

"About a year ago. He's only seen her once since then, at a conference late last year. They talked on the phone every now and then."

The food arrived and they both went through the ritual of reassuring one another that everything was very good. Simco, though, seemed suddenly preoccupied.

"I take it Bennet's heard about Weiss," he said finally.

"He mentioned it right away. I told him about Catherine and he sounded shocked. Then he asked me if I'd ever heard of Richard Weiss. I said I had, from Catherine. That's when he told me about meeting her through him. At the end, he told me that Weiss had been killed during a robbery in Pittsburgh."

"What did you say?"

Nancy smiled. "I lied. I acted surprised."

"He didn't remark about the coincidence?"

"About Weiss and Catherine, only a week apart? No. Neither did I."

Simco ate quietly for a few minutes, poured wine for both of them from the bottle he had ordered and waited patiently while the waiter ground pepper onto their salads. Finally he leaned forward. "How did he sound?"

"Bennet? Shocked at the disappearance. Concerned. He spoke very freely. I didn't have to pump him for information. He was very nice, really. I liked him. He wants to help."

"You trust him, then?"

"I don't know. Yes, I guess I do. There's no reason not to. I'll know more Wednesday."

Simco looked up quickly. "What's Wednesday?"

Nancy poked through the bread basket and selected a warm whole wheat roll. She took a bite of it and put it on her plate. "I'm meeting him in Boston. For lunch. He's coming up on business and said that between now and then he'd go through his file on Catherine, see if there's anything that might help." Nancy was consciously trying to keep her tone casual and it annoyed her that she felt she had to do that.

Simco studied his plate. "Do you think that's wise?"

"I think we should take help from wherever it's offered. Bennet worked closely with Catherine, at least for a while, so in some respects he knew her very well. It's certainly worth hearing what he has to say."

Simco did not look up.

"Is there something wrong?"

"Yes, I'd say there is," he said, finally. "How will you get to Boston? I'm afraid Wednesday's a bad day for me."

"I'll take the bus to Cotchpinicut tomorrow and pick up Catherine's car. I found a spare set of keys in the kitchen. She must have taken the others." She smiled at him. "Is that what's worrying you?"

Simco sat up straight, reached into his inside jacket pocket and took out a neatly folded piece of yellow paper. "This is what's worrying me," he said, unfolding the paper. "I told you that I reached that friend of mine at the State Department today. I think you'd better listen to this." Simco brought the paper closer to his face, squinting at it. "In this light, it's hard to read my own handwriting. I think I remember most of it. The guy I roomed with in college—Jack Bellinger—he's an expert on the Middle East, which doesn't help us very much, but he's been in the State Department for fifteen years and knows a lot of people. I gave him the names and dates and places from the newspaper stories and asked him to do what he could to check them out. He called back late this afternoon. The guy he knows at the India desk wasn't in. He'll reach him as soon as he can."

Simco looked up at Nancy, then back down at the piece of paper. "Joseph Dunlop. Dublin. They don't have much on that one. Anytime anyone in Ireland with political connections turns up dead, people think of terrorists. The IRA, that sort of thing." Simco turned the page. "But two things ruled that out: no one claimed responsibility and no one could nail down a cause of death."

"I'm not sure I follow you," said Nancy. "What about the cause of death?"

"Murder tends to be an obvious kind of business," said Simco. "Dunlop was a pretty young guy and they found him without a mark on him. They did a pretty thorough autopsy, I guess, and couldn't find a thing."

"Is that unusual?"

"I guess it is. At least Bellinger thought it was. It makes the next part all the more interesting."

Nancy's dessert arrived, a slab of dark cake with a thick red sauce artfully poured over it. She pushed it toward the middle of the table and invited Simco to share it with her. He shook his head. "Too rich for me," he said.

He looked back at the paper. "Cesar Valenzuela," he said. "Banker. Member of the Regional Council. We know all that. Here. He was found dead on the kitchen floor of his estate outside Antofagasta. It was assumed he'd had a heart attack, but the autopsy showed no heart damage." He looked up at Nancy. "The autopsy showed nothing at all. His wife is an American and apparently she raised hell with the Chileans. When that didn't get her anywhere, she went to our embassy. In a quiet way, Cesar wasn't much of a fan of the Pinochet government and the wife claimed that the autopsy was a coverup. To keep her quiet and to avoid any more embarrassment, we got the Chileans to agree to have the autopsy results reviewed by a couple of American pathologists in Santiago. But they came to the same conclusion—they couldn't find a cause of death." Simco folded the paper and put it back in his pocket.

"That's it?"

"Essentially, until Bellinger can check with the guy about India."

Nancy sat back and began to laugh quietly.

"You find this funny?"

"I was thinking about what I said the other day—about how when we learn something new we look at one another and say 'well?' " She gave Simco a long look. "Well?" she said.

Simco didn't smile. "There's something very odd here. Bellinger, when he called back, was very curious about what I was up to. He wanted to know what the connection was between Valenzuela and the guy in Ireland. I told him I didn't know, but I don't think he believed me."

"You think there is a connection?"

"Of course there is. We've been told there is."

"By Catherine?"

Simco nodded. "I'm willing to bet right now that when we find out more about the India case, it will turn out to be just like the other two. We know he was a minor official and we know he died suddenly. I'll bet there's no cause of death there either."

"But what did Catherine have to do with it? She was right here in Devon."

Simco signaled for the waiter to bring a check. "Maybe your friend Bennet can help you out on that one," he said.

When Simco pulled up in front of Catherine's house, Nancy wondered, vaguely, what the good night protocols should be. She hoped that they could simply say good night and thank you, but if Simco wanted to kiss her, she decided that she would go along—chastely, closed-mouthed, of course—if only to avoid embarrassing him. When he turned toward her, she braced herself. "Please be very careful around Bennet," he said.

"I'm sure he's fine, Frank."

"Please."

"I'll be careful."

He kept looking at her. "He's still the connection. He knew Weiss and Catherine. Keep in mind, there are four people dead."

Nancy opened the door. "Thanks for dinner," she said. "I'll call you Wednesday, when I get back from Boston."

She walked up the front path, unlocked the door and went inside. She felt along the wall for the light switch. When she couldn't find it, she stood there in the hallway, waiting for her eyes to adjust to the darkness. From somewhere in the house came a faint, metallic pinging, slow but regular, almost rhythmic. It was only the pipes, she knew, or perhaps the radiators, but still she recognized that lumpy heaviness inside her chest that seemed to squeeze against her lungs, making it more difficult to breathe. She found the lights. The heaviness receded, but it didn't disappear entirely and she wondered if Simco's caution might be justified.

MARCH—1987						
S	M	T	W	T	F	S
1	2	3	4	5	6	7
8	9	10	11	12	13	14
15	16	17	18	19	20	21
22	23	24	25	_26_	27	28
29	30	31				

DAY THIRTEEN

APRIL—1987						
S	M	T	W	T	F	S
			1	2	3	4
5	6	(7)	8	9	10	11
12	13	14	15	16	17	18
19	20	21	22	23	24	25
26	27	28	29	30		

DAY THIRTEEN

TUESDAY, APRIL 7, 1987

Bethesda, Maryland
Morning

Maggie Dacey put a shopping bag in the closet behind her desk and hung her raincoat carefully on a thick wooden hanger. She arranged herself on her leather chair and pressed a button on the intercom.

"Maggie?" she heard Bennet say, surprise in his voice.

"I'm here."

"So soon? I told you to take the morning."

She looked at her watch. "It's almost eleven. That is the morning. And there's so much to do."

"Come on, Maggie, there's more to life than work." He was teasing her again, but she heard the smile in his voice. "But since you're here, could you come in for a minute?"

Maggie pressed some buttons on her telephone so that incoming calls would be directed into Bennet's office and picked up her notebook. At Bennet's door, she ran her hand quickly through her hair and studied her reflection briefly in the polished brass nameplate. She knocked twice lightly, then opened the door.

Bennet was at his desk, in shirtsleeves, studying some papers.

His dark blue foulard suspenders, Maggie noticed, exactly matched the color of the thin stripes of his shirt. He looked up when Maggie closed the door and grinned at her, leaning back in his chair. "How did your morning go?"

"It was nice. I did a little shopping," said Maggie, entering the room, her gaze half lowered, not quite meeting Bennet's. A strand of her shoulder-length, loosely curled hair strayed across her forehead and she combed it back with her fingers. Bennet cocked his head to one side. "You've done something to your hair."

Maggie went to one of the windows and adjusted the blinds. "Let some light in," she said. "It's a beautiful spring day."

Bennet followed her with his eyes. "You've colored it," he said. "It's lighter, isn't it?"

She looked down at her notebook. "Just a little. It was getting so dull." She hesitated. Gradually, her mouth curved into a shy smile. "What do you think?" she asked tentatively, darting a glance at Bennet.

He was sifting through papers in his briefcase. "What?" He looked up at her. "Oh, very nice. Sorry. I was looking for my notes on the Paris meeting. Do you have them?"

Maggie's smile faded. "Yes," she said, "in my desk file."

"Ahead of me again. Already have them typed, I suppose. I need to go over them." Bennet closed his briefcase. "One other thing." Maggie sat down by his desk, opened her notebook and began taking notes. "With this Lakey business," Bennet continued, "I'm going to have to put someone in charge while I'm gone. Tony's been running that operation. I think he should be the one."

Maggie said nothing.

"You'll look after him, won't you?"

Maggie closed her notebook and stood up. "If that's what you want."

Bennet leaned back in his chair and smiled at her warmly. "It's what I want."

Maggie reached across his desk and picked up a mug half filled with coffee. "I'll get you a refill," she said, without looking at him.

Instead her gaze was directed to the silver-framed photograph on the corner of his desk, to the hair of the tanned woman who was smiling out at her. It was longer than hers and not as curly, but its color, a very light blond, was a near perfect match.

Devon, Connecticut
Midday

The faculty dining room at Stonington College had been shrinking for nearly thirty years. It had once occupied the entire second floor of North Reunion Hall with its muralled walls, its elegantly draped windows, and every day at lunch and dinner its tables had been set with fresh, white linen. Times had changed, however, and so had the dining habits of the faculty. There weren't many who found the starched formality of the room inviting and fewer still saw atmosphere as a substitute for decent food. In the late 1960s, the admissions office had gained a foothold on the floor and had been slowly moving westward ever since. By the 1980s, the room had been pushed off into a corner, then undressed: the tables were now Formica-topped, the chairs aluminum and the food, now served from large, square pans as one slid one's tray along a counter, had not improved.

Simco, single and caring little about food, still ate there when he could. There was a group of them—Simco, Bill Shields from Biology, Carlos Alvarez from History, Jim McElwee from English—who would get together two or three times a week for lunch and the sort of academic gossip that gives texture to life in a small New England college.

Today, only three of them convened—McElwee had the flu— and they sat at their usual table in the corner by the window, well placed for keeping an eye on things both in the room and outside in the courtyard. The talk was sporadic and desultory—the term was still too new to have spawned much that was interesting—and Simco had hardly said anything at all. He took a sip of milk, studied his glass, then turned to Bill Shields. "Bill," he said, "what do you know about autopsies?"

"Jesus, Frank," said Alvarez.

Shields looked at Simco. His fork, mounded with macaroni and cheese, stopped midway between his plate and mouth. "Autopsies? Not much."

"You went to med school, didn't you?"

"Just two years, and a long time ago." Shields took a bite of food. "Odd question."

"On television," said Simco, "on those detective shows, they do autopsies all the time to determine cause of death or time of death, that sort of thing. That's true enough, isn't it?"

Alvarez looked first at Simco, then at Shields. "Could we talk about baseball?" he asked. Alvarez hated baseball.

Shields smiled at him. "I guess so," he said to Simco.

"I just wondered how easy it is. You cut open a body, but with all that stuff in there, is it always so obvious what went wrong?"

Alvarez got up from the table. "Charming, gentlemen, but I'm going to have to tear myself away."

"Bye, Carl. We'll talk politics tomorrow," said Simco.

"I don't know," said Shields. "Probably not. On TV, things have to be neat, fit into a half hour."

"How often would it happen that they don't find anything, that the coroner, or whoever it is, has to shrug and say, 'Beats me what killed him'?"

"Sorry, Frank, can't help you." Shields looked at Simco and raised one eyebrow. "Planning on killing someone?"

"It's crossed my mind."

Shields got up and looked over at the serving counter. "Got time for dessert? My treat."

Simco looked at his watch. "Sure," he said. "What's the special?"

Shields walked over to the counter. "Pie."

"What kind?"

Shields picked up a plate wrapped tightly in Saran Wrap and

looked at it closely. "Red," he said, then picked up another, "and yellow."

"Red," said Simco.

Shields returned to the table and slid the plate across to Simco. "It just occurred to me that twice in my life I've been asked about autopsies and both times by you people in chemistry."

Simco was turning the plate over in his hands, trying to unravel the wrapping.

"It's easier if you just eat the plastic, too," said Shields.

"Fattening," said Simco. He put the plate down and began poking at the plastic with his fork. "Who else?"

"Catherine."

Simco looked up quickly. "Catherine Lakey?"

"Four or five years ago, she came to me with a bunch of birds in Ziploc bags. She said she found them by her feeder, somewhere on Cape Cod. She asked me to autopsy them, see why they died."

"And did you?"

"I did a couple, but, hell, Frank, I'm not a pathologist. I couldn't find anything."

"You mean you couldn't tell what killed them?"

"That's right," said Shields. "Catherine seemed so disappointed that I called a friend of mine at Harvard, a specialist in bird anatomy and physiology, and asked him if he would take a look. It made me feel better when he didn't find anything either."

Simco put down his fork. "Bill, this other guy, this expert, he didn't find anything? That's just what I was talking about."

"I know," said Shields. "That's why I thought of it."

"And then what?"

"And then nothing. Maybe six months after that, I asked her if she was still collecting dead birds and she said she wasn't. I don't think she mentioned it after that." Shields stopped eating his pie and looked closely at Simco. "Frank, what the hell is this about?"

Simco looked at his watch again, then slid his chair out from under the table and stood up. "Thanks for the pie, Bill," he said. "I've got to make a phone call."

Queens, New York
Afternoon

Carla Valenzuela sat at the living room window of her apartment, looking out over the postal annex across the street and the elementary school playground beyond it. A handsome woman on the edge of middle age, she wore her dark hair sleeked back into a tight bun—a style that accentuated the elegant curve of her nose, her high forehead, her bright, nearly black eyes.

She wasn't sure that she had done the right thing on the telephone this afternoon, but she had had no warning, no time to think. A man had called, a man who said he was Frank Simco, who claimed to be a professor at a college in Connecticut—one that she'd never heard of. She could check on that, she supposed, if she wanted to go to the trouble. He had told her—putting it very gingerly—that he'd "heard about Cesar"; then he'd made his request—apologetically, haltingly—would she mind talking to him about what had happened? When she had asked why a professor in Connecticut would be interested, he had stumbled through an awkward explanation: he was doing something for someone at the State Department, following up on things. Maybe she'd made a mistake, but that's when she'd decided to say nothing. These days, she hardly trusted anyone she knew. She certainly wasn't going to trust a stranger.

Yet, if she put aside, for a moment, the question of why the man had called, the fact remained that, after six months of silence and indifference, someone was actually interested in Cesar and in what had happened. And, although he'd been unconvincing on the telephone—his story about the State Department was transparently made up—perhaps that was reason enough to trust him. With the others, always so smooth and practiced, she could never tell when they were lying.

She remembered the American doctors in Santiago—how they had sat with her, dressed in their green surgical gowns, speaking to her slowly, condescendingly, as though she didn't understand English. It was surprising, they'd said, to find no cause of death, but surprising or not, they couldn't manufacture one just to satisfy her. There was no trauma, no heart damage, no evidence of stroke and all the blood chemistry was within normal limits. They were sorry, but they could do nothing other than confirm what the Chilean doctors had already found in Antofagasta. She had thought of arguing, but there was something in their faces that told her not to bother.

Instead, she had returned to Antofagasta and had begun trying to persuade someone—anyone—in the American embassy that her husband had been murdered, and that a growing number of people, both Chilean and American, were trying to cover it up. Finally, after weeks of being shunted from one minor embassy official to another, an aide to the American ambassador had called on her. He had seemed, at first, to be a very nice young man, impeccably mannered. He'd told her how sorry the ambassador was about what had happened, that he was there to assure her that the ambassador, personally, stood ready to do whatever he could to assist her. Then, without changing the warmth of his smile or the tone of his voice, he had informed her that despite the ambassador's great sympathy for her plight, the embassy had to insist that she stop making the reckless and unsubstantiated charges that were adversely affecting relations between the Chilean and the American governments. The point of the message had been very clear. A month later she'd moved back to the United States.

Carla Valenzuela got up from her seat by the window and went to the telephone, where she'd left the envelope. She studied the number that she had written on it, then dialed Connecticut information. Stonington College was listed. The number wasn't what he had given her, but that might not mean anything. It could be the number that connected her directly to his office and not what she suspected—some phone number for a bogus office smoothly answered by a mere girl who'd been paid to speak her lines. She dialed the main number for the college, still wondering if she had been duped again, but when she asked for Professor Frank Simco, she was put through to his office and she relaxed.

His secretary told her he had stepped out for a few minutes, but would call her back, if she left her number.

Carla crossed the room to the black grand piano in the corner. It was a Steinway that she and Cesar had given to one another on their tenth anniversary and, while it seemed to overwhelm the small living room of this apartment, it had fit very nicely into the music room of their estate in Chile. She sat down at the keyboard and with one finger picked out the beginning notes of the "Moonlight Sonata," the first piece that Cesar had taught her to play, and she thought that if this Professor Simco did call back, and if he agreed to come to New York to meet her, she would make one last effort to convince someone that what she said had happened was the truth. And, if she could trust this man, this time she would hold nothing back. She would tell him about the American and she would tell him about the spot of blood.

Cotchpinicut, Massachusetts
Evening

Nancy unlocked the back door of the cottage and stepped inside. It was cool in the house, cooler than it was outside, and with the sun now well down in the western sky, it was gloomy too. She dropped her duffel on the sofa, went into the kitchen and stood by the door for a moment, looking out at the dunes, then went outside and made her way along the path to the beach.

At the ridge of the dune, she removed her shoes, then plunged down its face in three or four big bouncing steps and ran across the beach to the water, dodging the debris washed up by winter storms. Although there was only a slight breeze and the surface of the ocean was almost oily smooth, big swells, slow and rhythmic, were rolling in from the northeast, hardly visible until the water mounded up all at once and collapsed, hissing at her feet. Alone on the beach, she was struck by the immensity of sand and dune and ocean stretching out in all directions, vast planes of earth and air merging seamlessly into a picture where she was nothing at all, and she began to understand why Catherine had been drawn here and why this was such a perfect place to disappear from.

Turning north, she began walking along the beach, staying on the firm, damp sand and skittering away from the icy outwash of the biggest breakers. She tried to keep her mind on the meeting with Bennet the next day, but the sea and sky intruded. The rhythm of the surf was mesmerizing and the sky, washed with the colors of sunset, was beautiful.

As the bottom of the sun touched the horizon, Nancy stopped to watch, then took a last, long look up the beach before returning to the cottage. A hundred yards away, a solitary figure was coming toward her. As it drew nearer, Nancy saw that it was a woman bundled in a heavy wool cardigan, her head lowered, her hair wrapped in a bandanna. She was approaching in short, brisk steps that had a slight bounce to them, and there was something familiar about her gait. Nancy took several steps toward her, then remembered, at the airport in Bloomington, at Christmas, Catherine coming down the concourse, loaded down with bags of presents, her head down, walking just that way.

"Catherine!" she shouted.

The woman stopped, looked up. Her mouth and nose were completely wrong, not even a resemblance. She smiled at Nancy, took in the entire sky with a sweep of her eyes. "You never get tired of the sunsets," she said.

It was nearly dark when Nancy got back to the cottage. She turned on some lights and stood in the middle of the kitchen, smoking a cigarette, trying to remember where she had seen the bottle of brandy the last time she had gone through the cabinets. Quickly she moved around the room, opening doors and closing them, until, above the sink, she found it. She half filled a small glass, took a swallow and shivered. "Come on, Nancy, get a grip," she said aloud, shaking her head.

She went back to the cabinets and looked through them to see what there might be for dinner, but found only a few cans of soup, a can of peaches and two or three packages of Jell-O. She went into the living room, opened her duffel and took out the white blouse and blue skirt that she had brought along for her meeting in Boston. In the bathroom she changed her clothes, then sat on the edge of the bathtub and washed the sand off her feet. She combed her hair, brushed a touch of pink blush onto her cheeks and lined her eyes with a soft gray pencil. In Catherine's bedroom, she looked at herself in the mirror. OK for Cotchpinicut on a week-night, she thought.

She drove slowly along the dark roads, wishing she had paid more attention to Simco's driving; it had dawned on her that she had only a vague idea of where the village was. When she found the main highway, she had to guess which way to go and decided to turn north. A few minutes later a large green sign appeared. COTCHPINICUT, it said, above an arrow pointing left.

Although it was still early evening when she arrived, the village seemed to have gone to bed already. Only the Village Market, the Ebb Tide restaurant across the street and the Mobil station on the corner had their lights on. Nancy parked the car in front of the market and went in to buy a magazine, knowing from experience that a woman eating alone in a restaurant needed to look occupied.

The Ebb Tide was just as dark as she had remembered it, its dim lights producing a murky, orange glow that gave the place the look of a funeral home or a church at night. She chose a small booth at the rear of the almost empty dining room and took the menu from its metal holder. From somewhere in the gloom above her a man's voice said, "Hello again."

She looked up with an uncertain smile, then recognized the waiter as the same one who had served them the week before. "You've got quite a memory," she said.

He looked around the nearly deserted room. "At this time of year, one remembers customers."

She laughed, asked what to order and, taking his advice, settled on scallops and a split of white wine. When he returned and was uncorking the bottle, he asked if she were staying in Cotchpinicut and seemed more than casually interested in her answer.

He had nice eyes that crinkled when he smiled, and a couple of weeks ago Nancy would have flirted with him, but that was then. Now she dismissed him politely and turned to her magazine.

Nancy finished her dinner and left a generous tip for the waiter. Outside, the village had grown even darker with the only lights now coming from the Ebb Tide's neon sign and the cold fluorescent glow from the phone booth on the corner by the Mobil station. Nancy crossed the street to her car, started it, then hesitated as she wondered if she should turn around and go out the way that she had come. She decided that she didn't need to. Simco had left the village driving in this direction and he'd found Pilgrim's Trace easily enough.

Outside the village there were no lights at all and the darkness, dense and enveloping, seemed to be not just the black of night, but something thickly oppressive and alive. She switched on her high beams and crept along the narrow road until she reached the highway. She hesitated, then turned right and began looking for the road that led to Pilgrim's Trace. She spotted it too late to make the turn and had to pull over to the shoulder of the highway to double back to it. After she'd gone about a mile, she began to worry. Wasn't this road narrower and sandier than the one she'd come out on? And before, hadn't there been houses? The road rose and dipped, then swung to the left and ended in a large asphalt parking lot. As she made her way around it, her headlights picked out a wooden sign with black lettering:

NATIONAL SEASHORE
MUSSEL POINT BLUFFS SCENIC AREA
NO OVERNIGHT PARKING

Irritated, she went back up the road and as she reached the crest of the first rise, she saw in the distance a pair of headlights coming toward her, rising and falling as the road rolled gently over the sandy hills. She dimmed her lights and pulled over to the right as far as she could to let the other car pass. It did—too fast, she thought, and too much in the middle of the road. She watched in the mirror as it receded rapidly into the darkness, only a single tail-light glowing dully. Kids, she thought, going parking.

When she reached the highway, she turned north, and shortly afterwards another road appeared on her right, leading off toward the ocean. She turned onto it and was immediately encouraged when she passed a house she was sure she'd remembered seeing on the way out. She sat back in her seat and turned the radio on. Soon, on the left, there would be another house, a small one, then the beach parking lot and, three or four roads after that, Pilgrim's Trace.

But, after several minutes had gone by, there was still no house, no parking lot—just emptiness and a road, suspended in inky space, unraveling into the night. Impatiently, she clicked the radio off, turned the car around and pulled over to the side of the road. She turned on the overhead light and opened the glove compartment to look for a map. There was one of Connecticut, another of southern New England, but nothing local enough to be of any use. "Shit," she muttered and slammed the glove compartment shut. She sat there, staring out the windshield, trying to think of where she might go to ask for directions. That house she'd passed, it had been dark, hadn't it . . . ? She heard something in the distance, then saw a glow of lights approaching. They grew brighter, disappeared as the road slipped behind a hill, then reappeared, closing in on her. They slowed, then sped up again and went by her with a whoosh and a soft patter of sand hitting her door and windshield. She turned in her seat and watched as the car moved rapidly away from her, swaying slightly from side to side. It had only a single taillight.

Nancy swung her car onto the road and headed back toward the highway, keeping an eye on the rearview mirror. In the last twenty minutes she had passed only two cars, and both times—was she imagining things?—it was the same car. It was an unsettling thought and suddenly she was very aware of how alone she was. She pressed down harder on the accelerator and relaxed her grip on the steering wheel only when, at last, she reached the highway.

Back in the village, she turned the car around so she could re-trace the way she had come in earlier that evening. She drove cautiously and continued to check the rearview mirror. She passed the houses she'd remembered, rounded the curve by the parking lot, then, four roads later, as she was turning onto Pilgrim's Trace, she saw the glint in the mirror. Distant headlights were moving slowly along the road behind her. She pressed the accelerator until she was going faster than she liked. The lights were farther behind her now, just a yellow glow in the mirror, but when they turned onto Pilgrim's Trace, she knew they were coming after her.

As she approached Catherine's cottage, she wondered about the road. Did it loop back to the highway? If it did, she could keep going—drive to Provincetown where there would be lights and people. But if it didn't . . . What if it was a dead end? She didn't like that idea at all.

Ahead on the left, she could see a dim rectangle of yellow light coming through the window of Catherine's living room. On an impulse, she reached down and turned off the headlights. She was startled by the darkness, but could still make out the edges of the roadway, marked by borders of white sand. When she reached the cottage, she stopped, backed into the parking area, turned the engine off and waited. She locked the doors, rolled down the right-hand window and hugged herself against the shivering that had taken hold of her.

When she looked back up the road, the glow was there, slowly growing brighter until, at the top of a gentle rise about a quarter of a mile away, it became two headlights, yellowish eyes staring straight ahead. They stopped, crept forward again, then stopped and blinked off. As the night went black again, Nancy clutched the steering wheel and waited, hoping her eyes would adjust to the sudden darkness all around her. She looked through the open window, saw nothing, then leaned toward it and listened. There was the whisper of a breeze working its way through the beach grass and, from behind her, the muffled, rhythmic crumping of the surf against the beach, but that was all.

She started the car and eased back onto Pilgrim's Trace, headlights off. She leaned over, rolled the right-hand window up and slowly began to make her way back up the road toward where the lights had been. It seemed darker now than it had been before. She leaned over the steering wheel, trying to will herself to see the road, then felt the thumping of the right front wheel as it thudded over clumps of beach grass. She swerved to the left, felt smooth pavement for a moment, then the left wheels were wallowing in sand. She swung the wheel back to the right, reached down and found the lights, pulled the knob and suddenly, six feet ahead, there was a car, sitting half off the road, half on, directly in front of her headlights. She swerved, pulling hard on the steering wheel, and felt the rear end of her car breaking free, sliding. She yanked the wheel the other way and thought she'd made it past the car when she felt a solid thud behind her and heard the muffled sound of broken glass. Her car lurched to the left, but she managed to steady it. She pressed the gas pedal to the floor. The car hesitated for a fraction of a moment, then sped off up Pilgrim's Trace.

When she reached the darkened village, she swung the car into the Mobil station, turned off her lights, coasted past the gas pumps around the building to the back and stopped the car. It was dead quiet except for the raspy sound of her breathing. She forced herself to sit in the car, to count slowly to a hundred, just to be sure that she hadn't been followed.

Then, taking her purse, she got out of the car and made her way along the side of the building. When she got within ten feet of the telephone booth, she looked up and down the deserted Main Street, then ran, hunched over, to the booth and opened the door. She grabbed the receiver off the hook, cradled it between her cheek and shoulder, opened her change purse and emptied it on the metal shelf in front of her. She found a dime and was about to put it in the slot when she stopped. At the far end of the street, headlights were moving slowly toward her. She stared at them, knowing that she should do something—make the call or run back to the car—but she simply stood there, frozen, watching. The lights came closer, eased slowly to the curb and stopped. A door opened, a man got out and started walking toward the phone booth. Nancy closed her eyes, heard the rapping on the glass panel, heard the door sliding open. She turned and found herself looking at a silver shield. Cotchpinicut Police, it said. She began to tremble and when she tried to speak, she burst into tears.

MARCH—1987						
S	M	T	W	T	F	S
1	2	3	4	5	6	7
8	9	10	11	12	13	14
15	16	17	18	19	20	21
22	23	24	25	<u>26</u>	27	28
29	30	31				

DAY FOURTEEN

APRIL—1987						
S	M	T	W	T	F	S
			1	2	3	4
5	6	7	(8)	9	10	11
12	13	14	15	16	17	18
19	20	21	22	23	24	25
26	27	28	29	30		

DAY FOURTEEN

Cotchpinicut, Massachusetts
Morning

Billy Cahoon sidled cautiously to his desk, carrying three large paper cups of coffee and two bags of Danish and doughnuts. A newspaper was tucked under his left arm. "Coffee," he shouted.

Beakey got up from the dispatcher's desk and sauntered over, grinning broadly, holding up a piece of paper. "You gotta see this," he said, handing it to Cahoon.

Cahoon took it and looked around the room. "Where's Enfield?" he asked absently.

"Don't know," said Beakey. "Would you read it?"

"What is it?" said Cahoon, glancing at the paper, not much interest in his voice.

Beakey sighed. "It's Cartwright's report about last night. Read it."

"Last night?" Cahoon reached into one of the bags, took out a doughnut, then began to read. After a minute or two, he looked up at Beakey. "Cartwright's not making this up?"

"Swear to God."

"Ten o'clock at night and Mulholland's in the phone booth crying?"

"Keep reading."

Cahoon turned the paper over and shook his head. "And Mulholland was sober?"

"Guess so."

"Somebody follows her out to the Bluffs, then back to Lakey's. She tries to run past him, smacks him, runs into town."

"Serves 'em right," said Beakey.

"Serves who right?"

"Damn kids," said Beakey. He took a big bite of a jelly doughnut, then licked some sugar off his fingers. "Even money says it's that Sears kid and his buddies from North Cotch. They got nothing to do so they find somebody out driving around and decide they'll scare the shit out of them."

"Maybe," said Cahoon, still reading. "Cartwright went back out to Lakey's with her?"

"She wouldn't go alone," said Beakey. "Tough duty."

"So she locks up the place, comes back here." Cahoon laughed. "Cartwright makes her fill out an accident report?"

"Regulations."

"So where is she?" asked Cahoon, raising his eyebrows.

Beakey got up and went back to his desk. "Boston, according to Cartwright. Said she wasn't going to stay around here."

"Jesus," said Cahoon, "and it's still the off-season."

The door opened. "Enfield!" shouted Cahoon. "Your coffee's getting cold."

"Where you been?" asked Beakey.

"Out to Voke-Tech, talking with Danny Sears," said Enfield, taking the lid off his coffee cup.

"Great minds," said Beakey.

"Yeah?" said Cahoon.

"He denied it," said Enfield. "So we took a walk to the parking lot to see his car. Either the kid's clean or he's found the fastest body shop on the Cape."

East Providence, Rhode Island
Morning

The two men stood in the parking lot of the Red Kettle Motor Inn, staring at the car. The older of the two, short and paunchy, ran his hand over the jagged remains of the right headlight, then back along the dented fender. He took a handkerchief out of his pocket and sneezed into it.

The younger man dropped his cigarette on the pavement, stepped on it, walked around to the driver's side and sat on the hood. From time to time he looked up at the sun and squinted.

"For Christ's sake," said Woody.

The younger man looked back over his shoulder. "Don't start, Woody. I'm not some goddamn kid."

Woody rubbed his nose with the handkerchief, then folded it with exaggerated care and put it back in his pocket. "You still don't know how to tail?"

The younger man sighed and looked at the ground.

Woody began to pace slowly back and forth in front of the car. "I got a kid at home in the eighth grade. I got a mother who's seventy-one. Neither of 'em ever been on a tail in their life. If I asked them, maybe they wouldn't be so good at it; maybe they'd get sloppy and let the tail see 'em. That happens." He stopped pacing, went over to the car and stood next to the younger man. "What do you think the chances are, Dink, they'd get fucking run over?"

"OK," said Dink. "You feeling better now?"

"Shit," said Woody. He went over and kicked the front tire. "She see the car?"

"Yeah, she saw it, but not to get a make on it. Not enough time."

Woody went back around to the front and surveyed the damaged fender. "You can't use it anyway. Not this way. You take mine. I'll get this fixed."

He scratched the back of his head. "She didn't see you, did she?"

"No." Dink slid off the hood and lit another cigarette. "No way."

"Sure?"

"I was scrunched way down in the seat. Even if there'd been time—"

"Taking a goddamn nap?"

"OK, Woody. I got it. I fucked up. Can we drop it?"

Woody put his hands in his pockets and shook his head. "Don't let her out of your goddamn sight," he said, mostly to himself. He looked around the parking lot, then opened the front door and slid in behind the wheel. "Get in," he said. "I want you with me when I tell O'Connell."

Boston, Massachusetts
Midday

Seeing the car in the daylight, the crumpled fender, the smudges of blue paint, the shattered taillight, brought back the reality of the night before. Dreams, she knew, or imaginings, did not leave dents. The police had been reassuring, telling her that she was reading too much into it, that it was probably just some local kids with time on their hands, trying to spook her. Possibly. But even so, she no longer dismissed the idea of danger quite so casually. Thoughts of Weiss and Pittsburgh had wedged themselves between her dreams the night before, and now, this morning, the prospect of meeting Bennet unsettled her, but it was too late to change her plans. She warned herself to be very careful.

She arrived at the restaurant early and waited in an elegant foyer, which was hung with a series of old lithographs depicting the history of Boston. She moved slowly from one to the other, studying each of them, and was startled when she heard someone behind her say, "Miss Mulholland?"

She turned and saw a man in the stiffly formal dress of a maître d', smiling, beckoning to her. "Yes," she said.

He made a small bow and moved a step closer. "Mr. Bennet called and asked me to show you to his table. He'll be a few minutes late. Would you follow me?"

He led her into the long and narrow dining room, its far wall a floor-to-ceiling window that provided sweeping views of the harbor, and beyond it, the airport. He stopped at a small table, at the far end of the room, window-side, and slid out a chair. "May I get you something from the bar?"

"Coffee would be fine."

He made another little bow and left. Nancy looked out at the harbor, which to her looked rather like a river. In the channel, a tugboat shoved a long, black barge through choppy water and off to the right an airliner descended, slow and silent, its wheels extended like legs, looking like an enormous silver duck. The coffee arrived and the waiter handed her a menu. Nancy was surprised to see that she could spend more for lunch here than she could for dinner at a good restaurant in Bloomington.

She didn't hear Bennet approach, and sitting the way she was, her view directed outward, toward the harbor, she couldn't see him, but she knew he was there behind her, nevertheless. She heard the words "I'm terribly sorry" and felt the brush of a hand on her shoulder. She found herself standing up, looking into a smiling face, and saw immediately that it was the remarkably handsome one that had caught her attention in Weiss's photo album.

"Gil Bennet," he said, extending his hand.

"Nancy Mulholland," she said, taking it.

They sat down and looked at one another with undisguised interest. Nancy was used to being looked at by men, appraised really, and had, over the years, learned to ignore it. Because she had them, looks failed to impress her and she was surprised, therefore, to find herself so taken by the physical appearance of the man who sat across the table from her.

"Been waiting long?"

"No," said Nancy. "But I wasn't quite expecting a place like this. I'm not really dressed for it."

"You're fine," he said, smiling, and he said it in a way that

Nancy felt she could take at face value. There wasn't any leering there, no flattery, just a simple statement of fact. She liked him and settled back in her chair, relaxed. He gestured toward the window. "Quite a view," he said, and he turned slightly in his chair and began an unhurried narrative, describing the landmarks of the harbor.

"You're from Boston, then," said Nancy when he had finished.

"Born in Missouri," he said. "Spent most of my life in Washington, D.C. But this is my favorite city."

A waiter appeared and hovered expectantly. They ordered, Nancy simply choosing the first thing that she could recognize— something with chicken and asparagus. Bennet asked for a bottle of white wine.

They chatted for a few minutes and Nancy busied herself with a roll from the basket that the waiter had brought, trying to break it without producing a blizzard of crumbs. Finally Bennet paused. "Would you mind telling me again how all this happened?"

"I'm not sure there's very much to tell. Eight days ago, last Tuesday, I got a call from the college asking me if I knew where she was. She had missed the first day of classes—simply hadn't shown up to teach. The week before, she'd gone to her place on Cape Cod for spring break and that's the last anyone saw of her."

The waiter brought the wine and Bennet tasted it. "That's it? She simply vanished?"

"Essentially, yes. The way she left the cottage—with the door open and the table set for breakfast—made it look like she expected to return, or at least wanted to make it look that way; and the police found a sandal on the beach, about the right size, but no one can be sure it's hers. Other than that, nothing."

"What do they think?"

"The police? I'm not sure. Suicide, probably, but I don't buy that."

"Why not?"

"I don't know. No motives, for one thing. There was absolutely nothing in Catherine's life or in her personality that would lead to suicide. For another, there's no indication—no notes, no hints, and, most of all, no body. Not many people kill themselves so discreetly."

Bennet took a sip of wine and looked out at the harbor. "If it wasn't suicide, what was it?"

Nancy leaned forward and shook her head. "That's just it. That's the thing I simply can't understand."

He chose a roll from the basket. "From what you've said, I gather it's occurred to you that she engineered this thing herself, that she disappeared because she wanted to?"

The question startled Nancy. What had she said? She studied Bennet for a moment before she answered. "It did occur to me, but that doesn't make any more sense than any other explanation. Less, actually."

"Why less?"

"Motive. There wasn't any, at least as far as I can see. I've read in the papers about people who make themselves disappear. They're usually desperate: money problems, family problems, things like that. Catherine wasn't that way. She was happy with her life, her job ... " Nancy let her voice trail off and then shrugged. "It just wouldn't make any sense."

"You're sure?" said Bennet.

"I don't know what you mean by 'sure.' A week ago, I'd have said yes, absolutely, but that was before any of this. What I'm saying is that the Catherine I knew—and I knew her very well— wouldn't have had any reason to make herself disappear."

Bennet leaned very slightly toward her and dropped his voice just enough for her to notice. "Forgive me," he said, "but I think it's possible ... "

The waiter returned, and in front of Nancy put down a large white plate, which had a small, flowerlike arrangement of thinly sliced chicken, drizzled in an orange-colored sauce that was flecked with bits of green. Bennet's meal, ground beef and onion rings, looked more substantial and more appetizing. Nancy took a small bite of food. "Very good," she said, although it really wasn't. They ate in silence for a while and Nancy watched a plane take off, climb over them, the roar of its engines reduced by the windows to a muffled hum. She looked over at Bennet. "What is possible?"

He looked up at her, then dabbed at his mouth with a napkin. "The other day, after you called, after the shock subsided, I thought about Catherine. She was not a conventional woman. Not by any means."

"Not conventional? In what way?"

"Not in any obvious way, of course," said Bennet. "As you say, she seemed to be perfectly ordinary—I don't mean that in any disparaging way—a happy, well-adjusted college teacher, aunt?"

Nancy nodded.

Bennet busied himself with his food, and seemed preoccupied, as though he were debating with himself. When he looked up, he hesitated before he spoke. "I don't suppose that Catherine ever mentioned to you that there were parts of her life quite separate from Stonington?" Bennet gave Nancy a bland, handsome smile.

"No, she didn't." There was something odd about the question, or at least about the way he asked it.

"Nothing about the book?"

"Nothing. But we didn't talk much about work."

"And about Weiss?"

Nancy shrugged. "Not very much. I remember when she met him. It was obvious she liked him. After that, she mentioned him from time to time. No long conversations though."

Bennet looked out over the harbor. "I knew Dick Weiss pretty well. It's funny, but I remember when he met Catherine. There was quite a romance there for a while. Did you know that?"

Nancy nodded. "I guessed."

"Did you know that Weiss proposed to her?"

"No," said Nancy.

"Several times, but she always refused, always found some excuse, even though she told Weiss that she loved him. He never understood that. He offered to quit his job and take his chances on finding something in New England, but she said no, she couldn't take that responsibility. Finally, he told her that they didn't have to be married, that they could live together for a while, maybe for just a summer, to see if things would work, but she said no to that too because she thought it wouldn't look good. He finally ran out of suggestions and gave up."

"Gave up?"

"He stopped pursuing her. Too frustrating," he said. "But they stayed friends."

"I know that they stayed friends," said Nancy, "but I'm not sure I see your point."

"I'm sorry," said Bennet. "I'm being clumsy." He paused, obviously setting out on a new tack—a gentler one. "You were close to her, weren't you?" he said.

"Yes."

"Did you ever visit her on the Cape?"

"No. We talked about it, but something always seemed to come up."

"I see," said Bennet. "And at the college, have you run across anyone there who ever visited her?"

Nancy thought for a moment, then shook her head. She was about to say something about Weiss, but decided against it until she could see where Bennet might be leading.

"And did she ever mention having guests or entertaining friends in Cotchpinicut?"

"She never mentioned it, but . . . "

"Don't you find it odd that no one, not you, not me, no one from the college, not even Dick Weiss, was ever invited out there?"

At the mention of Weiss, Nancy's eyes widened and she wondered if Bennet noticed. She clearly remembered the pictures in the album, of Weiss painting the cottage, putting up an umbrella on the beach. Was Bennet lying, or had Weiss lied to Bennet? Neither made very much sense.

"Don't you find that odd?" repeated Bennet.

"I don't know," said Nancy, recovering. "The way you put it, I suppose, but over the years I never really noticed. We all have our private places. Maybe that was hers." Nancy pushed her plate aside, still feeling hungry. "But I'm still not sure that I see what you're getting at."

"I'm not absolutely sure either," said Bennet. He picked up the bottle of wine and offered some to her. She shook her head.

He refilled his glass. "But I think things begin to point to another kind of life she had, centered in Cotchpinicut. One that no one seemed to know about."

"You make it sound sinister."

"Sinister?" Bennet laughed gently. "I don't think so. I don't think she was running drugs or burying bodies."

"What, then?"

Bennet looked at her for a long moment. "You're sure she never said anything?"

"About a secret life? No. Positive."

"OK. Please don't be offended, but the only thing that I can think of is sex."

"Sex!" Nancy said it too loudly and was aware of heads turning to look at her. She picked up a napkin and dabbed at her mouth. "Sorry," she said, "you took me by surprise."

"What I mean," said Bennet, "is that it's possible that Catherine might have been carrying on a liaison, an affair . . . "

"But why hide it like that? She's an adult, single, and who would care?"

"If it was with another woman?"

"Another woman?" Nancy put her head back and rubbed her eyes, then looked at Bennet and shook her head. "No. Not Catherine."

"And why not?" said Bennet. "She's a professor at a women's college in a small New England town. Very respectable. At the Cape she can live the way she wants fairly openly. Have you been to Provincetown?"

"No," said Nancy. "But believe me, Catherine wasn't having an affair with another woman. I'm not sure why I know that, but I do."

"OK. But it would explain a lot of things."

"Would it explain her disappearance?"

"It could. She could have been afraid of being found out. Maybe she was tired of the duplicity and went somewhere for a fresh start. Someplace where no one would care."

"Without telling anyone? And walking away from her job, her students in the middle of the year? No. Not Catherine."

The maître d' appeared at the table, bent down close to Bennet and said something to him in a voice too low for Nancy to hear. Bennet asked her if she would excuse him while he took a telephone call.

When he had gone, she realized how tired she was and how disappointed. There was a certain kind of superficial logic to what Bennet had said, but it had very little to do with the Catherine she knew and, furthermore, it did nothing to explain the appearance of Stephen Lakey, the incidents abroad, the messages to Weiss, or Weiss's death. Perhaps it was last night, or maybe Simco's warning, but even though she instinctively liked Gil Bennet, there was something just a bit disquieting about him. She wanted to tell him what she knew—something might ring a bell with him, something that he hadn't thought to mention because it hadn't seemed important—but she decided that she'd better not, at least not yet.

Bennet returned and apologized. Nancy looked at her watch. "It's time for me to go anyway," she said. "I've got a long drive." She looked in her purse and found a piece of paper, wrote a number on it and handed it to Bennet.

"If you think of anything else, you can reach me there."

"Devon? For how long?"

"I don't know," she said. She closed her purse. "Until I find her. Or until there's no point in looking anymore."

"I'm glad you came," said Bennet. "Catherine spoke of you often."

Nancy stood up and held out her hand. "I appreciate your help."

Bennet stood up and took her hand. "Good-bye," he said, then watched her as she made her way between tables and finally disappeared around a corner. He sat down again and from an inside jacket pocket removed a small, black notebook. He opened it and with a gold ballpoint pen he wrote down the number she had given him and next to it her name and a question mark. He looked at the harbor and watched a fishing boat, low in the water and trailed by a cloud of gulls, slowly make its way to the pier just beyond the restaurant. He thought of Woody—what Woody had said about Nancy Mulholland—and he realized that all of them had underestimated her.

She had played her hand very well, almost professionally, giving away nothing, telling him very little of what she knew. Prudent caution? Or was it something more than that? Could it be that she somehow knew far more than he thought she did, that she knew about him, about OEP and where Catherine fit in? It was a sobering thought. He had been the hunter for so long that he had entirely forgotten what it was like to be the hunted.

Queens, New York
Afternoon

The small commuter plane thudded down through the cloudy sky, making it feel, to Simco, as though they were flying down a flight of stairs. He didn't like to fly and avoided it whenever he could; that he was doing so now in a flimsy twin-engined nine-seater was a measure of how much he wanted to talk to Carla Valenzuela. The left wing dipped suddenly, then recovered and out the window to the right he could see Shea Stadium and the Tennis Center. He took some comfort from knowing that in a few minutes he would be on the ground, one way or the other.

Inside the terminal, he found the coffee shop that she had described and, from the entrance next to the cashier, he could see her, in the bright red sweater she'd said she would wear, sitting at a table in the corner by the window. He introduced himself and apologized for being late. She listened solemnly, sitting erect in her chair, then motioned that he should sit down. A waitress appeared and Simco ordered coffee for both of them.

"Thank you for meeting me," he said when the waitress had gone.

"You're the one who's gone to all the trouble." Her voice was deep, with just a trace of an accent. She looked at him steadily, appraisingly. "I hope you won't mind if I speak plainly."

"Not at all."

"Professor Simco, I can only talk to you if we agree to be honest with one another. Yesterday, on the telephone, I said no to you at first because when I asked you why you were interested in Cesar your answer didn't satisfy me."

She was looking directly into his eyes and it made Simco uncomfortable.

"Now," she continued, "would you please tell me why a professor from Connecticut wants to talk to me about my husband?"

Simco gave her an apologetic smile. "I'm sorry. I'm a bad liar. I'm looking for a woman named Catherine Lakey." He watched her face carefully for any sign of recognition. There was none. "I gather that name doesn't mean anything to you."

"No," she said.

Simco outlined the story of Catherine's disappearance, then briefly described Catherine's carefully concealed references to Cesar Valenzuela's death and to the events in Ireland and India. For the moment, he did not elaborate. When he finished, the look of disappointment on her face was clear.

"I see," she said quietly. "I know nothing about any of these things. I'm sorry, but I don't think that I can be of very much help to you." She gave him a faint smile. "Or you to me."

"I hope that's not the case," said Simco. "Would you mind if I began by asking a few questions?"

"What questions?"

"Did your husband have any academic connections that you know of? Perhaps he had friends or associates who were professors or who had some involvement with a university."

Carla Valenzuela shook her head slowly. "I'm sorry, Professor Simco, my husband was a banker. We were married twenty years and, of course, I didn't know everyone he knew, but he wasn't an academic man. Well educated, yes, but not academic. There are academic people in Antofagasta, at the university, but I don't think that any of them were exactly friends. We knew some of them, but only casually."

"And he had no business in India or Ireland?"

"He was a local banker. Have you ever been to Chile?"

"No."

"Antofagasta is not Santiago. It isn't even Valparaiso. Cesar's bank was not a very large one and the international business was small. A little in Bolivia, maybe something in Peru. Certainly nothing in Europe or Asia. I'm sorry."

"It's all right," said Simco. "I didn't really think that there were those kinds of connections. I was pretty sure that Miss Lakey didn't know your husband or the others and I don't think that they knew one another. I think the connection might have something to do with who they were and how they died."

"I see."

"That's really why I wanted to talk to you. I know you weren't satisfied with the investigation."

"And how do you know that?"

"I have a friend at the State Department. You made an impression."

Carla Valenzuela shook her head ruefully. "Not enough of one, apparently."

"Would you mind telling me about it?"

"Mind? Don't worry. I've talked about it so much and for so long . . . " She sighed. "It's almost like a recitation you do in school."

"You told our people in the embassy that you thought your husband was murdered."

She sat up a little straighter and balanced her chin on her folded hands. "I know he was. I don't care what the autopsies say. Cesar was a healthy man. Two weeks before he died he had a physical examination. There was nothing wrong."

"But even very healthy people can die suddenly."

"I'm sure they can. But they die of something, don't they? The heart, or stroke. Something, anyhow. They told me that Cesar died of nothing."

"Like Joseph Dunlop."

"Joseph Dunlop?"

"In Ireland. Dublin. He was like your husband: young, an official in the government and he died suddenly. They found no cause of death."

"He was murdered?"

Simco shrugged. "I don't know. I don't think anybody does. There wasn't any evidence." He looked at her steadily. She returned his look. "Do you have evidence?" he said.

"I'm not a lawyer," she said. "I don't know what makes good evidence. I don't have a weapon, if that's what you mean."

"What do you have?"

"I have circumstances and events. I'm not a political person, Professor Simco, and Cesar and I rarely talked about the Council, but in the months before his death, he took positions which were not popular with the government. In the newspapers, there were suggestions that he should resign."

"Was he ever threatened?"

"I don't know. If he was, he never told me about it. Anyway, when you talk about a murder, you need to talk about a motive. There were people who would be happy to see him off the Council."

"I see, but I'm afraid that's not evidence."

"I know that. There are other things. About a week before he died, he began having meetings with an American businessman who called himself Pelsen. Stephen Pelsen. He had come to Antofagasta to negotiate some sort of deal on copper. I don't know the details. He had come to the bank to secure financing for his project and he and Cesar had several meetings. Cesar said that he was a difficult man to do business with, but that he liked him personally. He came to the house one night and I met him. I didn't like him."

"Why not?"

"It's difficult to say, really. There was something about him that wasn't ... I'm not sure. Perhaps genuine is the word. He wore a business suit, a nice one, but he looked uncomfortable, as though he wasn't used to being in a suit. It may sound funny, but he didn't have the build of a businessman, either. He was very muscular, with a thick neck. He looked like he would have been very much at home in a gymnasium." She looked up at Simco. "I'm not sure this is helping you. Do you want me to go on?"

"Please."

"I wouldn't give this Stephen Pelsen another thought," she said, her voice flat, tired, "except that on the night Cesar died, he was supposed to meet with him."

"Did he?"

"I don't know. I suppose I'll never know. Cesar called from the bank in the afternoon and said that he was going to meet Mr. Pelsen for dinner and that he would be home by ten o'clock. I decided that I would go into the city to do some shopping and fix a simple dinner for myself when I got back. When I came home, at a little before eight, I was surprised to see Cesar's car and to see the lights on in the house."

Simco looked uncomfortable. "And is that when you found him?"

She nodded. "In the kitchen. He was lying on the floor and I could tell right away that he was dead. I called the police and they came quickly." Her voice trailed off and she shook her head, remembering. "I didn't think of Stephen Pelsen right then. It was the next day, or perhaps the day after. I called the police and told them that my husband was to have met with this man that night and perhaps someone should talk with him. Of course, I didn't know where he was staying."

"And did the police talk to him?"

"Professor Simco, you asked me before if I had evidence that Cesar was murdered. When the police checked the hotels for Mr. Pelsen, he was not there. There was no Stephen Pelsen in Antofagasta then, or for the entire month before."

"You're sure?"

Carla Valenzuela shrugged. "The police are sure. I told you, Antofagasta is not Santiago. There are not that many hotels."

"He might have stayed privately, with friends or business associates."

She smiled. "You think like the police. They said the same thing. They checked the best they could, executives at Codelco—the national copper company—but no one had heard of him." She paused and slowly stirred her coffee with a spoon. "I know what you're thinking."

"What's that?"

"That I'm jumping to conclusions. But the one thing I know about Mr. Pelsen was that he worked for a company called Western Copper and Refining. Cesar mentioned that to me and I remembered it. I don't know why. In Antofagasta, you remember the names of copper companies, I suppose. Western doesn't have an office in Antofagasta, so the police called the headquarters in Salt Lake City. I think you can guess what they discovered. There was no record of any employee named Stephen Pelsen and, furthermore, the company had no plans for doing anything anywhere in northern Chile."

Simco wasn't quite sure what to say. He found the story fascinating and at the same time sad, but again it seemed to be drifting farther and farther away from Catherine and from the things he wanted to know. Even if Carla Valenzuela was right in thinking that Stephen Pelsen, whoever he was, was involved in her husband's death, Simco didn't see how that helped him. He decided to change the direction of the conversation. "I'm interested in why you asked for the second autopsy, the one done by the Americans."

"Because I thought the first one was a lie," she said immediately. "It was clear to me that someone was making sure that an investigation would go no further. If there is no cause of death, no weapon, no suspect that anyone can find, there is no murder."

"But to find nothing in an autopsy, isn't that unusual?"

"Yes, it is."

"If they wanted to cover up a murder," Simco hesitated, trying to choose his words carefully, "wouldn't it have been less risky to have simply made up something and say he died of a heart attack?"

"I don't know. I suppose so."

"Well anyway, didn't the American doctors come to the same conclusion—that they couldn't find a cause of death?"

She nodded wearily.

"Do you think they were involved as well?"

"I don't know. I asked for Americans because I didn't trust the Chileans. We talked beforehand, the doctors and I, and I explained to them why I wanted their opinions. I also told them what I thought they ought to look for."

"You told them what to look for? I don't understand."

"The night he died, when I found him, his shirt had come undone from his trousers and I noticed that right here . . . " she pointed to a place on her sweater just below her ribs on her left side, "there was a small spot of blood, no more than a few millimeters across. It was easy enough to see because his shirt was white and because of the way he was lying on the floor. I didn't think very much about it until after the first autopsy, when it wasn't mentioned."

"So you told the American doctors about it?"

"They said they found nothing except a small bruise, no bigger than the nail on my little finger. It was nothing. Almost anything could have caused it, they said, and they couldn't see what it had to do with his death."

"But you think there was a connection?"

"I don't know. I'm not an expert. I don't know why there would be blood on his shirt. I don't know why he would have a bruise down there. I don't believe that Cesar died of nothing."

Simco sat back in his chair and looked out the window over Carla Valenzuela's left shoulder. He tried to imagine the scene that night in the kitchen, of the man lying face down on the floor, his shirt pulled out from his trousers, billowing out from underneath him, a red smudge on one side. Now what they had was a vanished American who used a false name, a spot of blood, a bruise, dead birds in Ziploc bags—and he remembered a time when the most difficult thing he had to do was to draw up the departmental budget. He thanked Carla Valenzuela, assured her that he would let her know if he discovered anything, then he made his way glumly to the little airplane, wishing very much that he had the time to take the train. Not only was he far more certain that a train would deliver him safely to Hartford, but it would give him time to think as well.

Bloomington, Indiana
Evening

The warm spring evening hadn't made its way into the second-floor corridor of the west wing of the Emma Singer Nursing Home. Instead, there was a hollow, gloomy silence broken only by the soft *squish-squeak* of thick soled nurses' shoes on polished linoleum and the intermittent, far-off gritty noise of television laughter. Even the ceiling lights, glowing a cheerless yellow, seemed muffled.

At ten minutes of six, the rhythm of the corridor quickened; the day nurses finished their last rounds and made their entries in the daily log; the night nurses came through the doors in twos and threes, their voices not yet hushed, the smell of the outdoors still clinging to them. At the nurses' station on second west, Florence Brower, the daytime floor supervisor, checked through the notes and reminders that had accumulated throughout the day, found the envelope that she was looking for and put it aside.

"You missed a grand day, Flo," said Mary Hesketh, the night supervisor, taking off her scarf. "Spring is here."

"Maybe it'll stay 'til Wednesday," said Florence.

"That's not what they're saying on the TV," said Mary, coming over to stand behind Florence, looking over her shoulder. "Anything new?"

Florence scanned the notes. "Mr. Viedt went to the hospital this morning."

"God bless him," said Mary. "He won't be coming back."

"Everything else is about the same. Sarah Daigle kicked up a fuss about the food again tonight. Said that either she was going to talk to Miss Singer right today or she was calling her sister to take her home. And here's something." She picked up the envelope, looked at it again and gave it to Mary Hesketh. "What do you suppose we do with this?"

Mary held it up to the light. "Mrs. Ruth Lakey," she read. "Now who on earth?"

Florence went to the small locker at the rear of the nurses' station, opened the door and took out a coat. "No return address," she said, "but do you see where it's from?"

Mary squinted at the postmark, but it was smudged and unreadable. Then she looked at the stamps in the upper right-hand corner. "Well," she said. "I wonder who she knows in France." She slid the envelope into the deep side pocket of her dress and by six-fifteen had forgotten it was there.

Devon, Connecticut
Evening

"Well?" said Nancy, exactly the way that Simco knew she would, after he finished telling her of his meeting with Carla Valenzuela. It was after eight and both of them seemed to sag on the furniture in Catherine Lakey's living room, Nancy in the armchair, Simco on the sofa. More than two hours of talk about the events of the past two days had deflated them, like balloons the day after a birthday party.

Simco leaned forward, resting his elbows on his knees, and picked absently at the remains of a pizza in a cardboard box on the coffee table in front of him. "Did she like birds?" he said without looking up.

"Did who like birds?"

"Catherine."

Nancy yawned and stretched. "I don't know, she never mentioned it. I suppose she did."

"She had a feeder in Cotchpinicut. It's still there. I noticed it when we were there last week."

"And?"

"On the plane this afternoon," said Simco, "I kept going over what Carla Valenzuela had said and I kept coming back to the birds."

"The birds that your friend in Biology told you about?"

"She told Shields that she had found them dead by the feeder. I wonder if she did."

"What difference would it make?"

"I don't know. In airplanes I tend to have morbid thoughts. I wondered if she might have killed them."

"Catherine? What a bizarre thought."

Simco looked at her without smiling. "Maybe, but those birds, Cesar Valenzuela, that Dunlop fellow in Ireland aren't coincidences."

"But why on earth would she kill a bunch of birds? And what would it have to do with the other two?"

"I wondered about that, but something that Bennet said to you today struck me as important."

"You're not going to tell me you buy that story of his?"

"No, but that's not what I mean. He said there might have been a side to Catherine that nobody knew. He might be right, and I think that's why we haven't been getting anywhere. We keep assuming that we're dealing with the Catherine that you and I know, and that leads us into brick walls. The Catherine we know wouldn't have disappeared to begin with."

"And the Catherine that we don't know is a bird killer."

Simco ignored the remark. "Maybe she discovered a way to kill birds without leaving a trace. She was a chemist. It's not impossible that she devised some sort of poison."

"Oh come on, Frank." Nancy got up from her chair and went over to the fireplace. She lit a cigarette.

"Please, Nancy, stay calm."

"I am calm," said Nancy rather too loudly. "It's just that you've got Catherine killing birds. And then what? She was having so much fun she decided to try people?"

"I don't think sarcasm helps very much," said Simco. "Of course, that's not what I'm saying, but we've got some strange events and I'm trying to make connections. Several years ago, your aunt showed up with a bunch of dead birds and even an expert couldn't figure out what killed them. Now she's calling your attention to a series of deaths and nobody can find a cause for them either. I understand why you might not like what I'm saying, but I don't think that means it ought to be rejected out of hand."

Nancy looked up at the ceiling. "I think it should be," she said slowly, "because it's absolutely preposterous." She held up her hand. "OK, I'll grant you that there may be sides to Catherine that neither of us—maybe no one at all—knows about. And maybe it's not a bad idea to try to imagine things she might have done, even if they don't sound like her. But so far today, Bennet's suggested that she's a lesbian who's run off somewhere to have an affair, and now you're telling me that she concocts poisons, then kills birds, and God only knows what else as well."

"No. I'm not saying that at all. Look, Nancy, she's a scientist. She might have been doing some sort of research, stumbled across something that kills things without leaving a trace. That might explain the birds."

Nancy shook her head rapidly. "I'm sorry, but I don't think it does. Even if she'd discovered this poison—although how or why I can't imagine—she wouldn't have used it on anything. Jesus, Frank. She wouldn't even use a fly swatter." Nancy came back to the chair, flopped into it. "And anyway, none of this explains those three men."

Simco ran both hands back through his hair. "But there's got to be a connection," he said, exasperation in his voice. "Dead birds, Catherine, three dead men. She's telling us there is."

"I think we ought to drop it. We're both tired. And it doesn't get us any closer to knowing where she is." She folded her hands in front of her and leaned forward, looking at the floor. "Nothing seems to," she said. "On the way down from Boston it occurred to me that, for the first time since I got here, I don't have anything to do tomorrow."

"Do?"

"No leads to follow up. You've done what you can do with the State Department. We've talked to everyone around here. We've followed up on Bennet. That's it. I can't think of anything else."

"I can call Bellinger and see if he's found out anything about India."

"But you're not going to go there and neither am I. I can't just sit here and wait for something to happen. I can do that in Indiana."

"You're thinking of going back?"

"I've got a job, work piling up. I've been gone two weeks now."

"But without you, this whole thing . . . " Simco seemed lost, almost stricken. "It just stops."

Nancy gave him a weary smile. "But it's stopped anyway."

"That can't be true," he said. "I just don't believe that we're absolutely out of options."

"I could call Cotchpinicut." Nancy made the suggestion without conviction in her voice. "Maybe those weren't kids following me. Maybe they've found out who it was."

"Maybe, but they probably would have called here by now." Simco looked at her. "There's still Bennet."

"What about him?"

"He's still the only connection between Catherine and Weiss and all you know about him is what he's told you. It's possible he knows more than he told you today."

"It's also possible he doesn't, but I don't know how we find out. Whoever he is, the Gil Bennet I met today is a very polished character. If he knew more than he was telling me, he hid it very well."

"But he lied about Weiss being at Cotchpinicut."

"I don't know. He might have, or Weiss might have lied to him, although I can't imagine why."

"What if you called him and told him that you'd come across new information?"

"What new information?"

"Tell him what you know. The marmalade, the cookbook, Stephen Lakey, Valenzuela. Everything."

"What?" Nancy shot a startled look at Simco. "Wasn't it you who told me to be careful? I don't see what that buys us."

"If Bennet is who he says he is, it doesn't buy us anything. But if he's somehow involved in this and he finds out what you know, it could draw him out."

Nancy's eyes went wide. "Draw him out? But that's exactly—exactly—what I didn't want to do today. If Bennet is involved, and if he had something to do with Weiss, it wasn't because Weiss didn't know anything. Maybe Weiss drew him out. And now you're telling me I ought to do the same thing."

"It's an idea. I don't know what else we can do."

"If it's such a great idea, why don't you call him. I'm sure you can draw him out as well as I can."

Simco smiled. "All right, it's a bad idea."

"Thank you," said Nancy.

"Can I try one more?"

"One more what?"

"Idea. You mentioned Weiss. He's the only other one we know who could have told us anything about Bennet, which might explain why he's dead. Anyhow, if Bennet worked with him for such a long time, isn't it possible, even likely, that someone at the med school could confirm that?"

"Who?"

"I don't know. There must be a secretary, or someone else who worked with him."

"It's worth a call," said Nancy. "You really think that Bennet's involved in this, don't you?"

"I'd be willing to bet on it."

"What if tomorrow we find out that Bennet isn't who he says he is?"

"Then I guess I'd be right." Simco gave her a broad smile and Nancy, all of a sudden, saw what he must have looked like when he was a little boy. "And you'd have to stick around for at least a few more days," he said.

"Frank, come on," she said, but she couldn't help smiling back at him. "Really, what do we do?"

"I haven't any idea."

Bloomington, Indiana
Night

Mary Hesketh closed the front door as quietly as she could, not wanting to disturb her husband, who, soon enough, would be awakened by the alarm clock and have to go off to work. In the kitchen, she opened the refrigerator, took out the sandwich she'd made earlier and sat down wearily at the old wooden table. She had been the night supervisor at the nursing home for nearly three months, but she still hadn't adjusted to the schedule and it seemed that she was always tired. When the sandwich crumbled in her hand, a piece of it falling into her lap, then onto the floor, she sighed and pushed her chair back. Bending down to retrieve the bit of bread and bologna, she saw the long, brown stain of coffee that ran down the left side of her uniform. Lord, she thought, how did that happen? She wasn't a coffee drinker herself, so it must have been one of the other nurses who had spilled it on her, and she hadn't noticed until now.

She stood up, examined the stain and wished she hadn't put off hemming her other uniform, the new one that was still in her sewing basket. After trying unsuccessfully to remove the stain with a damp sponge, she went down to the basement, took off her dress and arranged it carefully in the drum of the washing machine. In the laundry hamper she found enough white things—some of her husband's undershirts and a few towels—to make a small load. She measured out detergent and bleach and pressed the button to begin the cycle. "Doing wash at two o'clock in the morning, and at my age," she said to herself as she turned out the basement lights and slowly climbed the stairs to the kitchen.

Inside the washing machine, the water flowed into the drum with a soft whooshing sound. It swirled around the bottom layer of laundry, around the stained white uniform, around the pocket which still contained the envelope addressed to Ruth Lakey. A stamp floated gently off the upper right-hand corner and then, in a watery slow motion, the envelope's seal dissolved and the flap lifted, exposing the the top part of the letter inside. "Dearest Nannie," it began. "Don't worry. I'm doing this . . . " For just a moment, the writing turned bright and vivid, then it swirled off the page, staining the wash an inky blue. Twenty minutes later, when the machine had shuddered through its final spin, all that was left was lumpy wads of soft, gray pulp.

MARCH—1987						
S	M	T	W	T	F	S
1	2	3	4	5	6	7
8	9	10	11	12	13	14
15	16	17	18	19	20	21
22	23	24	25	<u>26</u>	27	28
29	30	31				

DAY FIFTEEN

APRIL—1987						
S	M	T	W	T	F	S
			1	2	3	4
5	6	7	8	(9)	10	11
12	13	14	15	16	17	18
19	20	21	22	23	24	25
26	27	28	29	30		

DAY FIFTEEN

THURSDAY, APRIL 9, 1987

Bethesda, Maryland
Morning

Bennet was very much aware of the way that Tony was looking at him. One of Tony's strengths—and weaknesses—was his blunt, transparent honesty. He was one of the few men that Bennet had ever met who had not a trace of guile. What he saw on Tony's face this morning was disapproval and concern.

"We can't take her lightly," said Bennet casually, leaning back in his big leather chair. "Woody made her out to be some sort of bumpkin, but she certainly isn't that."

Tony sat across the desk from him, impassive, his hands held together, fingertip to fingertip, just beneath his nose. Bennet noticed that his broad frame looked costumed rather than clothed. Although Tony's shirt and tie and blazer were beautifully matched and obviously expensive, they didn't suit him. Bennet had always thought that Tony looked like a stevedore and now concluded that no amount of tasteful decoration could conceal that. He'd look much better in a T-shirt.

When Tony said nothing, Bennet, who did not like long silences, went on. "It's hard to say if she knows anything more than what they put on the blackboard last weekend, but it was fairly clear that she doesn't trust me." He smiled at Tony. "And I'm not sure the meeting changed that. I think she wanted to meet me for the same reasons that I wanted to meet her, to probe the opposition, find out what the other knows." He laughed quietly, almost to himself. "It was quite a dance."

"They know more," said Tony.

Bennet, who had been slowly rolling a gold pen between his fingers, stopped. "I'm sorry?"

"That friend of hers, Frank Simco, flew to New York yesterday. He spent an hour and a half in a coffee shop at La Guardia with Carla Valenzuela."

"Carla Valenzuela? And?"

"I don't think they talked about the weather."

"I'm sure they didn't," said Bennet. "I'm sure that Mrs. Valenzuela filled Mr. Simco in on all the fanciful details that her vivid imagination could provide." Bennet shook his head. "I admire her persistence. It's fortunate that it comes across as monomania."

"She could have told him about Pelsen."

"I'm sure she did. She's told everyone else."

"This doesn't worry you?"

"I can't see why it should. The woman has been screaming for almost a year now. It concerned me at first, but as time went on it was clear that no one was listening. She has passion, but passion is no substitute for evidence."

"But Simco knows about the others."

"And I'm sure he sees a pattern, although I very much doubt he can make much sense out of it. It must be frustrating."

"I've told Woody to cover Simco's phone. I don't think he's a minor player anymore."

"When?"

"As soon as we can. The office phone is pretty simple. The home is trickier."

"Be very careful."

"Tell me more about Mulholland. You said you thought she doesn't trust you."

"I think it was what she didn't say, or at least what she chose not to say. She seemed relaxed, at first, and I thought it would be easy, but after a few minutes, I realized that actually she was very controlled and very much on guard. That surprised me."

Tony thought of the idiocy in Cotchpinicut two nights ago. If Bennet ever found out . . . "Don't you think it may be time to reassess our strategy?"

"About what we do? I don't think so. The fact that she met me tells me that she doesn't know where Lakey is, and that is still the central fact in all of this. As long as she and Simco don't find her, I don't think there's very much that they can do and, therefore, there isn't very much we need to do."

"If they should find her before we can make a move . . . "

"I've thought of that. It's a risk, but the mail is covered and so is Lakey's phone. And now Simco's. It would be difficult for her to reach them."

"Do you really think so? She seems to have managed pretty well so far."

"But she hasn't told them where she is and I'm beginning to suspect that she isn't going to. She doesn't seem to want them to know about that any more than she wants us to."

"It doesn't make much sense."

"Of course it does. If no one knows, no one tells. She knew very well how interested we'd be and I'm sure she saw no sense in compromising the safety of her niece or of herself, for that matter." Bennet wagged the gold pen at Tony. "The reason that we are in the middle of all this unpleasantness is that every one of us—perhaps you less than the others—has underestimated Catherine Lakey."

"So we do nothing? She's like a time bomb."

"I prefer not to think of it that way," said Bennet, his voice pleasant. "We watch and listen, just as we always have. Mulholland and Simco have lives to lead and very soon, I think, they'll go back to leading them. Lakey can't stay hidden forever. Eventually she'll make an error and somebody will recognize her."

"And then what?"

"We'll deal with the situation."

"What the hell does that mean, Gil? Deal with the situation.

Are we going to sit her down and tell her not to do things like this anymore? That it makes us worry?"

"You know what I mean."

"I'm not sure I do. Sometimes I wonder if you've got the stomach for this business."

Bennet leaned forward in his chair and pointed the gold pen directly at Tony's forehead. "But you've got stomach enough for both of us, don't you? Understand something, Tony. I issued the orders on Valenzuela and the others. I will issue the orders on Lakey, not because I enjoy it, but because it's something that has to be done. Ends drive means around here, not the other way around. Is that clear?"

Tony nodded. Bennet sat back in his chair and his expression softened. "Remember, Tony, we hold all the cards. If we simply have the patience to let the game go on long enough, we'll win."

"I see," said Tony, his voice signaling neither agreement nor disagreement.

"You'll look after things while I'm gone?" said Bennet.

Tony nodded.

"Maggie will report to you. I've told the appropriate people that you're in charge. Lakey is top priority. If anything happens, I want to know about it right away."

"And you'll be back Tuesday?"

"Or Wednesday. This sort of negotiation is hard to predict, but if things drag on, well . . . " Bennet smiled broadly. "April in Paris isn't what I'd call a hardship." He sorted through some papers on his desk. "I suppose that's it. Anything from Woody?"

"Only the Simco thing. Even he couldn't miss that."

"I really think you underestimate him."

"I don't think that's possible."

Bennet got up and came around the desk to the leather sofa where Tony sat. He patted him gently on the shoulder. "You scowl too much," he said in the tone that older brothers use when talking to younger ones. "It's a beautiful day. Go out and play some golf and forget about this for twenty-four hours."

Tony stood up. "I don't think that golf is going to help us very much." He started toward the door, then stopped and turned around. "You know, Gil, we've been wrong so many times in this thing, and you still stand there with that goddamn smile on your face as if you have all the answers. You just said that we're where we are because we've always underestimated her. What happens when we do it again?"

Bennet's easy smile evaporated. "I'd appreciate it if you'd let me worry about that." He went back and sat down at his desk. "I think I understand Catherine Lakey now. There won't be any more surprises."

Devon, Connecticut
Morning

When she answered the phone and heard the person on the other end introduce herself as Elizabeth Singer, the director of the nursing home, Nancy immediately thought that something had happened to her grandmother. "Is something wrong?" she asked, her voice brittle with alarm.

"Wrong? Oh no. I'm sorry. I should have told you right away that Mrs. Lakey's fine. I'm calling about something else entirely. Has there been any progress with Mrs. Lakey's daughter?"

"Progress?" said Nancy, who then remembered that she hadn't spoken to Elizabeth Singer in more than a week. "No, I'm afraid there's been very little. Unless something happens, I'll be coming back to Bloomington this weekend."

"I'm sorry to hear that. I had hoped ... " Elizabeth Singer paused. "Miss Mulholland, I'm sorry, but I think we've done something rather stupid here."

Nancy was puzzled. "What is it?"

"Yesterday," said Elizabeth Singer, "a letter arrived for Ruth. I can't remember the last time she's had any personal mail. I think that's part of the problem. The day nurse didn't know what to do with it, so she put it aside."

"What sort of letter?" said Nancy. "Who was it from?"

"Well, that's part of what I'm calling about. When the night supervisor came on, she knew right away that Ruth simply doesn't get letters, but, of course, we're not authorized to open mail, you see."

"I'll authorize it," Nancy said quickly. "Please read it to me."

"I'd like to do that, but as I was saying, with us not being authorized, the night nurse thought the letter ought to come to me—"

"Please!" shouted Nancy. She was startled by the vehemence in her voice. "I'm sorry, this could be very important." There was a long silence.

"Hello?" said Nancy.

"I'm sorry, but I can't," said Elizabeth Singer, finally. "The letter, well, it no longer exists."

"What do you mean, no longer exists?"

"The night nurse was going to give it to me, but, of course, I'm not here in the evenings, so she put it in the pocket of her uniform and I'm afraid she forgot about it, as we sometimes do, and, unfortunately, last night, she put it in the wash."

"Oh my God," said Nancy softly.

"Yes. I'm afraid it was destroyed. I'm terribly sorry."

"And no one opened it?"

"I'm afraid not. We're not . . . "

"Authorized. I know." Nancy closed her eyes and tried to think. "Could you tell me about the envelope? Was there a return address?"

"I'm sorry. Could you hold the line a moment?" Nancy could hear muffled voices, as though Elizabeth Singer were holding her hand over the mouthpiece. "Miss Mulholland, I didn't see the letter, but the night supervisor is here with me. Would you like to speak with her?"

"Please."

"Hello? This is Mary Hesketh." The voice was small, frightened.

"Hello, Mary. This is Nancy Mulholland."

"I'm so terribly sorry about what happened. I always check my pockets, but it was so late . . . "

"Mary, could you tell me about the envelope. What color was it? Did it have a return address?"

"It was blue and it was one of those tissuey ones that you get from overseas. No return address, because I knew how unusual it was, a letter for Mrs. Lakey, that I wondered who on earth could be sending it."

"Did you notice a postmark, where it was from?"

"The postmark was smudged, but it must have been from France because the stamp was French. It's the only thing that came out of the washer in one piece. I have it right here. 'République Française. 4,05F.' "

"Damn!"

"Pardon me?"

"I was just thinking that France is a very big place."

"I suppose it is."

"Is there anything else you can tell me? Was it handwritten?"

"Yes, in blue ink. And the writing was a little unusual. It was sort of square, I guess you might say."

"Square?"

"Not loopy or scrawly like some you see. It was easy to read."

Nancy had to force herself not to scream. The writing that Mary Hesketh was describing was Catherine's. "Was there anything else?"

"I don't think so. I'm awfully sorry."

"It's all right. May I speak to Ms. Singer please?"

"We feel very bad about this," said Elizabeth Singer. "Mary's very upset."

"Yes," said Nancy. "If anything else should come in for Mrs. Lakey, please call me at once. I'll probably be here until Saturday or Sunday and I'll call you when I get back to Bloomington."

Elizabeth Singer apologized three more times before hanging up. When she finally did, Nancy slammed the side of her fist down on the kitchen counter hard enough for it to hurt. She flexed her fingers two or three times to reassure herself that she hadn't done any serious damage and then went out to the bookshelves in the living room. She scanned the book spines, then reached up and took out a thick green volume. "World Atlas" it said in bright, gold letters. She took it over to the sofa and opened it to the large map of France. She stared at it for a long time, trying to imagine Catherine doing the very same thing, and hoping—foolishly, she knew—that her eyes would somehow be drawn to the same point where Catherine last had looked.

Devon, Connecticut
Afternoon

"Before I go, should I get the car fixed?" asked Nancy. She was in Simco's office, standing at the window, looking at the brilliant spring sunshine, noticing the light green haze of new growth that blurred the outlines of trees that stretched across the campus. "If she should come back and find it that way . . . "

Simco sat on the edge of his desk, his arms folded in front of him, watching her. "I don't see why you're going back at all. We know Bennet's lying, and if Catherine's in France . . . "

Nancy turned away from the window. "We don't know any such thing. All you found out is that Weiss's—what was she?"

"Lab assistant."

"That she did Weiss's editing and that all she knew about Bennet was that he called the office every now and then."

"And that nobody around here ever heard Catherine say anything about a book. A textbook is almost always a collaborative effort. At the very least, you talk to colleagues, get their advice, bounce ideas back and forth. Catherine didn't talk about a book because there wasn't any."

"Then who is Bennet and why would he be lying?"

"I don't know who he is. It's interesting. I called his number last night, then early this morning, then about an hour ago. If you call outside business hours, you get a machine with his voice saying, 'Hello, you've reached Gil Bennet.' During business hours, a woman answers—a secretary—and she says, 'Mr. Bennet's office.' "

"I don't think I follow you."

"It's so anonymous. There isn't a hint of what Mr. Bennet does."

"Is that so odd? When you answer the phone, do you say, 'Hello, Frank Simco, college professor?' "

"No, but I'm not in private business, either. And the phone number prefix—768—that's Bethesda. I called information. There's no listing for a Gil Bennet or Bennet Associates or Bennet anything except Bennet Brothers Moving and Storage and that's a different number. How many businesses can you think of that don't list their phone numbers?"

"If not business, what?"

"I don't know. Whatever it is connected him somehow with Weiss and Catherine. In any case, it's clear he's lying."

"But that still doesn't get us anywhere. I'm almost sure he doesn't know where Catherine is. That's why he met me in the first place the other day. And even if he did, I don't know how we'd get it out of him. Kidnap him; put a gun to his head? And if Catherine is in France, so what? That doesn't narrow things down very much and it doesn't have very much to do with whether I'm in Devon or not. If anything, the letter to Grandma Ruth might mean she'll try to reach me that way, again. If so, I ought to be in Bloomington."

"They would call you here."

Nancy smiled at him. "I was thinking last night that I've known you for only a little more than a week, but it feels like I've grown up with you. I think you're being nice, wanting me to stay, but I'm very tired and I think I have to put my life back in order. I need to sleep in my own bed and get up in the morning and go to work. I think you understand that."

"What becomes of Catherine, then?"

"I don't know, but I think now that she's the only one who can answer that. She planned all of this very carefully and she seems to know what she's doing. If that letter was from her, she's safe somewhere, or at least she was a week ago. I think we wait. She'll let us know when she thinks the time is right."

"I've got a call in to Bellinger."

"About India?"

Simco nodded.

"Well," said Nancy, looking again out the window, "it's too nice a day to be inside. I think I'll walk back to Catherine's and get to work on the house, try to leave it something like I found it."

"When will you go?" said Simco, alarm in his voice.

"I think Saturday. I've got some cleaning up to do, loose ends. I've got to figure out what to do about the mail, her bills, her bank account, that sort of thing. Will you keep paying her?"

"I don't know. This hasn't ever happened before, but her contract runs through the end of the academic year."

"She has a lawyer in Bloomington. I'll need to talk to him."

Simco looked embarrassed. "I've got a meeting tonight," he said. "But tomorrow, could you come to dinner?"

"Yes," said Nancy. "I'd like that."

"I'll put a steak on the grill."

"And I'll bring dessert."

"That won't be necessary."

"The wine?"

"No, thanks."

"OK." Nancy picked her jacket up from the arm of one of the leather chairs and started for the door. Before she reached it, she turned to Simco. "I think you should know there's a part of me that doesn't want to go back either," she said, leaving Simco staring at the door she closed behind her, wondering exactly what she meant, but happier wondering than knowing.

Bethesda, Maryland
Late afternoon

Maggie Dacey sat back in her chair and closed her eyes. Even though it was only a little after five she had already turned on the answering machine. She was tired of telling callers that Mr. Bennet was out of the office and wouldn't be back until Wednesday; tired of trying to take messages for him only to have the callers ask her how they could reach him. In the end, she had to tell them that they couldn't and that made them unhappy and occasionally unpleasant, but it had long been understood that those who really needed to reach Gil knew how. The others simply had to wait.

She looked at the square mesh basket on the corner of her desk and tried to guess how long it might take to get Gil's handwritten notes transcribed onto a computer disk. Maybe an hour and a half? She looked at her watch and wondered whether she should leave a little early today. If she did some of the work now, she wouldn't have much to do tomorrow except act as a receptionist, and although she knew that Gil thought that was important, it wouldn't keep her busy enough and her mind would wander and the day would drag. She'd been thinking about things again and she didn't want to do that.

Nevertheless, she decided that leaving early wasn't right. She sighed and took the top paper from the pile, turned on her computer and inserted a disk. She scanned the first paragraph and was about to begin typing when the telephone rang. She stared at it, waiting for the machine to answer, trying to remember if she had set the ring selector switch.

"Go away," she said, but it continued to ring. She knew it wasn't yet five-thirty, knew that technically she should be answering, but . . . She reached for the telephone, feeling ambivalent again about the way she always did the conscientious thing. "Good afternoon," she said. "Gil Bennet's office."

The voice on the other end, a woman's, sounded startled. "Oh hello, is Mr. Bennet there?"

Maggie recited her lines, regretting already that she had answered.

"Oh, that's right. He's gone to France, hasn't he? I'd almost forgotten."

The voice was small and distant, as though the woman were standing too far from the receiver. "I'm sorry," said Maggie, "I'm having trouble hearing you."

"He's gone to France, then?" said the voice, a little louder.

"Who's calling, please? May I take a message?"

There was no reply and Maggie thought that the woman had hung up. "Hello?" she said. "Are you still there?"

"Is this Maggie?" The voice was much stronger now and more familiar.

"Yes. I'm sorry, who is this?"

"Maggie, I'm glad to hear your voice. This is Catherine."

"Catherine? I'm sorry but—"

"Catherine Lakey."

"Catherine! My God, where are you?"

"That's not important. I just wanted to check in with Gil. I didn't want him to worry."

It was at times like this, Maggie knew, that she was at her very worst. She could think of nothing to say or do—just sat there, gripping the telephone so tightly that her knuckles went white, staring stupidly at the wall in front of her, saying nothing.

"He's in France, then?"

"Yes," said Maggie, responding stiffly, almost tonelessly, as if she were a machine programmed to respond to any question with a one-word answer.

"That's fine. Tell him I called."

"Catherine, please, don't hang up. I need to talk to you."

"There isn't time, Maggie. We'll talk later."

"I never meant—" Maggie's words rushed out, but stopped when she heard the click at the other end of the line, followed by the hollow hum of the dial tone. She sat for what seemed like several minutes before she slowly, carefully put down the receiver. She got up from her desk and went into Bennet's office where she went around behind his desk and opened the top right-hand drawer. She took out a small, white telephone, stared at it for a long moment, then slumped heavily into Bennet's chair. Slowly, deliberately, as though her hand were made of lead, she punched in a number and waited. "This is Maggie Dacey," she said finally. "I need to reach Tony O'Connell. Please tell him that this is a code four."

Bethesda, Maryland
Night

Bennet had been gone for less than four hours and already Tony O'Connell was running into things that he neither fully understood nor liked. Of greater concern was the knowledge that he couldn't do very much about them. Woody had called and reported Mulholland's conversation with the nursing home in Indiana. It had never occurred to him that Lakey would try to reach Mulholland through the old lady, and only a stupid mistake by a nurse had stopped her. While it was interesting to discover that Lakey was probably in France, it wasn't very useful. What concerned him much more was the possibility that Catherine would try again, send another letter to the home, and he would be in no position to do anything about it. He didn't have enough people to cover Mulholland and Simco and the nursing home, too, and even if he did, he didn't have the time to set someone up to handle the mail.

Now there was the phone call. He turned the switch on the tape recorder and listened to the conversation once again. Tape hiss and noise in the line made the first part difficult to understand, but then Lakey's voice grew stronger and louder. When she said, "I just wanted to check in with Gil. I didn't want him to worry," Tony stopped the tape. There was a subtle tone there, a gentle, taunting sarcasm that seemed very different from what he would expect to hear from Catherine Lakey. Had he misjudged her? He had met her once, at a reception somewhere two or three years ago, and the impression she had made was hardly any impression at all. He recalled a plain, middle-aged woman with short hair who had said very little and who had seemed uncomfortable in a social setting. To him she had seemed indistinguishable from so many of the others in the odd collection of academics that Bennet had recruited.

Her disappearance had caught him off guard—he admitted that—but it was easy enough to understand. Weiss had said something to her and she had gotten scared, run away, gone underground—under a rock, as Woody had put it. Tony had agreed with Bennet that sooner or later she'd make a mistake and somebody would recognize her and then . . . But frightened little school-teachers hiding under rocks did not make phone calls to the people who were hunting them and tell them not to worry.

He looked at his watch, did the quick conversion to Paris time, then called the Hôtel Saint-Étienne and left the message that Mr. Bennet, when he checked in, should call Mr. O'Connell at the Savannah number.

MARCH—1987						
S	M	T	W	T	F	S
1	2	3	4	5	6	7
8	9	10	11	12	13	14
15	16	17	18	19	20	21
22	23	24	25	<u>26</u>	27	28
29	30	31				

DAY SIXTEEN

APRIL—1987						
S	M	T	W	T	F	S
			1	2	3	4
5	6	7	8	9	(10)	11
12	13	14	15	16	17	18
19	20	21	22	23	24	25
26	27	28	29	30		

DAY SIXTEEN

Paris, France
Morning

She took her time getting dressed, choosing black tights and a tan skirt, a white oxford cloth shirt, a plain blue cotton sweater and a well-worn pair of comfortable brown loafers. In the bathroom she applied her makeup, marveling at how quickly what had once been an arcane procedure had become almost automatic. She feathered the powder gently toward the borders of her face, then brushed on the barest touch of eye shadow. Finally she put on her lipstick, smoothing it with the tip of her little finger. She put on the black-rimmed sunglasses and studied herself in the mirror, finding it difficult not to smile. She wasn't beautiful, certainly, but she found herself to be intriguing-looking, perhaps just the tiniest bit exotic and certainly unrecognizable.

A light morning mist softened the outlines of the buildings along the Boulevard Saint-Germain and, at this hour of the morning, traffic was sparse and the city was nearly quiet. She walked slowly, as she usually did; she was in no particular hurry and she thought that a slow pace was less conspicuous than a rapid one. When she reached the Abbaye Saint-Germain-des-Prés, she made her way past the beggar woman who sat outside the church doors every morning keening in a high-pitched voice, her French rapid and incomprehensible. Inside she stopped and let her eyes adjust to the semidarkness, then walked to one of the folding chairs that had been arranged in ragged rows at the front of the nave. In the company of four or five other early morning worshippers, all women, all elderly, she sat listening to the organ, studying the stained-glass windows. After a few minutes she got up and left, pausing only long enough at the doors to drop a two-franc piece into the beggar woman's cup. As she always did, the woman broke off her stream of muttering and, without looking up, said, "Merci, madame. Ça n'est pas pour moi; c'est pour mes enfants." She spoke the words slowly, giving emphasis to every other syllable, which made it sound like she was reciting a poem or singing the first verse of a children's song.

Beyond the Abbaye, the boulevard began to change: the cafés became more substantial, the shops more decidedly sophisticated and expensive. At a newsstand she stopped and was about to buy an *International Herald Tribune* when she remembered and bought a *Figaro* instead. She tucked the paper under her arm and warned herself to be more careful and to think before she acted.

At the café, she seated herself at an outside table, even though the mist remained and the morning air was chilly. She ordered a glass of orange juice and a cup of coffee, then arranged herself behind her newspaper so that she could glance over the top edge of it from time to time, down the Rue de Solférino, to the entrance of the Hôtel Saint-Étienne.

She tried to make sense of the paper, but her rudimentary French allowed her to get only a vague drift of what she read and, also, she found it difficult to concentrate. The waiter came out and asked her if she would like more coffee, but she shook her head, and just to be sure he understood, she placed her hand over the top of her cup. Paris was frightfully expensive and she was down to her last two thousand francs. A second cup of coffee was a small luxury, but it was one she thought she should forgo.

Over the top of her newspaper she saw the black Mercedes taxi turn down the Rue de Solférino, and even before it stopped in front of the hotel, she knew it would be him. He'd said so often how much he hated limousines and she supposed he thought that taking taxis was democratic, a common touch, but she still found it hard to picture him arriving in an old Renault.

He got out of the cab, his back to her, and waited on the sidewalk, hands on hips, while the driver got his luggage from the trunk. A bellboy was already hurrying through the front doors of the hotel with a baggage cart. Bennet reached into his pocket, pressed some bills into the hand of the driver and patted him on the shoulder, talking all the while in what she knew would be flawless French. The driver gave him a cheerful salute and got back in the Mercedes and drove off.

The bellboy loaded the cart and headed back through the doors to the lobby. Bennet took two or three steps, following him, then stopped and turned slowly through a full circle, looking up at the city around him, a happy smile on his face. Catherine lowered the newspaper to the table in front of her and stared at him. So much time and distance lay between this street in Paris this Friday morning and the reception long ago in Pittsburgh when Richard Weiss had steered her through a crowd of strangers, leading her by the hand up to Bennet, where she had stood, dazzled by his smile, shaking his hand, and had heard Richard say, behind her, "Cat, Gil is just the man to help you."

She caught the waiter's eye and pointed at her cup. It was only four francs, after all, and she wouldn't be in Paris very much longer. When the coffee arrived, she lifted the cup to her mouth and, before taking a sip, tipped it very slightly toward the Hôtel Saint-Étienne. "Welcome to Paris, you bastard," she said to herself.

Devon, Connecticut
Evening

At six o'clock, Simco double-checked his list and saw that everything was done except the ice. He'd made the salad, marinated the steak and wrapped the French bread for the oven. The table was set, wine was on the sideboard and beer was in the refrigerator. Out on the deck, he'd set up the charcoal grill and had arranged the vinyl lawn chairs for the best view of the sunset. A bowl of peanuts sat on a small pile of cocktail napkins, anchoring them against the breeze. On the tray table by the lawn chairs was a shiny, black, plastic ashtray. Simco picked it up and, with his thumbnail, rubbed off the small, sticky label that said $2.99.

From the kitchen, he heard her car in the driveway and by the time she rang the doorbell, he was already in the front hall, wiping a wet hand on his trousers. He opened the door, stepped out to greet her, then stopped. It was Nancy, standing there, smiling at him, but instead of blue jeans or her all-purpose navy blue skirt and white blouse, she had on an emerald green dress, something very soft, that looked like a long turtleneck sweater. In one arm she held an open box of red and white carnations. "For you," she said, handing the box to him.

Simco took them, stared at them and stood there, trying to think of something to say, his eyes moving from Nancy to the carnations, then back to Nancy—to the dress, to the face above the deep fold of the cowl neckline and to the eyes that watched him patiently. Slowly a smile spread across his face. "I don't think anyone's ever brought me flowers before."

She waited. He gazed at her, puzzled, until she cocked her head to one side and asked if she could come in.

"Oh. Why yes. Sorry," he stammered, backing through the doorway. With a sweep of the flowers he motioned her inside, then led her through the hall to his living room where a few straight-back chairs, a large beige sofa and an Eames chair and ottoman were arranged in front of an immense picture window bracketed by two glass-paned doors. Nancy crossed the room to the window. A large deck with a built-in bench ran the length of the house and beyond it were rolling fields which sloped gently down to a line of trees along the Devon River.

"It's beautiful."

"College land," said Simco. "They bought it in the thirties for almost nothing. It runs all the way to the river. And out here," he said, opening one door to the deck, "is where I thought we could be before dinner. That is, if you'll be warm enough." He glanced at her dress.

"I'll be fine," she said, stepping through the doorway. "It's lovely out here."

"Now, what can I get you?"

"A beer, if you have it?"

"Coming right up," said Simco, heading for the kitchen.

Nancy heard the screen door slam, heard water running, then ice clattering out of metal trays. As she settled back in the chair, she noticed the peanuts, the napkins, the ashtray, and smiled to herself. She lit a cigarette and relaxed. Out by the river a flash of color caught her eye. It was a red-winged blackbird bouncing back and forth between branches in a stand of silver birch. The sun, which had begun its slow slide down toward the western hills, was backlighting the bird, the trees and the tall sedges at the edge of the river. In the lowering light, the water shimmered and sparkled.

Nancy heard the bang of the screen door and, turning, she saw Simco approaching with a beer in one hand, his drink in another, and between them, held by both wrists, was a silver cocktail shaker filled with the carnations. Nancy took the beer from him and Simco put the cocktail shaker on the bench. The carnations slid to one side and collected in a clump. Simco separated a few, but the overall effect remained the same. "Maybe I should've left them to you," he said.

"Maybe," said Nancy, smiling into her glass of beer, "but there's something about the arrangement, the way it conceals the hand of man. I'd leave it just the way it is." Simco went over to the grill and she followed him, watching as he puttered, preparing it for the steak.

"I told you about India," he said.

Nancy pulled the lawn chair closer to the grill. She sat down and lit another cigarette. "You said it was the same as the others. No cause of death, I take it."

Simco nodded. "According to Bellinger, the autopsy was inconclusive, which is another way of saying that no one could figure out what killed Narayan. It's what we expected."

"I'm still surprised that we were so sure of the pattern."

Simco struck a match and touched it to the charcoal; there was a burst of orange flame. "What else was there? The cause of death, or lack of it, was the only thing that tied the three together. What I can't understand is how Catherine could have known that you'd ever get far enough to see it. She didn't know about Bellinger. She couldn't have. And without him, we don't get the details, we don't even hear of Carla Valenzuela, let alone meet her."

"She didn't know. I'm pretty sure of that," said Nancy. "I think the things she left—the marmalade, the cookbook—were things she hoped I'd find and follow up on. What puzzles me is why she led me—us—to those three men without telling what they had to do with her. Why only part of the story and not the whole thing?"

"Maybe the answer was in the letter to her mother."

"Maybe." Nancy drank the last of her beer. Simco poked at the coals with a stick. They were perfect, glowing red beneath a dusty gray.

"The timing was right," said Simco. "The letter arrived at the nursing home just after we'd found the other things. It might have tied everything together."

"Maybe. It seems to be the only thing she tried that didn't work." Nancy held out her empty glass. "I'd like another, if it's all right."

When Simco returned, she was at the grill, warming her hands over the coals. She stood by him as he put the steak on the fire. "We've worked well together," she said. "I just wish it had led us somewhere."

"You don't think it did?"

"I mean I wish we knew what to do next. Having gone this far, you'd think we'd have a plan—something other than wait and see."

Simco poked at the steak and sparks flew upward into the night air. The light was fading. Once a pale yellow, the sky had turned to violet and was now deepening to a dark blue, almost black. For a while neither of them said anything. "You know," said

Nancy, finally, "this afternoon I thought about doing what you said we should have done all long, and I decided I'd come here tonight and tell you that I agreed with you—that it was time to go to the authorities." Nancy shook her head, then took a sip of beer. "But the same old arguments came back: What authorities do we go to? What do we say that's convincing? Catherine's clever. Why didn't she go to them, or at least leave messages that she wanted them to see? I ended up right where I started ten days ago."

"But you're still going back to Bloomington." Simco turned the steak on the grill. The coals hissed and more sparks flew into the air.

"Yes."

"I see."

At the tone of his voice, Nancy looked up at him. "Frank, what else can I do? There's nothing left in Devon or Cotchpinicut. We've followed the trail and it's stopped, and there's no point in tormenting myself, sitting around all day, waiting."

Simco studied the fire, said nothing.

"It won't be easy in Bloomington. I know that. I still won't know what's going to happen. Will she call me? When? What will she say? Will I need to go to her, take care of her, or will she be fine and we can all go back to the way things were before?" It was very dark out now. She looked at Simco. "How much longer to dinner?"

Simco poked the steak. "A few minutes."

Nancy went to the bench and looked at the carnations in the cocktail shaker. "Maybe on second thought," she said, and picked them up and disappeared into the kitchen.

Several minutes later, Simco tested the meat. Seeing that it was a perfect medium rare, he carved it, then carried it into the dining room. The salad he'd prepared was on the table. So was the bread. The candles were lit. The wine was poured and Nancy was seated, waiting. She smiled at him. As he forked steak onto their plates, he noticed that she had arranged the carnations in an old Wedgewood pitcher he'd forgotten he had.

"Not as original," she said, "but it fits better on the table." She raised her wineglass. "Thank you. For everything."

Simco looked down at the table and shrugged. "There were times when I wasn't much help."

"Don't argue," she said, waggling her glass at him "To you, to all you've done."

Simco touched his glass to hers. "To . . . " he said, his voice trailed off. He smiled at her self-consciously, avoiding her eyes.

During dinner, the conversation came in clumps separated by silences that seemed not to bother either of them. They traded childhood stories about summer camp and school and what it was like to grow up in Worcester and in Bloomington. Awkwardly, Simco talked about his first marriage, hoping to coax Nancy into the subject of relationships, to find out where she stood right now, and where he stood. When she didn't follow his lead, the conversation drifted back to Catherine, but that was ground that they had already gone over too many times before.

Nancy stood up and began collecting plates. "Let me clean up."

"Please, no. My meal, my mess."

She sat down again. "You're a difficult person to do anything for."

"No, I'm not, as a matter of fact, but I suppose it's too late to get you to change your mind about going back tomorrow."

"Why do you want me to stay?" Nancy leaned forward in her chair and studied Simco for a moment. "I'm sorry. That's an unfair question."

"No, but I'm not sure how to answer it. I've liked having you here, even under the circumstances."

"Yes," said Nancy, folding her napkin on the table in front of her, "there are the circumstances. They're hardly normal, are they?" She looked up again at Simco. "And that's another reason why I should go back to Bloomington. I need to let things sit, give them a chance to sort themselves out."

"What things?"

She smiled at him and looked around the dining room. "These

things," she said. "Candlelight and flowers in a cocktail shaker and a lovely dinner."

"Those don't need sorting out. You liked them."

Nancy laughed and stood up. "Of course I liked them, but I think you know what I mean." She leaned toward Simco and put her hand on his wrist. "Thank you, Frank, but I really have to go. I still have packing to do."

"It's not even ten yet."

"And in an hour it won't even be eleven, but nothing will have changed." She walked around to where he was sitting and tugged him gently to his feet. "And, no, you're not going to take me to the airport tomorrow. I've already called a cab. I'll call you on Wednesday and you call me the Wednesday after that. Now will you kiss me good night?" She leaned toward him and put her hand on the back of his neck, coaxing him toward her. He kissed her tentatively, not quite knowing what she was asking of him. She drew back slightly and brushed the backs of her fingers across his cheek, giving him a puzzled smile. She leaned forward and kissed him lightly on the lips, then shook her head. "I'll call you," she said, then walked quickly past him into the darkness of the kitchen.

Simco heard the front door open and shut; heard the car motor and the wheels in the gravel of the driveway. He hurried into the front hall and stood there in the sweep of her headlights.

	MARCH—1987					
S	M	T	W	T	F	S
1	2	3	4	5	6	7
8	9	10	11	12	13	14
15	16	17	18	19	20	21
22	23	24	25	<u>26</u>	27	28
29	30	31				

DAY SEVENTEEN

	APRIL—1987					
S	M	T	W	T	F	S
			1	2	3	4
5	6	7	8	9	10	(11)
12	13	14	15	16	17	18
19	20	21	22	23	24	25
26	27	28	29	30		

DAY SEVENTEEN

SATURDAY, APRIL 11, 1987

Paris, France
Morning

She sat at the same table outside the same café, reading her newspaper, sipping coffee, looking up from time to time, scanning the street and the passersby. It was a warm, sunny Saturday morning and the pace along the boulevard seemed much slower than it had been the day before.

When he came out of the Hôtel Saint-Étienne, she saw him right away. He was wearing a dark blue suit and carried a tan leather attaché case. He stopped at the curb, where he bent down and spoke to a cab driver. He gestured with one hand, then pointed down the Rue de Solférino and laughed. He tapped the taxi lightly on its roof and, as it drove away, he began walking up the street, toward the café. At the corner of the Rue de l'Université, he hesitated as if he were unsure of which way to go. He looked briefly to his right, then shielded his eyes with his left hand and looked up the Rue de Solférino toward the Boulevard Saint-Germain, running his gaze to the left, first to the café and then back down the street. He stopped and looked again at the café, and suddenly, she knew he was looking directly at her.

She tried not to look at him, lowered her face to the newspaper, and felt the first surge of panic beginning to build. She thought of the ladies' room. She could get up from the table and go inside the café to the ladies' room, where he wouldn't dare follow her and . . . Then what? She'd have to come out eventually. It had been a stupid idea to think that makeup and hair color and dark glasses could fool someone like Bennet. But it didn't help, she told herself, to think about that now. Slowly, she lifted her eyes from the paper and began to turn her head toward the corner, expecting to see him almost in front of her, that charming smile on his face, his hand outstretched in front of him, saying, "Why Catherine, of all people . . . ," but when her eyes reached the corner, he was gone.

Quickly she dug in her purse, put a ten-franc piece on the table and folded the newspaper under her arm. The panic was gone and she was angry with herself for almost having given in to it. She crossed the street and walked rapidly down the Boulevard Saint-Germain, keeping close to the curb where it was less crowded. When she reached the corner of the Rue de l'Université, she saw him half a block ahead of her, strolling along the sidewalk, stopping every now and then, looking in shop windows.

She waited patiently for the light to change, then crossed, careful to keep him in view, but lagging far enough behind to have as many people as she could in the line of sight between them. At the river, he crossed the street to the Assemblée Nationale, as she knew he would, and she walked along the quai for a while, then turned on to the Esplanade des Invalides.

Paris surged happily around her in the warm spring light. Dogs galloped up and down the Esplanade, lovers lolled on blankets on the grass, young men played impromptu soccer games. Catherine walked with her head down, not noticing, then stopped and looked up at Les Invalides. Finally she turned and made her way back to the river where she found an old stone bench near the Pont Alexandre which offered her a view of both the Seine and the Assemblée. She unfolded her newspaper and pretended to read, glancing up from time to time to scan the scene in front of her. The huge clock on the Musée d'Orsay said 9:48. The waiting had begun.

Hartford/Indianapolis
Morning

The seat belt sign went off, but Woody was too cautious a man and too timid a flier to unbuckle himself. Not very long ago he had read that a door had come off an airplane in flight and three or four people—their seat belts unfastened, he was sure—had been sucked out through the opening. He closed his eyes and tried to imagine what it would be like for the row of passengers—sitting in their seats, eating peanuts, sipping Cokes, listening to music in their headsets—to be tumbling through the air, all of a sudden, twenty thousand feet above the ground. He finally decided that it would be so unbelievable that the poor bastards would say to themselves: "What a goddamn dream this is!" and they wouldn't even flinch when they hit the ground because they'd still be thinking that, at any minute, they were going to wake up.

The problem for Woody was that he knew that sooner or later he'd have to get out of his seat if, finally, he was going to get a good look at Mulholland. She was sitting somewhere behind him, in the smoking section, and if he waited until the line for the lavatories shortened, he could walk all the way to the back and go right by her, probably without her even looking up. He turned in his seat to look down the aisle and was surprised to see that the line was already gone, that only two people were standing at the magazine bin, looking for something to read. He undid his seat belt and stood up, smoothed his shirt, then made his way down the aisle, scanning the seats left and right as he went. He saw her in the next to the last row, on the left, by the window, asleep with her head against the bulkhead. She had on a gray pullover sweater and, even though she wore no makeup and her dark hair fell carelessly over her shoulder, Woody thought she was much prettier than she was in the picture they had given him.

He walked past her and went into the lavatory where he filled the sink with cold water and splashed some on his face. Having seen her up close, he couldn't blame Bennet for not wanting to do anything, even though he thought letting Simco and her run around, sticking their noses everywhere, was risky. Then he looked in the mirror and reminded himself what Tony had told him—that he wasn't here to think; he was here only to watch and to wait.

Cotchpinicut, Massachusetts
Midday

April meant change in Cotchpinicut. The light changed; the colors of the sea and of the sky changed; and in the village, shop owners began to reappear and the air took on the smell of fresh paint and sawdust.

Saturday was his day off, but Billy Cahoon decided to go down to the station anyway because it was still too early to work on his boat and he didn't have much else to do. He found Beakey alone at the dispatcher's desk, patiently trying to explain to someone on the telephone that the police simply couldn't help him get rid of squirrels in his attic. Cahoon went over to his desk and sat down. There was a yellow message slip stuck to his telephone. He peeled it off and read it. Nancy Mulholland had called early that morning and was going back to Indiana. Too bad, he thought, her having to go back there without knowing what had happened. He wrote her home phone number on the front of the Lakey file and decided he'd take a ride out to the cottage, since nobody would be using it for a while, just to make sure that it was locked up the way it was supposed to be.

The wind was warm and gentle, out of the west, and from the pathway that led from Catherine Lakey's door down to the dunes, the sea seemed almost motionless, like an enormous blue-green pond. Cahoon checked doors and windows and peered in through one to see if there was anything out of place. In the parking area he'd noticed tire tracks and some footprints in the sand that had to have been made since the rain on Wednesday, but everything looked all right.

He walked down the path to the place where it began to drop sharply toward the beach. He could see a scattering of people walking along the sand, some alone, some with dogs, a few in groups with small children. One couple had even brought blankets and beach chairs and sat reading and occasionally gazing out to sea, as if it were July.

He sat down on a clump of beach grass and thought about Catherine Lakey. How long had she been gone? Two weeks, going on three? Not a damn sign of her and now Cahoon knew that there probably never would be, just like that woman on Nantucket a couple of years ago. What was her name? He couldn't remember. He wondered how long it would take to forget Catherine Lakey's name as her file drifted toward the back of the drawer he used for unsolved cases. A year was his guess. Maybe two.

Devon, Connecticut
Afternoon

After seven or eight attempts at beginning a draft of a grant proposal, Frank Simco gave up on the idea of getting any work done and decided to take a walk instead. It was a bright sunny day, the first truly warm day of spring, and he thought that it might be nice to walk up to the orchards on the hillside above the campus, but after crossing the College Common, he didn't turn right up the hill. He turned left and, before he had really thought very much about where he was going, he found himself turning onto High Meadow Lane and stopping in front of number 21, the small house that belonged to Catherine Lakey.

The car was in the driveway, the right rear fender still dented, the taillight broken, and, for a moment, Simco wondered if Nancy, at the last minute, had changed her mind and decided not to go back to Bloomington after all. He went up the walk to the front door, but before he rang the bell he looked up and down the street because he didn't want anyone to yell to him, "Hey, Frank, she's not there. She left this morning in a taxi." When he saw no one, he rang the bell and waited, and when no one came to the door, he went around to the back and sat down on the steps at the back door.

He was surprised at himself and thought that if this was the way he was going to act, perhaps he'd better learn to play golf or get a dog. He thought about the night before and winced at the squandered opportunity. She'd asked him—asked him!—to kiss her good night and he'd fumbled through it like a twelve-year-old, and what was even worse, he'd never gotten around to telling her how he felt, even though he'd promised himself that he would. He was going to say that he was a forty-two-year-old man and that he had been around the block once or twice and that he had never—Simco stopped and considered the word—yes, never been so impressed with a woman before. Impressed? Is that the word he'd just used? My God, he thought, I'm even a klutz when I'm talking to myself. What he should have said was that he had never felt about a woman the way he felt about her, given that he had known her for less than two weeks. But why qualify it? What the hell difference did the two weeks make? Why hadn't he, for once, done something completely un-Simco-like and simply said to her: "Nancy, whatever happens with Catherine, whether I ever see you again or not, I love you." He hadn't said it, he reminded himself, because he wasn't absolutely sure it was true. Nonsense. He was sure enough. He hadn't said it because that was the way he was, always careful not to expose very much of himself, always retreating to the high ground of dignity and safety. If he had said something like that, she might have laughed—not out loud, she was too polite for that, but in some other way—and then where would he be? He'd probably be sitting on the back steps of Catherine Lakey's house, feeling lonely, facing another Saturday night of beer and pizza in front of the television.

He got up and began walking back to his office, wondering what time Nancy would arrive in Bloomington. He could call her tonight. He was much surer of himself on the telephone. But tonight she'd probably be tired from the traveling and everything else. Let her rest. Tomorrow night would be better. That would give her time to sort things out and, by then, he would have had a little more time to think about what he was going to say. Tomorrow would be better. Definitely.

Bloomington, Indiana
Evening

Nancy Mulholland sat by the window in her old, green armchair, smoking, watching the day turn into twilight, thinking about the sun setting behind the trees in Devon. There had been no messages from Catherine in the mail and nothing on the answering machine, but she had expected that and was, in fact, relieved. She knew it was unlikely that Catherine would be open and direct, and for now, at least, she didn't want more clues.

She took a sip from the glass of wine that was on the table beside her and wished it were Sunday night, not Saturday, so that tomorrow she could go to work and have something else to occupy her. She could go anyway, she supposed, and begin to catch up on all the paperwork, but she really should do something about the apartment and her laundry. She thought, too, about Grandma Ruth, that she should visit her, but in the middle of that thought another one intruded, about Frank. Maybe she should call him. When she caught herself thinking about him again, she realized that that had been happening all day. It was natural enough, she guessed, considering what she'd just been through, and as time went on she was fairly certain that everything, including Frank Simco, would seem a little less immediate. It bothered her, however, that she couldn't be absolutely sure.

The phone rang and she ran to the kitchen to answer it, but it was only someone from the Kidney Foundation asking for a donation. She made a pledge of twenty dollars and when the kidney person had hung up, she held the phone in her hand a moment and punched in the area code for Connecticut, then stopped, relieved that she couldn't remember the rest of the number. She put the phone back in its cradle and looked up at the kitchen clock: 7:25. She still had time to get over to the university for the Saturday night film series and, by the time she got back, it would be too late for phone calls.

Alexandria, Virginia
Late evening

Maggie was at work. She had on a headphone, the type pilots used to wear, and extending from it, like long, black snakes, were trunk lines, a half dozen of them. She sat before an immense switchboard, and when a red light lit up on it, she had to plug one of the lines from her headset into the hole beneath the light. Two lights were glowing red hot. Her mother was talking in one ear and a laundry service rep was saying something in the other. Her mother wanted to move to Chicago. The laundry man was telling her slowly, as if instructing a very dense child, "You put it out on Tuesday—not Wednesday—and it comes back Friday. Unless, you put it out Wednesday. Then it comes back a week from Friday. Do you get it?"

"I get it," said Maggie. "Out on Tuesday . . . "

"Tuesday!" said Maggie's mother. "Tuesday we're moving. The van's coming. I've already called it."

"Mother, please! Wait a moment."

A third light lit up. Maggie plugged in another line.

"Maggie, Maggie, Maggie. It's Catherine Lakey. I'm here, dear. Downstairs. Was just stopping by."

"Catherine!"

"Maggie!" said her mother.

"Miss Dacey. You got the schedule straight?"

"Maggie!" It was her mother again. "I need you home NOW! The van's here, early."

"Catherine, are you there?" said Maggie.

"Just for a minute, dear."

"Don't go, Catherine. I . . . we . . . "

The board lit up—three lights on row 2, four on row 8, then all the lights on 5. Sirens sounded. Why was that happening? Maggie wondered . . . because she wasn't doing her job? The sirens got louder and louder. With her foot, she found a pedal on the floor—it looked like a piano pedal—and she stomped on it as hard as she could, as if she were braking a runaway car. She kept stomping on it. All the switchboard lights glowed red and the sirens grew louder. Then the switchboard died. She'd killed it and had lost all contact. She plugged her lines into vacant holes . . . nothing.

Was Catherine still downstairs? She opened the only door in her dark boxlike room and a green light, the color of lime Jell-O, shimmered and grew more intense. There was heat behind her. A fire? She was on the edge of the door sill, looking down into nothing but the green. There was no hallway, no stairwell. She realized she had to jump and she did, terrified, falling, waiting to hit bottom, not knowing whether it would be green lawn or cement.

Just at the end, she awoke. The faint sounds of sirens coming through her open bedroom window were receding. She was soaked with sweat and the cord from the glasses she wore when she read at night was twisted below her on her pillow.

She padded in bare feet out of her bedroom and put a wool cardigan over her nightgown. She found the bourbon and a juice glass and took them back to her room where, sitting in the dark, she sipped the bourbon and tried to shake the nightmare away.

MARCH—1987						
S	M	T	W	T	F	S
1	2	3	4	5	6	7
8	9	10	11	12	13	14
15	16	17	18	19	20	21
22	23	24	25	<u>26</u>	27	28
29	30	31				

DAY EIGHTEEN

APRIL—1987						
S	M	T	W	T	F	S
			1	2	3	4
5	6	7	8	9	10	11
(12)	13	14	15	16	17	18
19	20	21	22	23	24	25
26	27	28	29	30		

Paris
Midday

She was surprised at how calm she felt and wondered what it meant, but then reminded herself not to dwell on meanings, not today. She took a last sip of coffee, left a tip of a few francs on the table, then gathered up her coat and her umbrella from the chair next to her and went into the ladies' room, where she washed her hands, removing the gray smudges of newsprint. She studied her image in the mirror, inspecting it as she would a stranger whose face had attracted her attention. Absently, she ran her fingers through her hair, then headed for the door, turning once for a last, over-the-shoulder look at the mirror.

She left the café and crossed to the other side of the Boulevard Saint-Germain where she began walking slowly toward the river. She glanced at her watch once or twice, but her attention was focused on the other side of the boulevard. She continued for another block or two, then stopped suddenly, went to the curb and looked across the street, squinting slightly. It was Bennet, precisely on schedule, walking in the opposite direction, but he was with another man, tall, white-haired and gray-suited, and they appeared to be deep in conversation, Bennet doing most of the talking, the other man listening intently, his head down.

This was something she hadn't expected; it was, in fact, the first time that Bennet had varied even slightly from what she'd anticipated, and she found herself at a loss for what to do next. She continued for a few steps in the direction she had been heading, hesitated, then turning too abruptly, she began walking back the way she had come, telling herself that she must not show the agitation she felt. She forced herself to slow her pace, to be more in rhythm with the midday strollers, and stealing glances across the street, she made sure that Bennet and his companion were still in sight. They were only three or four blocks from the hotel and she tried to sort quickly through her options, but realized that she really had none. If Bennet's friend accompanied him to the hotel for lunch or for a meeting in his room, she would have to wait, even if it meant all afternoon or longer. If the waiting went on too long, there was tomorrow, of course, but that thought made her nervous because she wasn't sure how long Bennet planned to stay in Paris.

The two men turned down the Rue de l'Université and she lost sight of them while she waited at the corner for the light to change. She hurried across the street and found that the narrow sidewalks were so crowded that she had to walk in the roadway. At the corner of the Rue de Solférino, she crossed to the café and looked back down the street to the hotel. The two men stood in front of the entrance, talking, then Bennet put his hand on the other man's shoulder and guided him to the curb. They shook hands and the man bent down to say something to a cab driver, nodded, opened the rear door and got in. As the cab pulled away from the curb and Bennet, Catherine knew that now she had very little time.

She hurried across the street just as he turned and disappeared into the hotel. She followed as rapidly as she could without calling attention to herself. The lobby was quiet and nearly empty; an elderly lady dozed in a large armchair, a couple stood at the cashier's window, and Bennet was at the front desk, collecting his keys and messages. He crossed to the concierge's desk, stopped to say something, then continued on to the elevators. Catherine followed him, keeping her head tilted slightly down and to the left, the way she had practiced it. She heard the elevator bell ring, heard the doors slide open and felt, rather than saw, the two or three people getting out, brushing past her. Then, next to her, she heard Bennet's voice: "Vous montez, madame?"

She gave a little nod, stepped into the elevator and stood as close as she could to the bright brass plate with the two neat rows of floor buttons. He followed her in and stood somewhere behind her. "Onzieme, s'il vous plait," he said slowly enough so that she could understand. She pressed the button for the eleventh floor. He moved closer. "Vous aussi?" he said. She nodded. Motors and cables whirred and clanked and the elevator began its slow ascent. To herself, she began counting the floors as they slid by.

She inched backward until, out of the corner of her eye she could just see Bennet's far shoulder. With hardly any movement of her arm, she passed her umbrella from her left hand to her right and rested it gently on the elevator floor. When she saw the seventh floor go by, she turned around until she was facing him. He looked at her with that charming, open smile of his, but with puzzlement in his eyes. "Oui? Yes?" he said.

She dropped her gaze to the floor and lifted the umbrella slightly, no more than three or four inches, then plunged it firmly, but not violently, into the instep of his left foot. The tip was very sharp and passed through the thin Italian leather of Bennet's shoe easily, without a sound, as if it were penetrating butter. This was like high school biology, she thought, when she'd had to draw a drop of blood from her finger and the lance was so sharp and smooth that she hardly believed that she had done it until she saw the deep red bubble gather on her thumb-tip, and all she could do was giggle in wonder and relief.

"Jesus Christ!" It was a cry of confusion, surprise, but not of pain. He looked down at his foot, took two steps backward, then looked directly at her. His eyes went wide. "Catherine?" he said more softly, confusion in his voice, disbelief. She returned his look for just a moment and the awful thought occurred to her that, despite all her planning, she had miscalculated, used the wrong dose, that the needle had somehow passed between his toes, that . . .

His arm moved toward her, hung in front of him, then slapped against the side of the elevator. His hand groped the wall, looking for something to hold on to, then stopped. "What the hell?" He blinked his eyes slowly, trying to focus them, but they had already lost their sparkle and a thin line of spittle ran down his chin from the corner of his mouth.

Catherine let out a deep breath, turned away and opened the brass lattice door an inch or two. The elevator stopped. Looking over her shoulder, she saw that he had crumpled into the corner of the car, into a sitting position, his head sagging. She went to him quickly, bent down until her mouth almost touched the side of his head just above his ear. "Is that the way it was for them?" she whispered hoarsely. She stood up and forced herself to inhale deeply. She shut her eyes for a moment, then closed the elevator door.

As the elevator continued upward, she returned to Bennet and knelt down beside him. She counted to herself. Eight seconds until the eleventh floor, seven. If there were people waiting to get on, she knew her role. She took one of Bennet's hands in hers, began patting it lightly. "Sir, are you all right? What's wrong? My God! Sir! Are you all right?"

She felt the elevator slow, then stop, and heard the outer doors roll open. She braced herself, but heard nothing, then looked over her shoulder. There was no one waiting. Quickly, she stood up and slid open the inner brass grille door. From her purse she took a small block of wood, which she placed in the track of the door, at the end. Then she stepped into the hallway and carefully closed the inner door until it hit the wood. It wedged the door open just an inch or so, hardly enough to notice, but until it was removed, the elevator would go nowhere.

She looked up and down the hallway and tapped her foot impatiently. Finally, with a rumble, the outer elevator doors slid closed. She took a handkerchief from her pocket and dabbed at her forehead, then lifted the umbrella and examined its tip and the smudge of blood. She took a bit of cellophane and an elastic band from her pocket. Carefully she wrapped the cellophane around the tip of the umbrella and secured it with the elastic. Holding the umbrella under her arm, she walked to the end of the hallway and opened the door beneath the red illuminated sign that said SORTIE, then walked down three flights of stairs to the eighth floor.

She opened the door a crack, checking to see that the hallway was empty, then walked to the elevators and pressed the down button for the one that wasn't stopped at the eleventh floor.

The car arrived quickly and she entered, grateful that she was the only passenger. After she had closed the inner door and pressed the button, she rested her umbrella in the corner, handle side down, and put on her raincoat, turning up the collar. She removed her dark glasses and put them in her pocket, picked up the umbrella and waited.

In the lobby, there was a small knot of people who had been waiting for an elevator and when she stepped out of hers they hurried past her into the car. She wondered if any of them were going to the eleventh floor, and if they were, whether anyone would notice that the other elevator was there, apparently stuck, and then, would someone peer through the small oval window, see inside and begin pounding on the large outer door, shouting for help?

Careful not to hurry, she walked through the lobby, out the main entrance to the street and across the Rue de Solférino to the café, where she took an outside seat. She ordered a cognac from the waiter and for the first time in her life she wished she smoked. From a distance came the undulating wail of a rapidly approaching siren, and she wondered if they had found him already, but it wobbled past her down the Boulevard Saint-Germain.

She took a long sip of cognac and tried to sort out how she felt. Weary, certainly, but strangely detached, as though she had just watched everything on an enormous television screen. It surprised her that there was no satisfaction, no vindication. She didn't feel relief nor was she nervous. She felt disconnected and numb.

She heard the sound of another siren growing louder. A police car screeched into the Rue de Solférino and sped past her, narrowly missing an old man who was crossing the street. It slammed to a stop in front of the Saint-Étienne and two policemen jumped out and dashed through the front doors of the hotel.

She got up, left some money on the table, and noticed that a small crowd of passersby had gathered on the sidewalk outside the hotel, straining to get a look at what was going on inside. She stared at them, then abruptly reminded herself that she had to get going, that her day's work had just begun.

Bloomington, Indiana
Morning

When the phone rang at seven-thirty, Nancy had already been awake for an hour, just lying in bed, looking out the large window above her dresser. The view it framed of trees and patches of sky sometimes made her feel that she was a little girl again, camping at Fortune Lake, looking at the morning from her sleeping bag.

She let the phone ring five or six times, running through a mental list of who it could or could not be, debating whether to answer it at all, then finally allowed curiosity to settle it.

"Hello," she said. There was an odd hum in the receiver that she hadn't heard before and for a moment she wondered if anyone was on the line.

"Nannie?" The voice was thin and distant, but familiar. "This is Catherine. I was afraid you wouldn't be there."

Nancy felt a thick, tingly wave pass through her, as though the telephone had become a live electric wire. She swung her legs out from under the covers and stood up beside the bed. "Catherine?" It was a whisper, and all that she could manage.

"Nannie dear, I'm sorry, but there isn't much time right now, and it's terribly important you listen to me carefully. Do you have a pencil and paper?"

"Yes," said Nancy stupidly, still standing there. "No, wait." She put the phone down and tried to think where a pencil might be. She opened the drawer of the bedside table and found a ballpoint pen and an old paperback mystery. She tore its front cover off, turned it over and picked up the phone. "I'm back."

There was that hum again, making it difficult to hear. Nancy pressed the telephone closer to her ear when suddenly what should have been obvious struck her with almost physical force. "Catherine, wait. Let me call you back."

"Please, Nannie, there isn't time."

"But the phone, Catherine, it isn't safe . . ."

"Nothing's ever safe, dear, and now it's far too late to matter," she said gently, then paused. When she spoke again her voice was sharp, urgent. "Please listen carefully. I'm in Paris. At the Hôtel l'Europe, on the Rue de Poissy." She spelled the address. "Are you writing this down?"

"Yes. Rue de Poissy."

"I need you here . . . "

"But . . . "

"Please, Nannie, listen! I need you here tomorrow morning. There are tickets for you in New York, at JFK. Go to the TWA international terminal, not domestic. The ticket's being held at the passenger service counter. It's in your name. Your flight number is 141 and it leaves at six-thirty tonight. You have to be there an hour and a half before departure. Bring your passport. I've arranged to have a visa waiting with your tickets."

"Catherine, what the hell . . . "

"Please, I'm almost finished. From De Gaulle take a taxi to my hotel. There will be a message for you there on how to find me."

"But where . . . "

"I don't know. It's very hard to see that far ahead. There will be some money there, but not very much. Bring some of your own and I'll pay you back."

Slowly Nancy was regaining her composure. "Is everything all right?"

There was a long pause. "I don't think that I can explain, at least not now, not so you'd understand. Did you get the letter?"

"The one to Grandma Ruth?"

"Yes."

"It never got to me. It was accidentally destroyed before anyone could read it."

"It really doesn't matter. I'll explain tomorrow, when I see you. There will be plenty of time then. Right now, I have to ask you to do another favor for me. Do you remember Richard Weiss? I tried to call him, but there was no answer. I have his number. I need you to call him. Tell him that . . . "

"Catherine! He's dead. I'm sorry."

"Who is? What are you talking about?"

"Richard Weiss. A week, ten days ago." Nancy waited for her aunt to say something. "Catherine?"

"How?" Her voice was flat.

"A robbery. The police think it was a mugging. In a park. I don't know."

"Bastards." It was almost a snarl and it startled Nancy.

"Who?"

"Tomorrow, Nannie. We'll talk. I really didn't think . . . "

"Bennet?"

"How do you know about him?"

"Catherine, for God's sake, I've spent the last two weeks following your clues. The marmalade, the cookbook. I know lots of things."

"Bennet's dead."

"What? How do you know that?"

"Because, goddamn it, Nannie, I just killed him. About an hour ago, a mile from here, in his hotel."

Nancy put a hand out on the bed to steady herself, then slowly lowered herself to the floor. "You what?" she whispered.

"Nannie, there's no time right now for this. There are things I've got to do. JFK. Flight 141. Six-thirty. Hotel l'Europe. Rue de Poissy. Please. I'll see you tomorrow. I'm sorry." The line went dead.

Nancy reached up and put the phone back in its cradle, then turned until she was kneeling against the bed. She buried her head in the sheets and pillows and groaned.

Arlington, Virginia
Morning

The ceramic mug hit the sink with enough force to send a shower of blue shards into the air. When they landed on the floor and countertops, they made the pattering sound of sleet on a tin roof.

Tony O'Connell, dressed in a bathrobe, stood at the kitchen table, his hands gripping the back of a chair. His head was down and his breathing was labored.

"You stupid, arrogant, fucking, know-it-all, son-of-a-bitch," he said, spitting the words out one at a time. He picked up the glass sugar bowl and hurled it as hard as he could toward the sink, but his aim was high and it exploded against the backsplash in a spray of glass and sugar. "Stupid, goddamn ... " From the front hallway came the sound of someone knocking on the door.

"Mr. O'Connell? You OK? It's Jimmy."

"Yeah, Jimmy. Fine. Just dropped some dishes."

"OK. Just checking."

O'Connell slid the chair out from under the table and sat down. He leaned forward, his elbows on his knees, and held his head in his hands. He would go to France today and kill this fucking Lakey with his own two hands, strangle her and watch her face turn purple, and then Mulholland, while he was at it, before she became a bigger problem than she already was. Goddamn son-of-a-bitch school teacher. Don't worry, she's under a rock; she's harmless; we'll find her. "Well, we didn't find her, did we?" he said out loud, his voice thick, the words running together. "She found you, you poor bastard. You poor fucking bastard."

Tony sat quietly for several minutes, then wearily got to his feet. He went to a small closet and took out a broom and swept a pathway through the glass and china to the sink. He ran some cold water, splashed it on his face, then stood there, his head down, dripping. He tried to think what Bennet would have done. He would have been calm. Angry, yes, but steely calm and clever. Think things through. Why the hell kill Bennet? Revenge? For three poor bastards she didn't even know? For Weiss? But she hadn't known about Weiss.

He wiped his face with a dish towel, poured another cup of coffee and took it into the living room of the small apartment. He stood at the window, staring out through it, not really seeing anything. It wasn't revenge, he thought, it couldn't have been. At every turn they'd been wrong about her, had assumed that she was simple and predictable. When Weiss had told her things, six months ago, they had said—Bennet had said—that it wasn't important; that quiet, little Catherine Lakey wasn't what you'd call a risk. And then she'd disappeared. Scared, they'd said, gone underground. Don't worry, we'll get her. We'll find her soon enough. He'd found her, all right.

If not revenge, then what? A warning? Was she telling them that they'd better keep away, better leave her alone? This fucking little college professor acting like a Mafia hit man leaving bodies around, warning them? Impossible. None of this made any sense. And why did she want Mulholland there, and what had she meant about having so little time and having things to do? When you kill someone, you don't invite your relatives to come stay with you. You get the hell away, as far as you can, as fast as you can, unless, of course . . . Jesus!

Tony slammed his coffee cup down on the table and ran back to his bedroom. He opened his briefcase and took out a small leather-bound notebook, riffled through the pages, picked up the telephone and dialed. He waited. "Come on," he said impatiently. "Graham? Tony O'Connell, OEP. Are we secure? I'm afraid the lid's coming off the Lakey problem. I just got word that Gil Bennet's been killed in Paris. I know. This morning. Look, Graham, it was Lakey who killed him. No details yet. I think you've got to take this to the DDO and he might want to take it higher." He listened for a moment, then shook his head. "I'm not telling you what to do. I just don't think that we have very much time to circle the wagons. Of course I'm available. I'll be at the office." He put the telephone down. "Asshole," he said. "She isn't going to wait for you."

New York City
Morning

As a general rule, Creighton Price didn't answer the phone on Sundays. He'd unplug the telephone in his bedroom and the one in the kitchen, then turn the ringer off on the phone in his den. You couldn't answer the telephone, he reasoned, if you didn't know it was ringing. He didn't do this out of any unusual distaste for telephones, nor did he have any particular longing to guard his privacy; it was simply that as a reporter for *The New York Times,* he spent most of his working week on the telephone and felt that for one day, at least, he'd like to do something else.

On this Sunday morning, he would not have answered the telephone either had he not been standing at the small desk in his study when he heard his answering machine switch on. When his message had finished playing, he heard the voice of Rachel Lukins, a young reporter whom he very much liked and, in fact, had taken under his wing.

"Creighton, it's Rachel. Hate to bother you at home on a Sunday, but I'm at the office and just got a message for you that's odd enough that I thought—"

Price fumbled with the buttons on the machine and picked up the receiver. "Rachel, I'm here."

"Hi. Sorry to bother you. The call came in just a few minutes ago and I wasn't sure what to do about it."

"Who was it?"

"A woman. She said her name was Catherine Lakey. She said she's a chemistry professor at Stonington College in Connecticut."

Price took a pen from the holder on the desk and, from long years of practice, began taking notes. "Go ahead."

"She said she was calling from France and needed to talk to you about someone called Gil Bennet."

"OK."

"Don't laugh, Creighton, but she said she'd just killed him."

"Killed who?"

"Gil Bennet, whoever he is."

"Oh, for Christ's sake. A nut cake."

"That's what I thought at first, but this woman didn't sound that way. She said you should call the Paris bureau in an hour or so—that they'd have heard about it by then."

"I'm sure."

"She said that her niece would be flying to Paris from JFK, six-thirty tonight, on TWA, flight 141, and if you meet her there, you'll get more of the story. Her name is Mulholland. Nancy Mulholland."

"What story is that?"

"She wouldn't tell me. She said that she'd sent a package to you, FedEx, that should be here tomorrow. She said it would explain everything."

"Is that it?"

"Not quite. She said I should tell you that this is as big as Watergate."

"Right. Aren't they all."

"I'm sorry, Creighton. I didn't know what else to do."

"It's fine, Rachel. This sort of thing happens every now and then. You've got to check it out."

"See you tomorrow?"

"Sure. No more calls, though." He put the phone down and switched on the answering machine, then sat down at the desk and stretched and yawned. Gil Bennet. He knew him, but not very well. A very polished, handsome guy. Navy background, he remembered. He was with something called the Office of Emergency Preparedness. OEP. He'd never really been able to get a handle on what they did. Some sort of contingency planning group. Maybe connected to the CIA. He couldn't remember. He glanced at his watch and saw that he had more than an hour before he was supposed to pick his kids up at their mother's. He reached across the desk to a thick blue book marked "Directory," thumbed through it, jotted down the number he wanted and placed the call. He waited through several rings, then heard the recording cut in. "Shit," he said softly to himself, and hung up. He checked the time again, then flipped through his Rolodex, found the number of the *Times'* Paris bureau and dialed.

"Hello," he said. "This is Creighton Price in New York. Would you put me through to the city desk." He waited and felt through the papers on the desk, looking for a pack of cigarettes.

"Creighton, this is Ev Burch."

"Ev! What the hell are you doing working on a Sunday?"

"It's only the sabbath for you Gentiles."

"Ev, I need confirmation on a report I just got. I'm told that a guy named Gil Bennet was killed in Paris today. He's U.S. government, maybe a spook. Have you heard anything?"

"Hold on. I'll check."

Price found the cigarettes and lit one with the big black lighter on the desk. He looked around for an ashtray, and when he couldn't find one, he opened the top drawer and scooped the paper clips out of their little well.

"Jesus, Creighton, who's your source? This only came in five minutes ago."

Price sat up straight. "Go," he said.

"Not much. Only that Bennet was found dead in an elevator around noon. Hôtel Saint-Étienne. Pretty ritzy."

"What else?"

"That's it, I think."

"Does it say he was murdered?"

"No. Nothing. Just his name. And that he was found dead."

"Ev, do me a favor, would you? Check around and pull together anything you hear about this."

"OK."

"How long are you going to be there?"

"Eight my time. It's four now."

"I'll call you."

Price hung up and quickly dialed another number. "Rachel Lukins, please." He crushed the cigarette out in the desk drawer. "Rachel, it's me. I was a lousy reporter. That Lakey woman who called, what's the name of the niece again?"

"Mulholland. Nancy Mulholland."

"And she's flying TWA ... "

"TWA, 141, out of JFK, six-thirty tonight."

"Got it. Thanks, Rachel."

"What's up?"

"Don't know yet and I'd appreciate if you didn't say anything about this until I see you tomorrow. Bye."

Absently, he pushed a paper clip across the desktop. Its trail made a spidery design in the dust. He sighed, and reluctantly picked up the phone and dialed his wife's number. This would be the third Sunday in the last two months that he'd had to cancel his day with the kids at the last minute. "It's why you divorced me in the first place," he said aloud before she answered. "At least you were right about that."

Devon, Connecticut
Morning

When he'd answered the telephone and heard her voice, he'd been so happily surprised that he hadn't listened very carefully, hadn't caught her tone. Instead, he'd concentrated on what he was going to say to her, determined this time not to squander another opportunity. But then she had told him and he'd sat down heavily on the old wooden chair in the kitchen and had found himself only able to say "what?" every few seconds, as though the word were some sort of beacon, signaling to Nancy that he was still there.

He'd written some things down on his notepad, but wasn't sure why. "JFK. Six-thirty. Hôtel l'Europe." He had underlined "Hôtel Europe" several times and had drawn a box around "JFK" and "6:30," as though they held special significance for him, although they didn't. He had written MURDER in large block letters and had followed it with a string of question marks. He'd finally asked Nancy if she thought this could be some enormous hoax. She'd said "No," that Catherine wouldn't ever do a thing like that, then she'd told him that she would call when she got to Paris.

Simco pulled his chair up to the kitchen table, tore the top page off his notepad and made the beginnings of a list. "President," he wrote, because he knew the president of the college would have to know about this. When the story broke, someone at Stonington would have to say something about shock and sadness and regrets. He hoped it wouldn't have to be him.

Then he wrote "search" because he knew that whoever took Catherine's place, it wouldn't be an interim appointment. To replace her, he'd have to find an experienced, tenured professor, and that wouldn't be easy, not this late in the year.

He went out the back door onto the deck and looked down toward the river, taking little pleasure from the bright, warm April morning. Somewhere above him, he could hear the buzzing of a small airplane and he thought that tonight, between six-thirty and seven, he ought to come out here and watch for her. Years ago he'd noticed that at dusk, when the ground was in shadow, you could look up on a clear night and, high in the sky, in the last patch of sunlight, you could see the planes—glimmering dots of silver sprouting plumes of white vapor. They were out of New York, he thought, bound for London or Paris, and tonight, because she was going to be on one of them, she'd be closer to him than she might be for a very long time.

Langley, Virginia
Afternoon

A glance around the room told Tony O'Connell that he would not be the next director of OEP. For one thing, his clothes were wrong. He'd been summoned from Bethesda on an hour's notice, and even if it had occurred to him—which it hadn't—he wouldn't have had time to change, so he sat there in his white polo shirt and khaki trousers, while the others, in their dark business suits, appraised him with cool curiosity. He noticed, too, that he didn't have the look that the others had: the thin-body, thin-head, Brooks Brothers mannequin look of wholesome, plain vanilla handsomeness.

He was introduced briefly to the others in the room: to Graham Person, OEP's liaison officer, whom Tony already knew, but not well; to John Fawcett, an assistant to the deputy director for operations; and to the deputy director himself, James Sperle. Graham motioned for Tony to take the seat next to him, on one side of the conference table.

Sperle leaned forward and folded his arms on the table in front of him. "I think we should begin," he said, looking at each of the others in turn, but lingering a little longer on Tony. "I'll remind you that this is extremely sensitive." He paused and sat back in his chair. "Graham?"

Graham Person opened a thin, black attaché case and removed a yellow legal pad on which there were some handwritten notes. "Here is what we know," he said without preamble. "At about 11:45 hours GMT, Bennet was found dead in an elevator in his hotel in Paris. French authorities at the scene treated the incident as a death by natural causes."

"I thought . . . " began Fawcett, who sat directly across from Tony.

"I know, John," said Person. "But there were no other indications. No signs of violence, no witnesses." He paused and looked around the room. "At 7:30 Eastern time, OEP intercepted a communication from Catherine Lakey to her niece in Bloomington, Indiana. Professor Lakey stated that she had killed Bennet and she asked her niece to fly to Paris tonight on a flight from New York. I believe that is all we know."

No one said anything and Tony gave Person a surprised, sideways look. It was difficult to believe that with the means at the disposal of the others at the table, nothing new had been learned in the last six hours.

"Please continue, Graham," said Sperle from the end of the table.

"This is an unusual situation, and a dangerous one. At the moment, based on what we know, there has been no compromise and, therefore, there has been no need for a response from us. As I said, the French are treating this as a sudden death from natural causes—a heart attack, presumably. They are not aware of a murder and they are not aware of Catherine Lakey. Mr. O'Connell," he looked over at Tony and nodded, "has been following the Lakey case and he is in the best position, I think, to fill in some important blanks. Tony?"

"Has Graham given you background on this?" Tony looked first at Sperle and then at Fawcett. He saw the slight nods. "First, I think we should take Lakey at her word and assume she did kill Bennet. We know she was in France and she doesn't have any reason that we're aware of to lie to her niece."

"Did Bennet know she was in the country?" said Fawcett.

"He did. He was informed when he arrived in Paris Friday."

"And were precautions taken?" said Fawcett, a slight and not pleasant smile on his face.

"I don't know what you mean."

"You don't?" said Fawcett.

"Not now, John," said Sperle. "Mr. O'Connell, would you continue."

"It sounds to me like she used cis-Ornithon 60, probably with a syringe of some sort. That would be consistent with the background. She would have had no difficulty getting it—at least enough for a single application. It works quickly and leaves no trace."

"None?" said Fawcett.

"None, unless you know exactly what you're looking for, and that's unlikely."

Sperle leaned back in his swivel chair, clasped his hands behind his neck, and turned slowly to Tony. "There's a certain irony in all of this, Mr. O'Connell, wouldn't you say?"

"I think you could say that."

Sperle tipped his chair forward, sat up straight, and studied Tony for a moment. "You've watched her. Right?" Tony nodded. "So, tell us, what's she up to? What's her next move? What do we do next?"

Tony hesitated and looked uncertainly to Person, who slid the legal pad toward him. Tony scanned the notes and saw where Person had underlined some things in red. He looked back at Sperle. "That's speculation. I've been wrong too often about Lakey. We all have."

Graham Person smiled at Sperle. "I think Tony's being a bit too . . . " he hesitated, " . . . modest? As for what she's up to, there are, we think, a couple of possibilities. There's revenge—but Tony doesn't like that."

"And why is that, Mr. O'Connell?" said Sperle from underneath raised eyebrows.

"For one thing, it doesn't fit at all with her profile. For another, she had no way of knowing for certain who really gave the orders. And, besides, Bennet had her charmed. Completely."

"There's a variation," continued Person, "which relies a little less on passion and a little more on calculation." He looked at Tony.

"Go ahead," said Sperle.

"She felt betrayed by OEP, we're sure of that, and it's not difficult to understand. Bennet is the only one she knows, so he becomes a symbol of betrayal."

"But that's revenge again," said Fawcett impatiently.

Person held up his hand. "Please let me finish. By killing Bennet she does exact a measure of revenge, certainly, but she also kills the body by cutting off the head."

"An assassination?" said Fawcett.

"Exactly. The elimination of the leader brings about a change of policy. The end of Bennet means the end of Bennet's programs. It's not a new idea, of course." He looked around the room. "I can't imagine where she got it."

"And now?" said Sperle, looking at Tony.

"That's very hard to say," interjected Person quickly. "We're looking for her, of course. She's not at her hotel, and, so far, at least, she's left no messages of any kind for her niece, or anyone else. And we don't yet understand why she's asked her niece to come to Paris. Our best guess is that she's going underground, at least for now; although she's probably worried more about us than the French police. After all, she's gotten away with murder, hasn't she? Unless we decide to change that."

"And that wouldn't be wise, at least not now," said Sperle.

"It wouldn't at all," said Person.

"What you're saying, Graham, is that we really can't do anything until she does."

"I think that's right."

"Jesus!" said Fawcett, slapping his hand on the table. "Would someone please tell me how this happened?"

"Not now, John," said Sperle. He looked back at Person. "Worst case?"

"I don't know. She goes public, I suppose, but she can't do that without implicating herself. I think that's low risk."

Sperle looked at Fawcett. "Can we handle that, John?"

"Plausibly deny? I don't know. Depends on what she has."

"Mr. O'Connell?" said Sperle.

"We don't think she has anything. When we ended the contract a year ago, she signed off on everything and we cleaned up after ourselves. That was six months before she knew anything."

"But if she's got the Ornithon?"

"That could be a problem."

"A problem we can deal with, John?"

Fawcett thought for a moment. "I suppose."

"And I can tell the Director that?"

Fawcett nodded without enthusiasm. Sperle stood up and leaned forward, resting his hands on the table. "John asked a question a few minutes ago, about how something like this could have happened. It's not a question we can stop and consider now, but it's one that everyone in this place had better think about very carefully. There are things that people don't like, but will go along with because they don't see any way around them. And there are other things that people won't go along with no matter what." Sperle paused and looked at each of them around the table. "This is one of those. If it can't be contained, there's no telling how far it will go." He looked over at Fawcett. "You'll keep me informed?" He nodded then at Person and at Tony and left the room.

Fawcett stood up and took his jacket off and loosened his tie. "All right, O'Connell," he said, "we're going to pretend you're Lakey and you're going to tell me everything you know."

Paris
Afternoon

The police station squatted on the street like a bulldog, gray and jowly, small-windowed, unfriendly. Whoever had designed it had been very much aware of the city's long history of civil unrest; even its door, massive and black with an oversized brass knocker, seemed more a barrier than an entrance. Catherine Lakey had to push hard on it to enter the hallway, and once inside, she stood a moment, allowing her eyes to adjust to the dim light provided by a single three-globed lamp that hung on a chain from the high ceiling. At the far end, behind a battered wooden desk, sat a young woman in a dark blue uniform, sorting through an untidy pile of papers.

Catherine went up to the desk and waited. When the young woman failed to look up from her work, Catherine said, "Madame?" in a small voice.

Without looking up, the woman said something in a short burst of nearly seamless musical sound that Catherine found both beautiful and unintelligible.

Catherine took a small card from her pocket and read from it: "Je ne parle pas français. Je parle seulement anglais. C'est tres important." She read the words slowly, pausing between them, as if she were reciting a list. The young woman looked up at her, tilting her head to one side. Catherine gave her a weak, hopeful smile. After a moment, she slid her chair back and stood up with a sigh. "Attendez," she said, and when Catherine looked at her blankly, she said, "Wait," although she pronounced it, "Wet."

In a minute or two the young woman returned, followed by another blue-uniformed officer, this one a small, thin man with large, prominent eyes and a receding chin. The young woman gestured at Catherine and then resumed her seat behind the desk. The policeman gave her a small nod. "And how may I help you, madame?" he said, his English good, but the cadence of his sentence clearly French.

"There's an important matter I need to discuss with you," said Catherine.

"Yes?"

She looked around the hallway and then down at the young woman behind the desk. "I wonder, is there somewhere we can talk? It's rather private."

He looked at her for a moment, then nodded slightly and said, "Please." He turned and led her down a narrow corridor to a door that had the number 8 painted in black on its pane of frosted glass. He opened the door and indicated that she should enter. The room was small and dingy and smelled strongly of stale cigarette smoke.

There was a Formica-topped table in the center of the room and a few chairs that looked as if they had come from a school cafeteria. Overhead there was a single fluorescent light fixture and, in one corner, on a small wooden table, was a telephone.

The policeman pointed to a chair, indicating that Catherine should sit down. When she had seated herself, he took the chair opposite her. "I am Inspector Daumier," he said.

"My name is Catherine Lakey, Inspector. I am an American."

"You are a tourist?"

"No, not exactly." Catherine looked down at her lap. "Early this afternoon a man was found dead in an elevator at the Hôtel Saint-Étienne. His name was Gil Bennet, an American. Do you know about this?"

"The Saint-Étienne? That's the seventh, isn't it? Not our district. This is the fifth. I don't think so."

"I see, but I think you can check, anyway. The police, I believe, think the man died naturally, of a heart attack probably." She looked up at Daumier, who was watching her with some curiosity. "I'm here to tell you that that's not so. He was murdered."

Daumier shifted in his chair and leaned forward very slightly. "You are a witness?" he said gently.

Catherine smiled into her lap, then looked up at Daumier. "Yes. A witness. I was right there. I saw everything."

Daumier clapped his hands lightly together and stood up. "I see," he said. "Could you wait a moment? I will need a statement from you. I will be right back."

Catherine stood up quickly, her smile fading. "Yes, but before you go, I think I should explain something. The reason I was there, why I saw everything, was that I was the one who killed him."

New York
Late afternoon

Nancy was startled when she went to the passenger service agent in the TWA international terminal and found everything waiting for her, exactly as Catherine had said it would be. The day had had such a dreamlike quality about it that she had expected—had even hoped—that when she identified herself, she'd be met with a blank stare, a shrug, an "I'm sorry, but we have nothing for anyone of that name."

She wondered, vaguely, what she would do in the hour and a half before the flight boarded. She decided, finally, that it might be a good idea to have a decent meal before the flight, an insurance policy against airline food, and as she looked around for signs of restaurants, she heard her name—or thought she did—as part of an announcement coming over the public address system. She waited for the announcement to be repeated, and when it wasn't, she went to the passenger service counter.

"That announcement a minute ago, was that for a Nancy Mulholland?" she said to the tall, bored-looking woman behind the counter.

"You her?"

Nancy nodded.

With her thumb she pointed off to Nancy's left. "He's looking for you."

Nancy looked in the direction she was pointing and saw a man of about forty, a cigarette in the corner of his mouth, leaning against the counter, watching her. He had on a blue nylon windbreaker with "Mets" written across the front in orange script, faded khaki trousers, and dark blue running shoes. He had a round, pleasant face, although it needed a shave, and his long but thinning sandy hair seemed to swirl in every direction, as though he'd been standing out in a high wind. He looked slightly disreputable, but not dangerous.

"I'm Nancy Mulholland," she said.

"I know," he said, smiling. "I heard you at the counter. My name is Creighton Price. I wonder if we could talk."

"Do I know you?"

"I'd be flattered if you did. I'm a reporter for *The New York Times.*"

Nancy felt a flutter of anxiety. "What do you want to talk about?"

"First let's find a place where we can hear one another," he said, looking around.

"I hear you fine. What's this about?"

He looked at her and scratched his head. "I'm sorry, but I think that's my line. Do you have an aunt named Catherine Lakey?"

"How did you know that?" she said, searching his face.

"She called me this morning. From Paris. Pardon me, but would you mind terribly if we found a better place to talk?"

"What time?"

"What time what?"

"What time did she call you?"

"I don't know. Ten. Ten-thirty."

"What did she say?"

"I don't think that's something I want to talk about right here in the middle of a million people. Please," he said and motioned to her that she should follow him. He walked rapidly across the terminal and got on an escalator to the upper level. At the top he looked around for a moment, then, apparently seeing what he wanted, he set off at a pace that almost forced Nancy into a run to keep up. He stopped at a nearly deserted waiting area outside the gate of a flight that wasn't scheduled to depart for four hours, went over to a window and looked out across the airport, then turned and faced her. "All right, now we don't have to shout. I didn't speak to your aunt, not directly. She called my office and asked them to give me a message. She said she'd just killed a man named Gil Bennet. She said that you were coming through here tonight on your way to Paris and you'd fill me in on the rest of the story. She said it was bigger than Watergate."

"How do you know her?"

"Your aunt? I don't. I've never heard of her."

"Why did she call you, then?"

Price shrugged. "I don't know. You write for the *Times,* people know your name I suppose. What's this about?"

Nancy stopped and looked at him appraisingly. "I'm sorry, but do you have some sort of identification?"

Price looked down at himself and laughed. "Sorry," he said.

"Day off. Don't blame you." He reached into his back pocket and took out a worn leather wallet and handed Nancy a small plastic card. She studied it and gave it back to him.

"If I talk to you, what happens?"

"What do you mean, what happens?"

"Will there be a story in the *Times* tomorrow about my aunt?"

"I don't know."

"I don't want that. Not now."

"I can't write a story unless there is one. Right now, all I know is that this guy Bennet is dead, and that some woman that I never heard of claims she killed him."

"Will you write that?"

"I can't. It's not enough."

"Mr. Price, if I tell you what I know, I think you'll be disappointed, and I don't want you to use it. Not yet."

Price sighed and scratched his head. "OK. Off the record." He reached into his jacket pocket and took out a small notebook and a pen.

"Is that really necessary?"

"For me it is. No memory. Don't worry, nothing gets used without your say-so."

Nancy bit her lower lip and then, in a low voice, began to tell Creighton Price the story of the past two weeks. She was surprised at how rapidly he transformed her words into swirly marks and lines across the pages of his notebook, looking up at her from time to time, but never stopping the motion of his pen. When she finished, she sat back in her chair. "That's it," she said. "That's everything I know."

Price closed the notebook and put it back in his pocket. "Interesting," he said. "You were right about one thing. Bennet was lying."

"How do you know that?"

"I've known him, or at least about him, for several years. He's the head of something called the Office of Emergency Preparedness, in Bethesda. I'm not absolutely sure what they do, but it has to do with contingency planning. You know, if the bad guys do such and such, then we should do this and so. Gil Bennet was no more an editor than I'm an astronaut."

"But how does Catherine fit into all of this? That's the thing that simply makes no sense."

"Obviously I don't know. She could have been doing business with Bennet, with OEP, and—"

"Business? What sort of business?" There was alarm in Nancy's voice.

"I don't know that either. I'm just speculating."

"But what the hell kind of business would it be that would cause her to kill someone?"

"Could be there was a love angle." Price saw the look on Nancy's face and held up his hand. "Take it easy, but Gil Bennet, I understand, was a charming, handsome guy. She's single. They meet, get a number going. He's a married man, makes promises, the way guys do; then reneges. She feels betrayed and kills him. It's happened before."

Nancy laughed. "Good Lord, you ought to write novels."

"Why is that so funny?"

"You don't know Catherine. And anyway, why all the mystery about the deaths abroad? And what about Weiss? And why call you? Why not Ann Landers?"

"OK. We'll know soon enough."

"I suppose we will."

Price stood up. "Miss Mulholland, I want you to understand that what you've said is off the record. Other things aren't."

"What other things?"

"The last part of your aunt's message this morning was that she was sending something to me, Federal Express. A package, I think. She said it would explain everything. It should arrive tomorrow."

"And then you'll write the story?"

"If it does explain. If it's important. If it checks out. That's my job."

"I suppose." Nancy stood up and looked at her watch. "My flight should be boarding."

"Is there somewhere I can reach you in Paris?"

"I don't know. I won't know until I get there."

Price reached into his back pocket and took out his wallet. He removed a white card and gave it to her. "You can call me. Collect, of course."

Nancy took the card without looking at it. "I don't know why," she said. "You're going to write what you're going to write."

"I'm not an enemy. I want to get things right."

"I've got to go."

Price watched her as she made her way back into the stream of people flowing in both directions through the corridor. It was possible, he knew, that this whole thing was just some silly fantasy concocted by an unbalanced woman looking for publicity, or attention, or God knows what. But after meeting Nancy Mulholland, his instincts told him that it wasn't.

Paris
Night

In the late-night silence of the small lobby of the Hôtel l'Europe, the night clerk dozed on a stool behind the registration desk. At a few minutes after one, the front door opened and through it came an old man, slightly stooped, wearing a stained tan sweater and shiny blue serge pants, carrying a scuffed black briefcase. There was a haze of silver stubble on his chin.

He stopped in front of the desk and to the clerk said softly, "Monsieur?" When there was no response he tried again, a little louder, leaning closer. "Monsieur?" He reached across and tapped the shoulder of the clerk, whose eyes fluttered, then opened wide, surprised, not understanding. The clerk coughed, then smiled as if he'd been playing a joke on his visitor. "Are you a guest?" he said uncertainly.

The older man lifted his briefcase up onto the desk with some effort, then opened it and took out a package the size of a telephone directory wrapped in brown paper. "Gaspard Messenger Service," he said, putting on a pair of black-rimmed glasses and unfolding a slip of yellow paper that he had taken from his pocket. "This is for a Nancy Mulholland in care of Catherine Lakey. They are guests here, I take it?"

The clerk opened the large register and ran his finger down one page, then up another. "We have a C. Lakey, but no Mulholland."

"Lakey is good enough," said the older man. He put the piece of yellow paper on the desk and smoothed it with his hand. "Could you sign here?" He pointed to a line at the bottom. "Merci," he said, and slid the package toward the clerk. "Bonsoir."

The clerk put the package on a shelf underneath the desk, then made out a message slip for Catherine Lakey that would alert the day clerk that the package had arrived. He put the slip in box 22 and turned the lever so that the message light glowed red. When he turned around he was startled to see another man at the desk, thick-faced, wearing a dark raincoat, looking at him unsmilingly. "Monsieur?" said the clerk.

The man reached inside his raincoat and brought out a bill-fold, which he flipped open. "Interpol."

The clerk glanced at it. "Yes?"

"I believe the man who was just here left a parcel for a Nancy Mulholland or a Catherine Lakey." His French was clear and grammatical, but there was an accent. It was difficult to place.

"That's right," said the clerk, bending down for the package. He placed it on the desk.

"If you'd be so kind," said the man, extending his hand. "I have authorization." The clerk handed him the package. "If everything is in order, it will be returned." He put the package under his arm and went out the door and walked halfway down the block to a black Peugeot sedan that was parked at the curb. When he opened the passenger-side door and got in, the driver flicked on the overhead light. "Is that it?" he said in English.

The other man was already undoing the brown paper. "Right," he said. Then, "What the hell is this?" The package contained two thin, black looseleaf notebooks on top of which were two white, business-size envelopes. One said "Nannie." It was the other, however, that caught his attention. It said, simply, "OEP." He opened it, took out a piece of paper, neatly typed; held it under the overhead light and began to read:

> *Hello—I knew I couldn't get this to Nancy without it first going to you, so I didn't try. I really don't mind, because I've arranged it so it doesn't matter. There are two notebooks, one for Nancy and one for you. The contents are the same. I imagine you won't want hers to reach her. Suit yourselves, of course, but I have sent identical copies to various people in various places so, eventually, Nancy will learn what the notebook contains. And, I assure you that whether or not you believe me is of no consequence.*
>
> *Catherine Lakey*

He picked up one notebook, opened it, read for a moment, flipped forward a few pages, read again, then looked at the driver. "Jesus Christ, that goddamn cocky bitch."

	MARCH—1987					
S	M	T	W	T	F	S
1	2	3	4	5	6	7
8	9	10	11	12	13	14
15	16	17	18	19	20	21
22	23	24	25	<u>26</u>	27	28
29	30	31				

DAY NINETEEN

	APRIL—1987					
S	M	T	W	T	F	S
			1	2	3	4
5	6	7	8	9	10	11
12	(13)	14	15	16	17	18
19	20	21	22	23	24	25
26	27	28	29	30		

DAY NINETEEN

MONDAY, APRIL 13, 1987

Paris
Morning

Marmalade, thought Nancy as she watched the dull countryside slide by the taxi window in the drab gray light of early morning. She had always imagined that France, and especially Paris, would be quaint and small and charming and strikingly different—different most of all from anything she had seen before. Instead, so far at least, it looked like the gloomy outskirts of just about every American city she had seen. It depressed her and she leaned her head back and closed her eyes, trying to ignore the tired griminess she felt, the dull thudding headache brought on by lack of sleep and the clammy anxiety that came from not even being able to imagine what might come next.

The taxi slowed and she heard the driver mutter something; she opened her eyes and saw that they were in the city now, and it looked more like the Paris she'd imagined: old and elegant gray stone buildings lined the streets with their black wrought iron balustrades and brass nameplates on the doors. She looked up over the rooftops and searched for the Eiffel Tower, but couldn't find it. The taxi sped across a bridge and into narrow, twisting streets clotted with Monday morning traffic. It weaved from lane to lane for two more blocks, braking hard once and swerving suddenly around a double-parked car before, abruptly, it pulled to the curb and stopped.

The driver pointed through the window. "C'est ici, mademoiselle," he said. Nancy looked and saw a dark green facade, two large windows on either side of a cheerful yellow door, and overhead in yellow script, Hôtel l'Europe. She looked at the meter, calculated the tip, then opened her purse and sorted through the unfamiliar banknotes, one at a time, conscious that the driver was already on the sidewalk, standing next to her suitcase, waiting. As she got out and handed him the money, he was gesturing toward the hotel, saying something too rapidly for her to understand. She thought that he might be offering to carry her bag inside. She smiled and shook her head. "Ça n'est pas . . . " she began, but her high school French deserted her. She couldn't remember the word for heavy so she picked the suitcase up and simply said, "Merci." He nodded, got back into the taxi, and she went into the hotel.

Nancy crossed the small, deserted lobby to the reception desk and rang the bell. In a moment, from somewhere in the back, a stooped man in a worn blue coat shuffled toward her, nodding, saying in almost singsong cadence, "Bonjour, mademoiselle. Bonjour."

Nancy put her suitcase down. "Anglais?"

"Yes. A little."

"I'm Nancy Mulholland," she said, louder than she'd intended. "Catherine Lakey is a guest here."

The desk clerk nodded vigorously. "Ah, oui."

"She was supposed to leave a message for me."

The clerk turned toward the mailboxes on the back wall, saw the blinking light under number 22, reached up and removed a slip of paper. "Oui, mademoiselle. There is something for you. It arrived last night." He bent down and looked underneath the reception counter, then stood up, a puzzled expression on his face. "It's supposed to be . . . " he said, looking around the small area behind the counter, running his hand over surfaces. "I don't understand."

"What's the matter?" said Nancy.

"It's not here. The note says there is a package under the counter, but there is nothing."

Nancy stood on tiptoes and looked over the counter. "You're sure?"

"There is nothing." The clerk shrugged.

"Jesus Christ." Nancy's voice was tired, cranky. She pinched the bridge of her nose and closed her eyes.

"If you would like, I will call the night clerk. He is the one who left the message."

"Please. I've come all the way from New York."

The clerk disappeared into a room at the rear of the reception area and Nancy tried very hard to collect herself, to focus on what she might do if the night clerk couldn't help, if there wasn't a message.

"Excuse me?" said a voice close behind her.

Turning, Nancy saw a woman smiling at her expectantly. She was short and square, verging on stout, and her gray-and-white-checked business suit looked awkward on her, out of place. Her complexion was that of someone who spent a great deal of time outdoors and her face, though plain, was friendly. "You're Nancy Mulholland. The description was perfect. I'm Elizabeth Portiere and I represent your aunt. She sent me here to meet you." She held out her hand.

Nancy took it briefly. "Represent? Where is she?"

"I'm her lawyer. She's being held by the police."

Nancy sighed. "Goddamn it."

"I'm sorry. She asked me to take you to her. It isn't far."

Nancy turned back to the reception desk. "Monsieur?" she called out.

The clerk shuffled out of the back room. "I'm sorry, but there was no answer and—"

"Thank you for trying. I have to go out for a while. May I leave my bag here?"

The clerk nodded and Nancy followed Elizabeth Portiere out onto the street. They walked in silence for a few minutes. "When did this happen?" said Nancy.

"Yesterday afternoon. She called me and told me where she

was. She said she'd killed a man and had turned herself in."

"Turned herself in?"

"Miss Mulholland, I wonder . . . "

"Nancy."

"Nancy. I really don't understand what's going on here. I met Catherine two weeks ago. She called my office and said that she was visiting a friend in Paris and that she was afraid her friend might need a criminal lawyer and wondered if I would be prepared to represent her. When I asked what the case might involve, she said she wasn't sure, but assured me that it wouldn't be very complicated. At her invitation, we had lunch together—sort of an audition, I'm sure, but I'm used to that. I liked her. We talked mostly about fees. That seemed to worry her. She said her friend didn't have much money, and after that I didn't hear from her, not until yesterday."

"Did you see her?"

"I went to the police station, yes. She seemed calm, or perhaps serene is a better word. She said that now I could do the worrying. When I asked her to tell me everything that had happened, she said she would, eventually, but that the most important thing was for me to meet you this morning."

"So you don't know any more than I do."

"After I talked to her, I talked to the police, to an Inspector Daumier. The odd thing is she's not being charged with anything, at least not yet. She's being held on suspicion of murder."

"But she's admitted it."

"The police need more than that. They need evidence that a crime was committed. Gilbert Bennet is certainly dead, but Daumier said they weren't positive he'd been murdered."

"Will I be able to see her?"

"I think so. Here." She guided Nancy across the street to the police station, where she stopped in front of a door that looked ancient and rather forbidding. It was painted black. "Perhaps I'd better do the talking." Nancy nodded. They entered and walked slowly to the desk at the end of the corridor where Elizabeth spoke to the young policeman in rapid French. He picked up a telephone, spoke briefly, listened, then hung up. He spoke to Elizabeth, who nodded to Nancy. "A few minutes," she said.

They stood together in the corridor, not speaking, until a se-vere-looking woman in a dark blue uniform appeared and led them down another long hallway to the room where Catherine had met with Daumier the day before. The policewoman held the door open for them, turned on the lights, then left. Nancy sat down at the table and lit a cigarette.

After a few minutes, there was the sound of voices in the hall-way, then shadows on the frosted glass of the door. Finally, it opened, slowly. Nancy crushed out her cigarette in the black plas-tic ashtray that was on the table and stood up.

The curly, black, stylishly cut hair made Nancy hesitate for a moment, but there was no mistaking the eyes. And when she saw the smile and the laugh lines and heard the voice saying "Nannie" the way Catherine always said it, she ran to her, put her arms around her, held her as tightly as she could. They finally backed away from one another, still holding hands, and all that Nancy could think of to say was: "You look fine."

Catherine put a hand to her hair. "Do you like it?"

Nancy brushed away some tears and nodded.

Catherine looked over her shoulder at Elizabeth. "Thanks," she said.

"I'll wait outside."

"No. Please. You'll need to hear this. How much time will they give us?"

"A half hour. Maybe forty-five minutes."

Catherine turned back to Nancy. "Has this been terrible for you?"

Nancy shrugged, shook her head. "I've been fine."

"I'm so sorry, Nannie, but I don't think there was any other way."

"I just wasn't sure that I would see you again." A tear ran past the corner of Nancy's mouth and hung on the edge of her chin. She forced a smile. "The marmalade was perfect."

Catherine closed her eyes and smiled at the ceiling. "Good. It was all that I could think of to tell you not to worry. I had to be so careful because they were watching everything."

"They?"

"There's so much to tell." She sat down in one of the folding chairs and motioned that Nancy and Elizabeth should sit opposite her. Elizabeth took out a legal pad and pencil. "That won't be necessary," said Catherine. She looked at Nancy. "Did you get my package?"

"No, but the hotel clerk said there was something. It's gone."

Catherine smiled. "They aren't very thoughtful, are they? Well, no matter. It's all been written down." She looked down at her lap and folded her hands together. Without looking up she said, "I'm glad you got to Cotchpinicut, Nannie. It's beautiful, isn't it?"

"Yes, it is."

"The awful thing is that this whole business started there. In the last few months, I've often thought that if I hadn't found the cottage, none of this would have happened."

"I don't understand," said Nancy.

"I'm sorry, dear. I should start at the beginning. It was Thanksgiving 1981. I'd never been to Cape Cod at that time of year so I decided to spend the break at the cottage. I walked the beach, corrected papers, that sort of thing. And then I noticed the birds. They were outside the kitchen window, finches, cardinals, blue jays, and they were feeding on little red berries. Bearberries, I found out later. What interested me, though, was that there were other berries growing nearby—white ones that the birds seemed to ignore—and the scientist in me wondered why. When I came back at Christmas, the bearberries were gone, picked clean. There was snow on the ground, but even with food so scarce, the birds wouldn't touch the white ones. I did an experiment. I wanted to see if it was the color that made the difference so I dyed them red and sprinkled them on the snow. The next day, I went out to check and some of the berries had been eaten. I also found four dead birds."

Nancy leaned forward. "And you took them back to Stonington in Ziploc bags?"

"How on earth did you know that?"

"The biology professor, I forget his name, he told Frank about it."

"Frank Simco?"

"He's been a tremendous help, but go on."

"Well, it was Bill Shields in Biology. I asked him to examine the birds, find out what killed them. When he couldn't find anything, he sent them to a friend of his at Harvard, a specialist in bird anatomy and physiology, and he couldn't find a cause of death either. Not a thing. That puzzled me. I was sure it was the berries, but I couldn't imagine how they could work so powerfully and so quickly without leaving a trace so I began to do some research. I found very little about them in the literature and certainly nothing about them being poisonous. I began going to meetings and conferences about folk medicine, about the history of herbal home remedies, even about Native American pharmacology—anything I thought might be connected, even slightly. I also tried to do a chemical analysis, but I was pretty rusty and the equipment I had at Stonington wasn't right at all. I got nowhere. Then, in the fall of 1982, I met Richard."

"I remember."

Catherine smiled. "Yes." Her expression changed and her smile faded. She looked down at the floor and shook her head. "A bad day for both of us, I guess, although at the time . . . Anyway, he was a pharmacologist and he understood the problem. The college didn't have funds for that kind of research, so I needed a grant, but to get a grant, I had to show expertise in the field, which I certainly couldn't do. Catch-22. That's when he told me about OEP."

"So you met Gil Bennet through Richard?"

Catherine nodded. "Richard was interested in neurotoxins, nerve gas, that sort of thing. OEP was a government group that monitored the development of nonconventional weapons, mostly chemical and biological. The idea was that if we knew what was going on, we could come up with ways of defending against them. If we could convince the other side that their weapons wouldn't work, they wouldn't use them. It sounded very good. Anyway, Richard had been working with OEP for two years and said it was an ideal situation. They provided a small lab, any equipment he needed, and paid a small stipend. The best thing was that there wasn't any pressure. He asked me if I'd be interested in talking to them. I said yes and in a month or so I met the director, Mr. Gilbert Bennet."

"And you went to work for him?"

"Yes, but not right away. I had to submit a proposal, had to go through a security clearance, all of that. It took three or four months. That was in April or May of 1983. By June, they'd installed a small lab in my guest bedroom in Cotchpinicut and I started work that summer."

"Is that why I never got an invitation then?"

"To Cotchpinicut? I'm sorry, Nannie, but you would have asked questions and I didn't want to lie. I thought it would only be a year or two."

"And was it?"

"Actually, it took a little longer. The work was slow and tedious—at least for someone like me—and I could only work during vacations and on occasional weekends. But OEP was very patient. They never pushed."

"I'm still not sure I understand why they were so interested in you or your work."

Catherine smiled. "What they said . . . " she paused, " . . . and they were so convincing, was that if the toxin in the berries left no trace, it could be a very dangerous tool in the wrong hands. If I could isolate it, they could work on developing means to detect it, maybe even develop some kind of antidote. My work might save lives. Or so they said."

"I see."

"There were some technicalities to work out, but by late 1984 I had a fairly good handle on what the active fraction was and the next year I was able to synthesize it in small quantities. About a year ago, the work was done and that was to have been the end of it, or almost the end." Catherine paused, looked in her lap, then up at Nancy.

"But it wasn't?"

"No." Catherine shook her head. "When I finished, I went

through something called signing off. They came out, removed the lab and all the equipment so you couldn't tell that anything had ever been there. I turned over my records, my receipts, everything. I signed papers pledging never to discuss my work—all in the interest of national security. I thought the whole thing had been a good experience. I'd found a problem that interested me; I'd solved it and I thought that, as it had turned out, the solution was a useful one. I felt very good about what I'd done."

"And that was a year ago?"

"Yes. April '86. And it stayed that way until the fall. Then Richard called. It was early October and the school year had just begun. He said he had bad news." Catherine's voice dropped, lost its animation, and her hands, which had been still in her lap, began moving nervously, one stroking the other.

"Richard said that he'd found out . . . that he'd been told that OEP had lied to me . . . that Gilbert Bennet had. They weren't using the poison for what they said. They were using it on people. Killing them. To see if it worked. To see if it could be detected. They called it field testing."

"Chile?" said Nancy.

"You found the cookbook?"

Nancy nodded.

"I thought you would, but I knew the puzzle had to be difficult. Even if you solved it, I didn't want you to know everything. Not then. That would have been too dangerous for you." She looked up at Nancy. "You've got to understand about these people. They're killers." She shook her head. "Well, if I failed, I needed you to know enough to carry on. I had to be so careful. At least I thought I did."

"Because Richard said so?"

"Yes."

"What tipped him off?"

"I don't know. He said he couldn't tell me, but he assured me that, beyond any doubt, what he said was true. He showed me the clippings from the *Times* and told me how they'd done it." Catherine's voice dropped. " . . . all three with small syringes." Catherine paused, took a deep breath and continued, speaking evenly but with anger in her voice. "He said those men were simply target practice—human skeets he called them. Three minor officials in three friendly countries chosen because if something went wrong, suspicion wouldn't be directed at OEP. I was horrified. What was worse, Nannie, was that I was terribly afraid that this was just the beginning. Why would they test it that way unless they planned to use it whenever it suited them, whenever someone somewhere couldn't be dealt with any other way. I simply couldn't stand by and let that happen."

"And so you decided on this?"

"Oh no. Not right away. Richard told me what he knew only to warn me away from ever working with OEP again. He said that nothing we could do would bring those three men back. For months we argued bitterly about it. I wanted to go to someone in the government—I know my congressman slightly, worked on his campaign six years ago. I wanted to tell him what I knew—at least start an investigation—but Richard said no, that it wouldn't work, that they'd deny everything. We had no proof. He also said it could be dangerous, that you couldn't tell how people like that would react. Finally I agreed that I'd think things over carefully until the summer. Then, if I still felt strongly about it, he promised he'd help me do something."

"What happened? Why didn't you wait?"

"They found out we knew. We don't know exactly how, but Richard thought it must have been his telephone. Gil—Mr. Bennet—met with him two or three times and made veiled threats. He kept talking about how serious it would be if OEP's work were ever compromised, and how he was sure that Richard understood that, and how concerned he was that others, like me, might not understand. It was clear that he was using Richard to threaten me. And then Stephen Lakey appeared at the nursing home. Do you know about that?"

"I found out about it right away. I didn't understand it."

"He was from OEP, a signal to me which said they knew about me, knew where my family was, and could find my mother, you, me, any of us, whenever they needed to. It was a warning."

"I see."

"It frightened me, of course, but that's what made me absolutely certain I had to do something."

Nancy leaned forward. "But, Catherine, why this? There had to be some other way."

Catherine made a sound that fell between a brittle laugh and a sigh. She looked up at the ceiling. "Another way? Oh my God, Nannie, if there were, I think I would have found it. I went over everything a thousand times and at the end this was the only way I could see that had a chance of working. I knew that Richard was right, that I couldn't tell the world, not in the usual way. If I called a press conference and made charges, they'd sound strange, maybe even crazy, especially without proof. I might cause a little flap, make OEP uncomfortable for a week or so, but then it would die down and everybody would forget. No, I knew I needed something bigger, more dramatic, than just a story, and finally I hit on the idea of doing to them what they had done to those poor men, only I'd do it in the open. Show-and-tell. It's going to be hard for them to deny this, Nannie, over Gilbert Bennet's dead body and an autopsy report that shows how he died."

"But you said the poison was undetectable."

Catherine smiled. "It very nearly is—and no standard autopsy would ever find it. But if you know precisely what to look for, and where, you'll find traces in the spinal fluid."

Nancy shook her head. "This is so hard to believe."

"I hope not. It's got to be believed."

"But this plan, how did you ever . . . ?"

"I worked backwards. I knew that he came to Paris for meetings every year in April. It was the only place and time when I knew for sure he'd be out and away from Washington. I also knew I was being watched—that if I was going to get to him, I had to get away from them. And I remembered a newspaper story I'd read about a woman in Nantucket who simply walked out of her house one day and disappeared. I thought how perfect that would be, and how easy. I knew OEP couldn't be watching the cottage—it's too isolated out there, they'd be too obvious. So I began squirreling money away, small amounts, buying traveler's checks. I bought my plane ticket through a big travel agency in Dallas, and when I went to a conference in Boston in February, I left a suitcase of clothes in a storage locker. Then came that morning—when was it? Almost three weeks ago. I left, just walked out the door and down the beach. I threw my sandals into the ocean." Catherine laughed again. "I knew it was a long shot, but I thought if they were found, washed up on the beach, the search for me might stay in Cotchpinicut or stop altogether. Anyway, after that, when I was sure no one was watching, I doubled back. I changed my clothes in the garage of a house up the street, bundled up so no one could recognize me, then walked into town, got on the bus to Boston, and flew here."

"And killed Gil Bennet."

"Yes . . . with a syringe of cis-Ornithon 60 rigged inside the tip of an ordinary umbrella. Ornithon. It was named after the poor birds."

Nancy looked over at Elizabeth Portiere. "What happens now?"

"I can't be sure. The police are investigating. She'll be charged." Elizabeth looked over at Catherine. "And plead guilty?"

"Of course. That's the whole point. There won't need to be much of an investigation. I've already told them how I did it and why. They'll have to do an autopsy, of course, probably today. I've told them what to look for. By tonight, or certainly tomorrow, the police will be able to confirm how he died. I left the umbrella in my room—it's safer there—and a small sample of the poison. I told Inspector Daumier about them yesterday and he sent some men to get them. I even made sure that the blood stayed on the umbrella tip so they'll have the umbrella and they'll have the poison. I don't think they'll need much else."

Nancy looked at Elizabeth Portiere, a question on her face.

"I'm sorry," said Elizabeth. "Premeditated murder. Life."

"Jesus," said Nancy. "But can't it be justified? Won't the story count for something?"

"I don't know. I don't really think so."

Catherine got up and went over to her niece's chair, bent down and smoothed Nancy's hair. "Nannie, life in prison is better than it would have been if I'd done nothing. I killed those men. No, not me, I know that, but it was my work, Nannie, and at least part of the responsibility is mine. Now I've stopped it and there won't be any more of this killing. It's not a bad trade."

Nancy looked up at her. "But why couldn't you have told me all this before? Let me help you think things through?"

"And put you in the same terrible danger I was in? I couldn't have done that. I know I've done the right thing. I'm sorrier than anyone will ever know about Richard. I feel quite sure that it was my disappearance that frightened them, that got him killed. They probably felt they couldn't risk losing him, too. But, that's over with now; almost everything is. I need you to help me."

"How?"

"Did Creighton Price meet you in New York?"

"Yes."

"Good. In a few hours, he'll receive the package that I sent. It contains a notebook with the story I've just told you. Please call him, make sure he's received it. I doubt that he can do very much without some corroboration. Tell him to call Daumier in a few hours. The autopsy results should be in by then. That should be enough."

There was a sharp rapping on the door and the policewoman who had escorted Nancy and Elizabeth down the corridor poked her head in.

"Cinq minutes?" asked Elizabeth.

The policewoman nodded and closed the door.

"I'll call Mr. Price," said Nancy, "and book a room at the hotel."

"No, no take mine," said Catherine. "It's paid for through the end of the week. Now go get some rest."

Nancy stood up and hugged Catherine. "I'm glad I'm here."

"So am I."

Nancy ran her fingers down along Catherine's cheek. "You're very brave."

"I was very stupid and I'm trying to make up for it."

The door opened and Elizabeth Portiere stood up. She put a hand on Nancy's sleeve. "It's time," she said.

Nancy gave Catherine a quick, hard hug. "Don't worry," she said.

Catherine smiled up at her. "The worrying is over."

Langley, Virginia
Morning

"I don't understand why the fucking hell we can't get Lakey and Bennet out of France." John Fawcett spoke very slowly, as if by saying the words deliberately, one at a time, he could regain at least some of the composure he'd lost.

Graham Person stopped stirring what remained of the coffee in the bottom of the stained Styrofoam cup in front of him and looked up at Fawcett, who looked years older than he had the day before, and not entirely well. His open collar showed the sag of skin around his neck and the pallor of his face was set off by the blue-gray shadow of a day-old beard. His shirt had the limp, crumpled look of one that had been slept in. Person had been there with Fawcett since midnight, shortly after the duty officer had called and reported that a long facsimile message, marked top secret, was coming in from Paris.

"We're doing everything we can, John. We're dealing with the French. That's never easy," said Person. He'd weathered the night somewhat better than Fawcett had. Although his eyes looked tired, his voice was firm and calm. "Their line is that it's a domestic matter and, of course, they're right. It doesn't matter that they're both Americans. It happened on French soil."

"Sons of bitches. They wrap themselves in legal niceties when it suits them, don't they? They know goddamn well we're in trouble, and they're not doing anything to help."

"Come on, John, they're not some banana republic. They can't have it look like we're interfering. Lakey's admitted she killed him, for Christ's sake, and I'm sure that made the Paris papers. What the hell are they going to do?"

Fawcett rolled a soggy napkin into a ball and tossed it at one of the coffee cups that littered the table. It missed. "All right," he said finally. "Would it make a difference if we told them we'd settle just for Bennet?"

"Would we?"

Fawcett picked up the stack of papers that had rolled out of the fax machine the night before and waved them in Graham Person's direction. "This is a problem, Graham, especially since we don't know where else she sent it, but I think it can be handled as long as it's just her word. After all, who the hell is she?" He dropped the papers on the table. "But, if we don't get Bennet, and she tells them what to look for, there might be nothing we can do."

"You've cleared it with Sperle?"

"It was his idea. He didn't think we'd get both of them."

"Maybe you guys should talk to the French."

"Who's running this for them?"

"Senderens."

"Paul Senderens? He's a reasonable man. At least he used to be. But I want you to talk to him, Graham. I'd rather this were handled below the highest level. If you don't get anywhere with Senderens, I'll go to Sperle."

"How much can I say?"

Fawcett rubbed his eyes and thought a moment. "We can't be coy, but . . . " he pointed his finger at Graham Person, "everything is off the record. Nothing in writing."

"All right," said Person, getting up. "I'll see what we can do."

Devon, Connecticut
Morning

The thick manila envelope, sealed and crisscrossed with heavy packing tape, arrived at Simco's office at midmorning. It was addressed to him in the blocky, backward-slanting printing that told him right away that it was from Catherine.

Inside he found what he first thought was the typescript of a paper or an article: twenty or thirty neatly typed pages, single-spaced, held together by two thick rubber bands. Taped to the first page was a plain white envelope which said, simply, "Frank." He opened it and read:

Dear Frank,

There isn't time for me to say all the things I need to say to you and to all the others at the college. I'm terribly sorry for all the trouble I have caused, and if there had been some way I could have avoided it, I surely would have. When you have read the accompanying document, perhaps you will understand.

I do not want to alarm you, but you must follow my instructions precisely. Everything depends on it.

First, tell no one of this package. After you have read it, please put it somewhere that is secure, preferably under lock and key. Then you should call my niece, Nancy Mulholland, at the Hôtel l'Europe in Paris. If she isn't there, just leave a message that you called and the word "yes." She will call you back within twenty-four hours. I hope that that is all you'll have to do.

If you do not hear from Nancy within twenty-four hours, however, you must call Creighton Price at The New York Times in New York. He should confirm to you that he has received a package identical to yours, but if he has not, you must arrange to meet with him and to give him what I've sent you.

Thank you, Frank, and I'm sorry that I've had to impose on you. I've learned, however, that trust is a rare commodity, and you are one of the very few whom I trust implicitly.

Catherine

Simco undid the rubber bands and began to read.

An hour and a half later, he dialed the number of the Hôtel l'Europe and asked for Nancy Mulholland. When he was told that she was not in her room, he left the message that Frank Simco had called and that it was very important for Miss Mulholland to know that he said yes.

New York City
Morning

He read it for the third time, very slowly, jotting notes, and when he finished, Creighton Price picked up the telephone and dialed the number that he had for OEP. When a woman answered, Price introduced himself in a low, almost apologetic voice that suggested that he was one of them, a mourner and a friend, and that he had called to pay his respects. She told him that Mr. O'Connell was the one he should talk to, and that he was on another line and would be with him in a minute.

Tony O'Connell wasn't on another line; he was at Gil Bennett's desk, going through files, sorting through the memos and the field directives that Sperle and Fawcett had asked him to collect. When he picked up the telephone and Maggie told him who was calling, he was neither surprised nor particularly alarmed. Creighton Price was the *Times'* man on intelligence; he'd probably known Bennet, and it was only natural that Price would be the one to do the story. He pressed the button on the telephone. "Tony O'Connell."

"Mr. O'Connell, we've heard about Gil Bennet. Would you care to make a comment?"

Tony quietly slid open the top drawer of Bennet's desk and removed a legal pad covered with his tiny, cramped handwriting. "Everyone at OEP, of course, is shocked and saddened by what has happened," he read. "Gil Bennet was a consummate professional, a valued leader, a patriot, a friend. He devoted his life to the idea that vigilance is the price of liberty and he spared no effort to ensure that the forces of freedom across the globe would never be caught off guard, would never be forced to bargain from a position of weakness. All of us have suffered a great loss."

Price rolled his eyes. "Thank you. Mr. O'Connell, you are . . . ?"

"Director of field operations. I've been here since the start."

"Mr. O'Connell, I've found it difficult to find out very much about OEP beyond the generic. I wonder if you could connect some dots?"

"We monitor and evaluate trends in technology, usually weapons technology, and draw up contingency plans to deal with those developments as they occur."

"You're spies?"

"We are assessors, evaluators, planners."

"And you do this undercover."

"I'm sorry, Mr. Price, I'm not at liberty to discuss our methods of operation. I hope you'll understand."

"And Mr. Bennet was in Paris on OEP business?"

"He was. Yes, sir."

"And you can't discuss the nature of that business?"

"I'm afraid I can't."

Price sorted through some papers on his desk. "Mr. O'Connell, Catherine Lakey, the woman who's confessed to killing Bennet, can you tell me about her?"

There was the slightest change in Price's tone—a subtle sharpening—that Tony heard. He knew the ground was getting dangerous. "I'm afraid I can't, Mr. Price."

"You can't or you won't?"

"I can't because I don't know anything about her."

"Are you aware that she claims to be a former employee of OEP?"

Where did Price get that? Was it in the Paris papers? Had the *Times* gotten to her? "I'm sorry, I wasn't aware."

"Was she?"

"I'm sorry, Mr. Price, OEP has employed many people over the years. I don't have those records in front of me. I was told she was a college professor."

"So you don't deny it."

"Or confirm it. I have no idea."

"What can you tell me about cis-Ornithon 60?"

Tony stared straight ahead, suddenly understanding what had happened. He felt a trickle of perspiration run from under one arm, down along his side.

"Mr. O'Connell?"

"I'm sorry, Mr. Price, I thought this was going to be a call about Gil Bennet."

"It is. I'm trying to find out more about him. Catherine Lakey says that she developed cis-Ornithon 60 for you. She says it's a powerful poison that leaves virtually no trace. It sounds like something that might be a very useful instrument."

Tony O'Connell simply didn't know the rules. Bennet would have, or Sperle. Do you deny without denying, or say nothing, or get angry? "Mr. Price, I'm a field man. There are any number of things I'm sure I don't know about."

"But this stuff sounds like it would be right up your alley."

"Sorry."

"OK, another field question. Joseph Dunlop, Cesar Valenzuela, Moraji Narayan. What can you tell me about them?"

Jesus Christ, thought O'Connell. "I've never heard of them."

"And Richard Weiss?"

How much of this could they check out, O'Connell wondered. And if they checked it out and it was clear that he was lying . . . Weiss couldn't hurt them anymore, he decided, there couldn't be much risk. "I think that name's familiar."

"He worked for OEP?"

"I think so, some time ago."

"Neurotoxins?"

"You know I can't discuss that."

"Catherine Lakey says he was the one who found out about the cis-Ornithon 60. It was Weiss, in fact, who tipped her off how her discovery was going to be used."

"Mr. Price, look, I don't think that this conversation is getting us anywhere."

"Is that a denial?"

"Of what?"

"That Weiss tipped off Lakey and was killed for his trouble?"

"That's ridiculous."

"A denial, then?"

"Yes." O'Connell paused to try to collect himself. "Mr. Price, would you mind telling me where you're getting this?"

"Sorry. I've got to protect my sources."

"I see. Is there anything else?"

"Not unless you're willing to start telling me what's going on."

"There's nothing going on, beyond the fact that Bennet's been killed by some lunatic in Paris—"

"And you have no idea why?"

"None."

"Bullshit, Mr. O'Connell."

"Mr. Price, I'm very busy . . . "

"I'll bet you are."

"Good-bye."

O'Connell held the button down on the phone, released it, dialed a number. "Graham?" he said, loosening his tie. "I've just talked with Creighton Price of the *Times*. He's got the whole goddamn story."

In New York, Creighton Price leaned back in his chair and held up the pad on which he'd been taking notes. He was absolutely certain that O'Connell was lying, but he couldn't prove it, couldn't prove a single goddamn thing in Lakey's story. He thumbed through the pages of her narrative and shook his head. The telephone rang and he picked it up. "Price," he said.

"Mr. Price, this is Nancy Mulholland."

"In Paris?"

"Yes. Did you get the package from my aunt?"

"This morning."

"And you've read it?"

"Yes."

"And?"

"It's interesting reading."

"Will you print it?"

"I thought you didn't want me writing stories."

"Now I do. I spent an hour with her this morning. She told me everything."

"I don't think I can. What she's saying, these are very serious allegations. I need more than just her word."

"You don't believe her?"

"I didn't say that. I can't write a story—at least not this kind of story—just on someone's say-so. I need some sort of confirmation. I just got off the phone with OEP. They're denying everything."

"In the material she sent you I know she told you about the poison, but you may not know that that's how she killed Bennet."

"What?"

"She used the poison, the Ornithon, in a syringe concealed in the tip of an umbrella. She's told the police, and by now they'll have both of them, the umbrella and the poison. She's also told them what to look for at the autopsy. If you know what to look for, and you do the right tests, it can be detected. The person handling the case is named Daumier, Inspector Daumier. If you call him in an hour or so, he'll confirm all this. Will that be enough?"

"I'm sure it will."

"Thank you, Mr. Price. Some good will come of this."

Creighton Price thought about that for a moment. Surely something would, but he wasn't sure that "good" was quite the word.

Paris
Afternoon

The room where Catherine was kept in the police station—"kept" was Daumier's word, and it sounded so much nicer than others

she could think of—didn't look anything like any jail cell she'd
imagined. There were bars on the windows, old iron ones twisted
into scrollwork, and the door, reinforced with metal plates, had
two serious-looking deadbolt locks, but those were the only indications that she wasn't staying in the guest room of a comfortable nineteenth-century Parisian town house. The floor was worn
dark wood and the freshly painted light brown walls ran up to a
ten-foot ceiling. She had an iron bed, a writing table, a small chest
of drawers and, in one corner, behind a folding screen, there was
a toilet and a sink. The double windows looked out over a cob-
blestoned courtyard where several of the police officers—probably the highest ranking—parked their cars. In all, it was a nicer
room than the one she'd had at the Hôtel l'Europe.

Inspector Daumier knocked on the door and announced himself at a few minutes before three. The door opened and he strode
purposefully to the writing table, a black leather portfolio under
one arm. He looked serious and official. "I trust you have been
comfortable," he said, unzipping the portfolio.

It was the first visit he had paid and Catherine tried to read in
his face what its purpose might be. "Why yes, thank you."

"It is odd to say, but I think you will be pleased to learn that
you will be formally charged."

"With murder? I see."

"And you still intend to make a guilty plea?"

"Yes. Of course."

"In that case, I wonder if it would be convenient for you to
make a statement to that effect?"

"A confession?"

"Yes. You may write it or you may dictate it."

"I'd prefer to write it."

"Yes," said Daumier, smiling very faintly. "But I think we
should discuss what you are going to say."

"You know what I'm going to say. I said it to you yesterday."

"That you killed him with a poison in the tip of an umbrella?"

"Yes. What else would I say?"

Daumier ran his fingers along his chin and made a small sigh.

"Miss Lakey, I have here . . . " he reached into the portfolio and took out some papers, sorted through them, then handed one to her. "This is a copy of the autopsy report on Mr. Bennet. It was done this morning and I think that you can see quite plainly the statement of the cause of death. He died of a single bullet wound to the heart, very small caliber. Nine millimeters."

Catherine looked up quickly at Daumier, studied him for a moment, then smiled. "That's preposterous, Inspector. I'm afraid you were given the wrong report."

Daumier extended his hand toward her. "May I?"

She handed him the paper.

He studied it for a moment. "Gilbert Edward Bennet. Age forty-one. Chevy Chase, Maryland, U.S.A. Employed by Office of Emergency Preparedness, U.S. Government." He looked up at her. "Is all of that correct?"

"Yes."

He reached back into the portfolio. "I'm sorry to do this. It is indelicate, but I must ask you to look at something."

He took out what at first looked like a blank white piece of heavy paper and handed it to her. When she turned it over, she saw that it was a photograph of Bennet, of his upper chest and head. He was naked and his eyes were closed, which gave him the appearance of being peacefully asleep. On the left side of his chest, just beneath the nipple, was a brown-red dot, which someone had circled with a blue marker. "I don't understand."

"Is that Gilbert Bennet?"

"Yes," said Catherine, still staring at the picture.

"There are other pictures, but I don't think it is necessary to look at them. May I?"

Catherine handed him the photograph. "He wasn't shot," she said softly.

Daumier put the papers and the photograph back in the portfolio. "I'm afraid he was."

Catherine leaned forward. "If he was shot, Inspector, then why in God's name did it take your people almost a day to figure that out? And why did it take even longer than that to file charges?"

"I'm glad you asked me that because those were exactly the questions that occurred to me. Yesterday was Sunday, and there were no medical examiners available to make an official determination. It is true that the policeman on the scene observed the bullet hole in the shirt, but then there was the peculiar contradiction of your confession. It was decided that it would be better to wait until an autopsy could be performed."

"I didn't shoot him, Inspector. I don't own a gun. I've never even held one. I told you what happened."

"Miss Lakey, I don't understand why you are saying these things. This morning, as you asked, we went to your room to find the umbrella you described. We searched the room thoroughly, but could not find it. What we did find, however, in the top drawer of your bureau, was a nine-millimeter pistol that had recently been fired. The laboratory has confirmed that it is the same weapon used on Mr. Bennet."

Catherine stood up and went to the window. "Oh my God," she said, "I didn't think they could do this. Not here." She turned to face Daumier. "Who did the autopsy?"

Daumier shrugged. "René Bouchard, I suppose, but what does it matter?"

"It matters because they got to him," said Catherine, her voice rising. "I need to see him. I need to talk to him. Did he check the spinal fluid?"

Daumier shook his head and studied the autopsy report. "Apparently not. There was no need."

"There was a need! I told you that. Call him, please. Have him look. It shows up in the spinal fluid."

"I'm afraid that is quite impossible, Miss Lakey. Mr. Bennet's body is on the way back to the United States."

Catherine went over to her bed and sat down heavily. "Back to the United States . . . " She looked at Daumier. "May I use a telephone?"

He got up and knocked twice on the door. It opened and he spoke a few words to a policewoman. The door closed, and in a few minutes she returned with a telephone. Daumier plugged it into a jack on the wall. "I will be outside," he said.

Catherine got up off the bed and held on to one of its iron bars to steady herself. She picked up a piece of paper from the writing table and went over to the telephone. She dialed, waited. "Elizabeth Portiere, please." She waited again. "Elizabeth? It's Catherine. Yes, I'm afraid . . . " She stopped, cleared her throat. "Look, I'm afraid . . . " The sob came, deep and hollow, followed by another. She knew this was a terrible thing to do, on the telephone, with someone she hardly knew, but she couldn't stop, and even if she could, she didn't want to.

Langley, Virginia
Afternoon

Graham Person thought that James Sperle's office looked like a private library with its dark wood paneling and walls of expensively bound books. He wondered if any of them were ever read, and by whom.

"Graham?" Sperle was looking directly at him. "You're our press expert. What will Price do with this?"

Person hesitated. He hated questions like that, having been in the game long enough to know that predicting what the press would do was always a crapshoot. "Assuming he's got Lakey's story?"

Sperle nodded.

"That might depend on what he thought of Tony."

"Assume the worst," said Fawcett.

Person ignored the remark. "If Tony was convincing and if Price has nothing other than what we've seen, I think he's got a problem."

"Please, Graham. I need you to be clear. Will he write the story?"

Person thought for a moment. "What do you want? My hunch or the facts? If it's facts, then the answer is that I don't know. I'm not the editor."

"Stick your neck out."

"He'll write the story. He'd be a fool not to."

"Even without confirmation?"

"He'll have to make it soft—he'll use the word 'allege' a hundred times—and they'll bury it somewhere in the middle of the paper."

"Doesn't sound so bad," said Fawcett.

Person said nothing. Sperle looked at him. "What's the matter, Graham?"

"It won't end with the *Times*. What worries me is what will happen when some of the others pick this up. What about the *New York Post*? How do you think they'll play it? I'd even be worried about the networks."

"We can't stonewall, then?"

"No. Too dangerous. If there's a fire in the basement, you don't sit in the living room and hope that it goes out."

Sperle turned away from Person to Fawcett. "It looks like your turn, John."

Fawcett snapped open the attaché case on the table in front of him and took out two thin, blue binders. He handed one to Sperle, one to Person. "The script," he said.

Sperle and Person read in silence for a few minutes. "That's very good, John," said Sperle. Person nodded. "When?"

"Tomorrow. I think we've got to take the initiative."

"And we'll need the Director, I assume."

"He's the best in the world."

Sperle stood up. "I'll take this to him now. He'll have to clear it with the higher-ups, but that shouldn't be a problem. Will you make the arrangements?" Fawcett nodded. "And Graham, please go see O'Connell. Tell him not to worry about the documents right now. We'll do that later. Tell him we think it would be best if he got away from Washington for a while. Have him take some time off. And tell him that we don't want him to talk to anyone—anyone at all."

Paris
Evening

"They're going to move me tomorrow, Nannie." She sat on her bed, cross-legged, twirling the fringe of the blanket around and around in her fingers. As the light outside faded, the room was drained of color until everything was black or white or gray.

Nancy turned away from the window. "Where?"

"I don't know. Lithviers? Does that sound right? I'll miss it here. It reminds me of a convent, or what I always thought a convent might be like. It's a place for penance, don't you think? For contemplation too. I was thinking this morning that there's a part of me that's sorry for what I did. Not because it hasn't worked out, but about Gil. He was doing some terrible things, wasn't he? But was he evil? Maybe he got caught up in something. I don't know. Maybe I did, too. Do you think I should write his wife?"

"Catherine, stop it!" Nancy crossed quickly to the bed and sat down beside her aunt.

"What should I stop?"

"That tone that says you've given up."

"But I have, Nannie. This afternoon, they won, didn't they? They came three thousand miles across the ocean to a foreign country and they changed everything around. They told me that I wasn't big enough or smart enough to hurt them. Maybe no one is."

"But Creighton Price is going to write the story."

"Not the story that we wanted. His story will be about the ravings of an unbalanced woman. Do you remember a few years ago when somewhere in the South a man shot a congressman, I think it was, and he said that voices made him do it? That's the kind of story this will be. People will shake their heads and wonder what the world is coming to. Then they'll forget about it."

Nancy shook her head. "I'm sorry, Catherine, but I won't let them. Not after everything you've done."

Catherine reached out and grabbed Nancy by the wrist.

"That's exactly what you won't do. Haven't you learned anything from all of this? What do you think will happen if you won't let this thing alone? Do you think they're dumb enough to leave things sitting in the open so you can find them? And what if you do? Do you think this is some sort of game where if you somehow score more points, they'll shake your hand and say, 'Nice going, Nannie, you sure got us that time.' Is that what they said to Richard? Leave it alone, Nannie, please."

"And just leave you here?"

"You have to leave me here, and that would have been true no matter what. It's my choice." She looked at Nancy and gave her a small smile. "I'll finally have to learn French." She noticed that Nancy's eyes were brimming. "Please, none of that. I do want you to do a favor for me when you get back."

Nancy nodded.

"This summer, please use the cottage in Cotchpinicut. Mother is taken care of through the end of this year, but if she goes on beyond that, the cottage will have to be sold. I so much wanted you to have it."

It was nearly dark in the room by now and Nancy got up from the bed, went behind the screen in the corner and ran some water in the sink. When she came out, she was dabbing at her face with a towel. "It's getting late. I have to go."

"Have you called Frank?"

"No. I got his message."

"Call him when you get back to the hotel. Tell him what's happened. Thank him for me."

Nancy went over to the bed, bent down and kissed the top of Catherine's head. "I will," she said. "What time will they move you?"

"The afternoon, I think."

"I'll see you in the morning, then."

Catherine heard Nancy make her way slowly to the door, rap lightly on it, and when it opened, briefly saw her outlined in the yellow rectangle of light. When the door closed again, she felt relieved to be in darkness, and alone.

Devon, Connecticut
Evening

Frank Simco sat with the telephone pinched between cheek and shoulder, listening. He pushed an open can of beer slowly back and forth across the desktop, studying the trail of moisture that it left. He said little; an "um-hum" now and then, a nod. Finally, he sighed, "Jesus, Nancy, I'm sorry."

"It hasn't been a good day." Her voice was sad, but composed and remarkably clear. When he had answered the phone, he was sure she was back in the United States, perhaps New York, and he'd had to fight the impulse to tell her that she sounded as if she were in the next room, like his mother always did.

"There's nothing you can do?"

"Here? No. I don't know anything about the country. I barely speak the language. There are legal angles to pursue, but Elizabeth is taking care of those. Anyway, Catherine worries. She thinks OEP is all over Paris and she doesn't want me to be anywhere near them."

"I don't see why OEP would do anything, not now."

"I know, but it's hard to tell Catherine that."

"Maybe Price's story won't be as bad as you think."

"Maybe, but when I talked to him, he told me I'd be disappointed. Frank?"

"What is it?"

"I don't know what to do. I've thought of going back to Washington and finding someone who'll believe all this, but I don't know how to do it. We've got no goddamn proof, and they're so powerful. I don't know who'd listen." Nancy paused. "It wouldn't be possible for you to come here, would it?"

"To Paris? Why?"

"To be here." She sounded like a little girl about to cry.

"Nancy, I can't. Not now. How long will you be there?"

He could hear her struggling for control. "I'm sorry. I'm being stupid. Maybe the end of the week. Saturday. Frank, you're not going to walk away from me now, are you?"

"Of course not."

"I really need you. I need your help. I miss you."

"Will you come through New York?"

"Maybe. I don't know. I don't have a ticket yet."

"But you'll have a stopover, if not New York, then Boston."

"I suppose."

"And I could meet you."

"That's too far to come to sit in an airport for an hour between planes."

"Not in the airport for an hour. We could stay somewhere for the night." He said it before he'd thought about it and the sound of his words stupefied him.

"I have to get back to Bloomington."

"One more night won't make a difference."

"You're right, it won't. I'll call you when I get my ticket."

They said good-bye, gently, awkwardly, like teenagers lingering on the doorstep, not wanting the night to slip away from them. Finally, Nancy said that she simply had to go, that it was after midnight and she was desperately tired. He put the phone down and stared at it while he finished the now warm beer. He thought of Catherine sitting in a prison somewhere in Paris and he felt sad and angry and helpless all at the same time. And then he thought of Nancy—the way she'd looked the last time he'd seen her, how her hand had felt as it brushed along his cheek—and he wondered how he could possibly wait until Saturday to see her.

MARCH—1987						
S	M	T	W	T	F	S
1	2	3	4	5	6	7
8	9	10	11	12	13	14
15	16	17	18	19	20	21
22	23	24	25	<u>26</u>	27	28
29	30	31				

DAY TWENTY

APRIL—1987						
S	M	T	W	T	F	S
			1	2	3	4
5	6	7	8	9	10	11
12	13	(14)	15	16	17	18
19	20	21	22	23	24	25
26	27	28	29	30		

DAY TWENTY

Alexandria, Virginia
Evening

Her mother wanted her again. She got up wearily, even a little unsteadily, and went down the hallway to the bedroom. The old woman was propped up on a hill of pillows, tiny, frail, blue-skinned, looking more and more each day like a baby bird, but her eyes were bright and alert as they darted from the plate on the tray in front of her to the television set.

"This is cold, Maggie," she said, prodding the scrambled egg with her fork.

"No it isn't."

"You're drinking. I can smell it."

"I'm having a drink before dinner, Mother. I'm thirty-four."

"Hm." The old woman swung her eyes away from the television and studied Maggie carefully. "You've been crying again. What's gotten into you these last two days?"

"I'm fine, Mother. There are things at the office. Things that aren't going well."

"Things that make you cry? A man?"

"Can I get you anything?"

The old woman looked back at the television screen and was

instantly absorbed, as though Maggie weren't there.

Maggie returned to the kitchen and made herself another drink, putting the ice cubes in the glass carefully so her mother couldn't hear. She took a paper towel from the roll and blew her nose. The clock above the sink said 6:00. She turned on the small portable television that sat on the countertop and swung the antenna back and forth until the picture sharpened, stabilized. She almost never watched the news and, therefore, didn't know which of the stations would be most likely to carry the story. It didn't matter, she supposed. It was big enough so that all of them would. She turned up the sound and watched a toothpaste commercial, then saw the news anchor reappear, smiling handsomely, perfectly. On a screen behind him was a picture of Henry Fullerton, the Director of the CIA, with the words "CIA DENIAL." They cut to a reporter, a woman, standing in front of the headquarters in Langley.

Maggie pulled a kitchen chair from under the table and slid it over close to the counter. She sat down, and suddenly there he was, glaring at the camera as if it had offended him, his blue eyes clearly angry, his hands gripping the edges of the lectern. Henry Fullerton looked like Moses.

"This morning," he began, slowly, his voice a rumble, "in *The New York Times,* there appeared a story . . . " Maggie tried hard to concentrate, but found the eyes of Henry Fullerton disconcerting, as if all the intervening layers of glass and cable and air between them weren't really there at all, and he was in the kitchen talking to her. She looked away, out the window.

" . . . scurrilous . . . " she heard him say, "impugn the integrity . . . ," " . . . Gilbert Edward Bennet . . . " She felt her eyes begin to fill again and she thought of the funeral tomorrow and wondered how she would get through it, with his wife there, whom she had never met, and his children, and she would be the only one in the entire overflowing church who'd know. " . . . senseless act of violence . . . "

She made herself look up at the television screen to see if his eyes betrayed anything. They didn't. It was marvelous and frightening how they could do things like that, every one of them. But never Gil, she was sure. He cared about people. He cared about her—not in that way, of course, although once when she'd worn a low-cut summer dress to work and had bent down over his desk to show him something, she had caught him looking, and she hadn't minded. He would never have allowed the killing unless there was something or someone forcing him to. And that's why she'd told Richard Weiss. Gil liked him and respected him. Richard would talk to him, find out what was wrong, help him.

She'd never understood why he hadn't done it. He'd never said a thing to Gil. He'd told Catherine instead. And then everything simply came apart in front of her, like those slow-motion movies of buildings being blown up. Catherine disappeared. Richard. Gil.

" . . . a tragedy compounded by the callousness, the unconscionable irresponsibility of the press." His eyes glared at her from the television screen. The twenty-minute statement had been seamlessly edited to three for national evening news consumption, and now they cut to a congressman being interviewed, saying that he doubted there would be the need for an investigation, unless, of course, any of the allegations could be substantiated.

She turned off the television and went back down the hallway to check on her mother. The old woman seemed to be asleep, but opened one eye when Maggie stepped into the room.

"I'm going out. I won't be long."

"Had anything to eat?"

"Yes," Maggie lied.

"Gotta eat if you drink," she said, closing her eye.

Maggie made sure the emergency pager was on the bedside table, went back to the kitchen and found her keys. It was after the rush hour; the trip to Bethesda wouldn't take long.

She signed in with the night man, checking the book to see whether anyone else was in. There wasn't. Upstairs, she turned her desk light on, then activated the television camera that surveyed the hallway. She let herself into Bennet's office with the key that he had given to her years before, and went over to the desk, which was still strewn with the memos and field directives that Tony O'Connell had been going through.

After forty minutes she was finished. She flipped through the large rolodex on Bennet's desk, jotted down a number, then left the room, making sure the door was locked behind her. She turned off the light on her desk and the television camera, then folded the small stack of papers neatly in half and slipped them in her purse. At the front desk she signed out.

When she entered the apartment, she called out, "Mother, it's me," put her purse down on the table and went down the hall to check on her.

"I'd like some tea," said the old woman, almost fiercely, glaring at the television as though she had been arguing with it.

"I'll put on some water."

"Who is he?" she said without looking up at Maggie.

"He?" Maggie smiled. "No he. Just some work at the office."

She went back to the kitchen and put on the kettle, then took out the number she had copied down and picked up the wall telephone beside the door. She waited, tense, then relaxed when someone answered. "Mr. Price?"

"Hello. It's not important who this is, not now. I'm calling because . . . " She paused, "because I've discovered documents that support every detail of Catherine Lakey's story. They're here with me and I want you to have them, all of them. I'm in Washington. Yes. Tomorrow would be fine. There's a restaurant I know . . . " The kettle gave a short chirp, then another, then broke into the piercing, steady whistle that had always seemed to say to her, so long ago, when she was just a little girl, "It's done, it's done!"